Dean Koontz was born into a very poor family and learned early on to escape into fiction – though books were scorned by his parents as a waste of time. He won an *Atlantic Monthly* fiction competition in 1965 at the age of twenty. Since then eighteen of his novels have appeared in the national and international bestseller lists and have sold over a hundred million copies worldwide.

He lives in southern California with his wife Gerda.

The Voice of The Night

Dean Koontz

Previously published as
THE VOICE OF THE NIGHT
by Brian Coffey

Previously published as
THE VOICE OF THE NIGHT
by Brian Coffey

The right of Dean Koontz to be identified as the Author of
the Work has been asserted by him in accordance with the
Copyright, Designs and Patents Act 1988.

First published in Great Britain in 1981
by Robert Hale under the name of Brian Coffey

First published in paperback in 1985
by Star Books
the paperback division of W H Allen & Co

Reprinted in this edition in 1990
by HEADLINE BOOK PUBLISHING

A HEADLINE FEATURE paperback

20 19 18 17 16 15 14 13 12

ISBN 0 7472 3519 8

Printed and bound in Great Britain by
Clays Ltd, St Ives plc

HEADLINE BOOK PUBLISHING
A division of Hodder Headline PLC
338 Euston Road, London NW1 3BH

To old friends—
Harry and Diane Record
Paul and Mary Ann Perencevic
Andy and Ann Wickstrom
—who, like wine, get better
year by year.

A faint cold fear
thrills through my veins.
—*Shakespeare*

Part One

1

'You ever killed anything?' Roy asked.

Colin frowned. 'Like what?'

The two boys were on a high hill at the north end of town. The ocean lay beyond.

'Anything,' Roy said. 'You ever killed anything at all?'

'I don't know what you mean,' Colin said.

Far out on the sun-dappled water, a large ship moved northward toward distant San Francisco. Nearer shore stood an oil-drilling platform. On the deserted beach a flock of birds relentlessly worked the damp sand for their lunch.

'You must've killed something,' Roy said impatiently. 'What about bugs?'

Colin shrugged. 'Sure. Mosquitoes. Ants. Flies. So what?'

'How'd you like it?'

'Like what?'

'Killing 'em.'

Colin stared at him, finally shook his head. 'Roy, sometimes you're pretty weird.'

Roy grinned.

'You like killing bugs?' Colin asked uneasily.

'Sometimes.'

'Why?'

'It's a real popper.'

3

Anything that Roy thought was fun, anything that thrilled him, he called a 'popper'.

'What's it like?' Colin asked.

'The way they squish.'

'Yech.'

'Ever pull the legs off a praying mantis and watch it try to walk?' Roy asked.

'Weird. Really weird.'

Roy turned to the insistently crashing sea and stood defiantly with his hands on his hips, as if he were challenging the incoming tide. It was a natural pose for him; he was a born fighter.

Colin was fourteen years old, the same age as Roy, and he never challenged anything or anyone. He rolled with life, floated where it took him, offering no resistance. Long ago he had learned that resistance caused pain.

Colin sat on the crown of the hill, in the spare dry grass. He looked up admiringly at Roy.

Without turning from the sea, Roy said, 'Ever kill anything bigger than bugs?'

'No.'

'I did.'

'Yeah?'

'Lots of times.'

'What'd you kill?' Colin asked.

'Mice.'

'Hey,' Colin said, suddenly remembering, 'my dad killed a bat once.'

Roy looked down at him. 'When was that?'

'Couple of years ago, down in Los Angeles. My mom and dad were still together then. We had a house in Westwood.'

'That where he killed the bat?'

'Yeah. Must've been some of them living in the attic. One of them got into my folks' bedroom. It

4

happened at night. I woke up and heard my mom screaming.'

'She was really scared, huh?'

'Terrified.'

'I sure wish I'd seen that.'

'I ran down the hall to see what was wrong, and this bat was swooping around their room.'

'Was she naked?'

Colin blinked. 'Who?'

'Your mother.'

'Of course not.'

'I thought maybe she slept naked and you saw her.'

'No,' Colin said. He could feel his face turning red.

'She wearing a negligee?' Roy asked.

'I don't know.'

'You don't *know*?'

'I don't remember,' Colin said uneasily.

'If I was the one who saw her,' Roy said, 'I'd sure as hell remember.'

'Well, I guess she was wearing a negligee,' Colin said. 'Yeah. I remember now.'

Actually, he couldn't recall whether she had been wearing pajamas or a fur coat, and he didn't understand why it mattered to Roy.

'Could you see through it?' Roy asked.

'See through what?'

'For Christ's sake, Colin! Could you see through her negligee?'

'Why would I want to?'

'Are you a *moron*?'

'Why would I want to stand around gaping at my own mom?'

'She's built, that's why.'

'You gotta be kidding!'

5

'Nice tits.'

'Roy, don't be ridiculous.'

'Terrific legs.'

'How would you know?'

'Saw her in a swimsuit,' Roy said. 'She's foxy.'

'She's what?'

'Sexy.'

'She's my *mother*!'

'So what?'

'Sometimes I wonder about you, Roy.'

'You're hopeless.'

'*Me*? Jeez.'

'Hopeless.'

'I thought we were talking about the bat.'

'So what happened to the bat?'

'My dad got a broom and knocked it out of the air. He kept hitting it until it stopped squealing. Boy, you should have heard it squeal.' Colin shuddered. 'It was awful.'

'Blood?'

'Huh?'

'Was there a lot of blood?'

'No.'

Roy looked at the sea again. He didn't seem impressed by the story about the bat.

The warm breeze stirred Roy's hair. He had the kind of thick golden hair and the wholesome freckled face that you saw in television commercials. He was a sturdy boy, strong for his age, a good athlete.

Colin wished he looked like Roy.

Someday, when I'm rich, Colin thought, I'll walk into a plastic surgeon's office with maybe a million bucks in cash and a picture of Roy. I'll get myself totally remade. Totally transformed. The surgeon will change my brown hair to corn yellow. He'll say, *Don't want this thin, pale face any more, do you? Can't blame you. Who would want it? Let's make it handsome.* He'll take care of my ears, too. They won't be so big when he's done. And he'll fix these damned eyes. I won't have to wear thick glasses any more. And he'll say, *Want me to add a bunch of muscles to your chest and arms and legs? No problem. Easy as cake.* And then I won't just *look* like Roy; I'll *be* as strong as Roy, too, and I'll be able to run as fast as Roy, and I won't be afraid of anything, not anything in the world. Yeah. But I better go into that office with *two* million.

Still studying the progress of the ship on the sea, Roy said, 'Killed bigger things, too.'

'Bigger than mice?'

'Sure.'

'Like what?'

'A cat.'

'You killed a cat?'

'That's what I said, didn't I?'

'Why'd you do that?'

'I was bored.'

'That's no reason.'

'It was something to do.'

'Jeez.'

Roy turned away from the sea.

'What a crock,' Colin said.

Roy hunkered in front of Colin, locked eyes with him. 'It was a popper, a really terrific popper.'

'A popper? Fun? Why would killing a cat be fun?'

'Why *wouldn't* it be fun?' Roy asked.

Colin was skeptical. 'How'd you kill it?'

'First I put it in a cage.'

'What kind of cage?'

'A big old birdcage, about three feet square.'

'Where'd you get a thing like that?'

'It was in our basement. A long time ago my mother owned a parrot. When it died she didn't get a new bird, but she didn't throw away the cage either.'

'Was it your cat?'

'Nah. Belonged to some people down the street.'

'What was its name?'

Roy shrugged.

'If there'd really been a cat, you'd remember its name,' Colin said.

'Fluffy. Its name was Fluffy.'

'Sounds likely.'

'It's true. I put it in the cage and worked on it with my mother's knitting needles.'

'Worked on it?'

'I poked at it through the bars. Christ, you should have heard it!'

'No thanks.'

'That was one damned mad cat. It spat and screamed and tried to claw me.'

'So you killed it with the knitting needles.'

'Nah. The needles just made it angry.'

'Can't imagine why.'

'Later I got a long, two-pronged meat fork from the kitchen and killed it with that.'

'Where were your folks during all this?'

'Both of them at work. I buried the cat and cleaned up all the blood before they got home.'

Colin shook his head and sighed. 'What a great big load of bull.'

'You don't believe me?'

'You never killed any cat.'

'Why would I make up a story like that?'

'You're trying to see if you can gross me out. You're trying to make me sick.'

Roy grinned. 'Are you sick?'

'Of course not.'

'You look kinda pale.'

'You can't make me sick because I know it didn't happen. There wasn't any cat.'

Roy's eyes were sharp and demanding. Colin imagined he could feel them probing like the points of that meat fork.

'How long have you known me?' Roy asked.

'Since the day after Mom and I moved here.'

'How long's that?'

'You know. Since the first of June. A month.'

'In all that time, have I ever lied to you? No. Because you're my friend. I wouldn't lie to a friend.'

'You're not lying exactly. Just sort of playing a game.'

'I don't like games,' Roy said.

'But you like to joke around a lot.'

'I'm not joking now.'

'Sure you are. You're setting me up. As soon as I say I believe you about the cat, you'll laugh at me. I won't fall for it.'

'Well,' Roy said, 'I tried.'

'Hah! You *were* setting me up!'

'If that's what you want to think, it's OK with me.'

Roy walked away. He stopped twenty feet from Colin and faced the sea again. He stared at the hazy horizon as if he were in a trance. To Colin, who was a science-fiction buff, Roy appeared to be in telepathic communication with something that hid far out in the deep, dark, rolling water.

9

'Roy? You *were* joking about the cat, weren't you?'

Roy turned, stared at him coolly for a moment, then grinned.

Colin grinned too. 'Yeah. I knew it. You were trying to make a fool out of me.'

2

Colin stretched out on his back, closed his eyes, and roasted for a while in the sun.

He couldn't stop thinking about the cat. He tried to conjure up pleasant images, but each of them faded and was replaced by a vision of a bloody cat in a birdcage. Its eyes were open, dead yet watchful eyes. He was certain the cat was waiting for him to get too close, waiting for a chance to strike out with razor-sharp claws.

Something bumped his foot.

He sat up, startled.

Roy stared down at him. 'What time is it?'

Colin blinked, looked at his wristwatch. 'Almost one o'clock.'

'Come on. Get up.'

'Where we going?'

'The old lady works afternoons at the gift shop,' Roy said. 'We've got my house to ourselves.'

'What's to do at your place?'

'There's something I want to show you.'

Colin stood and brushed sandy soil from his jeans. 'Gonna show me where you buried the cat?'

'I thought you didn't believe in the cat.'

'I don't.'

'Then forget it. I want to show you the trains.'

'What trains?'

11

'You'll see. It's a real popper.'

'Race into town?' Colin asked.

'Sure.'

'Go!' Colin shouted.

As usual, Roy reached his bicycle first. He was fifty yards away, racing into the wind, before Colin touched foot to pedal.

Cars, vans, campers, and lumbering motor homes jostled for position on the two-lane blacktop. Colin and Roy rode on the oiled berm.

Most of the year, Seaview Road carried very little traffic. Everyone except local residents used the interstate that bypassed Santa Leona.

During the tourist season the town was crowded, teeming with vacationers who drove too fast and recklessly. They seemed to be pursued by demons. They were all so frantic, in a great hurry to relax, relax, relax.

Colin coasted down the last hill, into the outskirts of Santa Leona. The wind buffeted his face, ruffled his hair, and blew the automobile exhaust fumes away from him.

He couldn't suppress a grin. His spirits were higher than they had been in a long, long time.

He had a lot to be happy about. Two more months of bright California summer lay ahead of him, two months of freedom before school began. And with his father gone, he no longer dreaded going home each day.

His parents' divorce still disturbed him. But a broken marriage was better than the loud and bitter arguments that for several years had been a nightly ritual.

Sometimes, in his dreams, Colin could still hear the shouted accusations, the uncharacteristically foul language that his mother used in the heat of a

12

fight, the inevitable sound of his father striking her, and then the weeping. No matter how warm his bedroom, he was always freezing when he woke from these nightmares – cold, shivering, yet drenched with sweat.

He did not feel close to his mother, but life with her was far more enjoyable than life with his father would have been. His mother didn't share or even understand his interests – science fiction, horror comics, werewolf and vampire stories, monster movies – but she never forbade him to pursue them, which his father had tried to do.

However, the most important change in recent months, the thing that made him happiest, had nothing to do with his parents. It was Roy Borden. For the first time in his life, Colin had a friend.

He was too shy to make friends easily. He waited for other kids to come to him, even though he realised they weren't likely to be interested in a thin, awkward, myopic, bookish boy who didn't mix well or enjoy sports or watch a lot of television.

Roy Borden was self-confident, outgoing, and popular. Colin admired and envied him. Nearly any boy in town would have been proud to be Roy's best friend. For reasons that Colin could not grasp, Roy had chosen him. Going places with someone like Roy, confiding in someone like Roy, having someone like Roy confide in him – these were new experiences for Colin. He felt as if he were a pitiful pauper who had miraculously fallen into favor with a great prince.

Colin was afraid that it would end as abruptly as it had begun.

That thought made his heart race. In an instant his mouth went dry.

Before he'd met Roy, loneliness was all he had ever known; therefore, it had been endurable. Now that he had experienced comradeship, however, a return to loneliness would be painful, devastating.

Colin reached the botton of the long hill.

One block ahead, Roy turned right at the corner.

Suddenly Colin thought the other boy might duck out on him, disappear down an alley-way, and hide from him forever. It was a crazy thought, but he couldn't shake it.

He leaned forward, into the handlebars. *Wait for me, Roy. Please wait!* He pedaled frantically, trying to catch up.

When he rounded the corner, he was relieved to see that his friend had not vanished. In fact, Roy had slowed down; he glanced back. Colin waved. They were only thirty yards apart. They weren't really racing any more because they both knew who would win.

Roy turned left, into a narrow residential street that was flanked by date trees. Colin followed through the feathery shadows that were cast by the wind-stirred palm fronds.

The conversation he'd had with Roy on the hill now echoed through Colin's mind:

You killed a cat?

That's what I said, didn't I?

Why'd you do that?

I was bored.

At least a dozen times during the past week, Colin had sensed that Roy was testing him. He felt certain the gruesome story about the cat was just the latest test, but he couldn't imagine what Roy had wanted him to say or do. Had he passed or failed?

14

Although he didn't know what answers were expected of him, he knew instinctively *why* he was being tested. Roy possessed a wonderful – or perhaps terrible – secret that he was eager to share, but he wanted to be certain that Colin was worthy of it.

Roy had never spoken of a secret, not one word, but it was in his eyes. Colin could see it, the vague shape of it, but not the details, and he wondered what it might be.

3

Two blocks from his home, Roy Borden turned left, into another street, away from the Borden house, and for a moment Colin again felt that the older boy was trying to lose him. But Roy pulled into a driveway in the middle of the block and parked his bike. Colin stopped beside him.

The house was neat and white with dark blue shutters. A two-year-old Honda Accord was parked in the open garage, facing out, and a man was leaning under the raised hood, repairing something. He was thirty feet away from Colin and Roy, and he was not immediately aware that he had company.

'What're we doing here?' Colin asked.

'I want you to meet Coach Molinoff,' Roy said.

'Who?'

'He coaches the junior-varsity football team,' Roy said. 'I want you to meet him.'

'Why?'

'You'll see.'

Roy walked toward the man who was working under the hood of the Honda.

Reluctantly, Colin followed. He was not much good at meeting people. He never knew what to say or how to act. He was sure that he always made a terrible first impression, and he dreaded scenes like this one.

Coach Molinoff looked up from the Honda's engine as he heard the boys approaching. He was a tall, broad-shouldered, sandy-haired man with gray-blue eyes. He grinned when he saw Roy.

'Hey, what's up, Roy?'

'Coach, this is Colin Jacobs. He's new in town. Moved up from L.A. He'll be going to school at Central in the fall. Same grade as me.'

Molinoff held out one big calloused hand. 'Really glad to meet you.'

Colin accepted the greeting awkwardly, his own hand disappearing in Molinoff's bearish grip. The coach's fingers were slightly greasy.

To Roy, Molinoff said, 'So how's the summer treating you, my man?'

'It's been OK so far,' Roy said. 'But I'm mainly just killing time, waiting for preseason practice to start the end of August.'

'We're going to have a terrific year,' the coach said.

'I know it,' Roy said.

'You handle yourself as well as you did last year,' said Molinoff, 'and Coach Penneman might just give you some fourth-quarter time in varsity games later in the season.'

'You really think so?' Roy asked.

'Don't give me that wide-eyed look,' Molinoff said. 'You're the best player on the junior-varsity team, and you know it. There's no virtue in false modesty, my man.'

Roy and the coach began to discuss football strategy, and Colin just listened, unable to contribute anything to the conversation. He never had shown much interest in sports. If asked about athletics of any kind, he always said that sports bored him and that he preferred the excitement of stimulating books and movies. In truth, while novels and films gave him endless pleasure, he sometimes wished he also could share the special camaraderie that athletes seemed to enjoy among themselves. For a boy like him, on the outside looking in, the world of sports was intriguing and glamorous; however, he did not waste a lot of time daydreaming about it, for he was fully aware that nature had given him less than the necessary equipment for a successful career in sports. With his myopic vision, his skinny legs, and his thin arms, he would never be more involved in sports than he was at that moment – a listener, watcher, never a participant.

Molinoff and Roy talked football for a few minutes, and then Roy said, 'Coach, what about the team managers?'

'What about them?' Molinoff asked.

'Well, last year you had Bob Freemont and Jim Safinelli. But Jim's folks moved to Seattle, and Bob is going to be one of the varsity teams' managers next season. So you need a couple of new guys.'

'You have somebody in mind?' Molinoff asked.

'Yeah,' Roy said. 'How about giving Colin a chance?'

Colin blinked in surprise.

The coach stared at him appraisingly. 'You know what's involved, Colin?'

'You get a team jacket of your own,' Roy told Colin. 'You sit with the players on the bench at every game. And you get to travel on the team bus with us to all the out-of-town games.'

'Roy's painting only the rosy part of the picture,' the coach said. 'Those are just the benefits of being a manager. You'll have duties, too. Like collecting and bundling the uniforms for the laundry. And taking care of the towel supply. You'll have to learn how to give the players good neck and shoulder massages. You'll run errands for me. A lot of other things. You'll be taking on a good bit of responsibility. Think you can handle it?'

Suddenly, for the first time in his life, Colin was able to picture himself on the inside instead of the outside, moving in the right circles, mingling with some of the most popular kids in school. Deep down, he knew that a team manager was a glorified messenger boy, but he pushed all the negative thoughts out of his mind. The important thing – the *incredible* thing – was that he would be a part of a world that previously had been completely beyond his reach. He would be accepted by the players; at least to some extent, he would be one of the guys. One of the guys! His mental image of life as a team manager was dazzling, enormously appealing, for he had been an outcast all of his life. He couldn't quite believe this was really happening to him.

'Well?' Coach Molinoff asked. 'Do you think you'd make a good team manager?'

'He'd be perfect,' Roy said.

'I'd sure like to try,' Colin said. His mouth was dry.

Molinoff stared at Colin, his blue-gray eyes calculating, weighing, judging. Then he glanced at Roy and said, 'I guess you wouldn't recommend anybody who was a complete washout.'

'Colin's right for the job,' Roy said. 'Very dependable.'

Molinoff looked at Colin again, finally nodded. 'OK. You're a team manager, son. Come with

20

Roy to the first practice. That's August twentieth. And be ready to work hard!'

'Yes, sir. Thank you, sir.'

As he walked with Roy to the bicycles at the end of the driveway, Colin felt taller and stronger than he had felt only a few minutes ago. He was grinning.

'You'll like traveling on the team bus,' Roy said. 'We'll have a lot of laughs.'

As Colin got on his bike, he said, 'Roy, I . . . well . . . I think you're just about the best friend a guy could ask for.'

'Hey, I did it as much for me as for you,' Roy said. 'Those trips to out-of-town games can be boring sometimes. But with you and me together on the bus, there won't be a dull minute. Now come on. Let's go to my place. I want to show you those trains.' He pedaled away.

Following Roy along the tree-shaded, sun-speckled pavement, elated and somewhat dazed, Colin wondered if the team manager's job was the thing for which Roy had been testing him. Was it the secret that Roy had been harboring for the past week? Colin thought about that for a while, but by the time he reached the Borden house, he decided there was something else that Roy was concealing, something so important that Colin had still not proved himself worthy to hear it.

4

They entered the Borden house through the kitchen door.

'Mom?' Roy called. 'Dad?'

'I thought you said they weren't home.'

'Just checking. I better be sure. If they caught us . . .'

'Caught us doing what?'

'I'm not supposed to mess around with the trains.'

'Roy, I don't want to get in trouble with your folks.'

'We won't. Wait here.' Roy hurried into the living room. 'Anyone home?'

Colin had been here on only two other occasions, and as before he was amazed at how spotless everything was. The kitchen gleamed. The floor was freshly scrubbed and waxed. The counters shone almost like mirrors. No dirty dishes waited to be washed; no overlooked crumbs marred the table; and there was not even a single vague stain in the sink. The utensils were not hung on wall racks; all pots and pans and spoons and ladles were secreted away in drawers and dust-free cupboards. Mrs Borden apparently did not appreciate knickknacks, for there was not a single decorative plate or plaque or piece of needlepoint wisdom on the walls, no spice rack,

23

no calendar, no clutter at all – and no sense that this was a place where real people cooked real food. The house looked as if Mrs Borden spent all of her time performing an elaborate series of cleaning operations – first scraping, then scouring, then scrubbing, then washing, rinsing, polishing, buffing – much the same way that a cabinetmaker sanded a piece of wood, beginning with coarse sandpaper and working up gradually to the finest grain.

Colin's own mother didn't keep a *dirty* kitchen. Far from it. They had a cleaning woman. She came in twice a week to help keep things neat. But their place didn't look like this.

According to Roy, Mrs Borden refused to consider a cleaning woman. She didn't think anyone else in the world would have standards as high as hers. She wasn't satisfied with a neat house; she wanted it to be sterile.

Roy returned to the kitchen. 'No one's here. Let's play with the trains awhile.'

'Where are they?'

'In the garage.'

'Whose are they?'

'The old man's.'

'And you're not supposed to touch them?'

'Screw him. He'll never know.'

'I don't want your folks mad at me.'

'For Christ's sake, Colin, how are they ever going to find out?'

'Is this the secret?'

Roy had started to turn away. Now he looked back. 'What secret?'

'You've got one. You're almost ready to explode with it.'

'How do you know?'

'I can see . . . the way you act. You've been testing me to see if you can trust me with a secret.'

Roy shook his head. 'You're pretty smart.'

Colin shrugged, embarrassed.

'No, you really are. You've just about been reading my mind.'

'So you *have* been testing me.'

'Yeah.'

'That dumb stuff about the cat—'

'— was true.'

'Oh sure.'

'Better believe it.'

'You're still testing me.'

'Maybe.'

'So there *is* a secret?'

'A big one.'

'The trains?'

'Nah. That's just a tiny part of it.'

'So what's the rest of it?'

Roy grinned.

Something in that grin, something strange in those bright blue eyes made Colin want to step back from the other boy. But he didn't flinch.

'I'll tell you about it,' Roy said. 'But only when I'm ready.'

'When will that be?'

'Soon.'

'You can trust me.'

'Only when I'm ready. Now come on. You'll like the trains.'

Colin followed him across the kitchen and through a white door. Beyond, there were two short steps and then the garage – and the model railroad.

'*Wow!*'

'Isn't it a popper?'

'Where's your dad park the car?'

'Always in the driveway. No room in here.'

'When did he get all this stuff?'

'Started collecting when he was a kid,' Roy said. 'He added to it every year. It's worth more than fifteen thousand dollars.'

'Fifteen thousand! Who'd pay that much money for a bunch of toy trains?'

'People who should have lived in better times.'

Colin blinked. 'Huh!'

'That's what my old man says. He says people who like model railroads are people who were meant to live in a better, cleaner, nicer, more organised world than the one we've got today.'

'What's that supposed to mean?'

'I'll be damned if I know. But that's what he says. He can ramble on for an hour about how much better the world was back when there were trains but not airplanes. He can bore your ass off.'

The train set was on a waist-high platform that nearly filled the three-car garage. On three sides there was just enough room to walk. On the fourth side, which featured the master-control console, there were two stools, a narrow work-bench, and a tool cabinet.

A brilliantly conceived, incredibly detailed miniature world had been constructed upon that platform. There were mountains and valleys, streams and rivers and lakes, meadows dotted with minuscule wildflowers, forests where timid deer peered out of the shadows between the trees, picture-postcard villages, farms, outposts, realistic little people engaged in a hundred chores, scale-model cars, trucks, buses, motorcycles, bicycles, neat houses with picket fences, four exquisitely rendered train stations – one Victorian-style, one Swiss, one Italian, one Spanish – and shops and churches and schools. Narrow-gauge railroad tracks ran everywhere – alongside the rivers, through the towns, across the valleys, around the sides of the mountains, across trestles and drawbridges, into and out of the stations, up and down and back and forth in graceful loops and straightaways and sharp turns and horseshoes and switchbacks.

Colin slowly circled the display, studying it with unconcealed awe. The illusion was not shattered by a close inspection. Even from a distance of only one inch the pine forests looked *real*; each tree was superbly crafted. The houses were complete in every detail, even down to rain spouting, workable windows in some of them, walkways made from individual stones, and television antennae secured by fine guy wires. The automobiles were not merely toy cars. They were carefully crafted, tiny but otherwise exact, replicas of full-size vehicles; and except for those that were parked along the streets and in the driveways, they all boasted a driver, sometimes passengers as well, and occasionally a family dog or cat on the back seat.

'How much of this did your dad build himself?' Colin asked.

'Everything but the trains and a few of the model cars.'

'It's fantastic.'

'It takes a whole week to make just one of those little houses, sometimes longer if it's really something special. He spent months and months on each of those train stations.'

'How long ago did he finish it?'

'It isn't finished,' Roy said. 'It'll never be finished – until he's dead.'

'But it can't possibly get bigger,' Colin said. 'There isn't any more room for it.'

'Not bigger, just better,' Roy said. His voice held a new note, a hardness, an iciness; his teeth were very nearly clenched tight, but he still smiled. 'The old man keeps improving the layout. All he does when he comes home from work is tinker with this damned thing. I don't think he ever takes time to screw the old lady any more.'

That kind of talk embarrassed Colin, and he didn't respond to it. He saw himself as being considerably less sophisticated than Roy, and he tried hard to change himself for the better in every way he was able; however, he simply could not learn to be comfortable with strong curse words and sex talk. The hot blush and the sudden thickness of tongue and throat were uncontrollable. He felt childish and stupid.

'He squirrels himself away in here every damn night,' Roy said, still using that new, cold voice. 'He even eats supper in here sometimes. He's a nut case just like she is.'

Colin had read a great deal about many things but only a little about psychology. Nevertheless, as he continued to marvel at the miniatures, he realised that the uncompromising attention to detail was an expression of the same fanatical insistence on neatness and order that was so evident in Mrs Borden's endless battle to keep the house as clean as a hospital operating room.

He wondered if Roy's parents really were nut cases. Of course, they weren't a couple of raving lunatics; they weren't certifiable. They weren't so far gone that they sat in corners talking to themselves and eating flies. Maybe just a little bit crazy. Just a tiny bit nuts. Perhaps they'd get a lot worse as time went on, gradually crazier and crazier, until ten or fifteen years from now they *would* be eating flies. It sure was something to think about.

Colin decided that if he and Roy became lifelong friends, he would hang around Roy's house only for another ten years. After that he'd maintain his friendship with Roy but avoid Mr. and Mrs Borden, so that when they finally went completely insane they wouldn't be able to get their hands on him and force him to eat flies or, worse yet, chop him up with an ax.

He knew all about lunatic killers. He'd seen the movies about them. *Psycho. Straitjacket. Whatever Happened to Baby Jane?* A couple dozen others, too. Maybe a hundred. One thing he learned from those films was that crazy people favored messy killing. They used knives and scythes and hatchets and axes. You'd never catch one of them resorting to something bloodless like poison or gas or a smothering pillow.

Roy sat on one of the stools in front of the control console. 'Over here, Colin. You'll be able to see more of it from here than anywhere else.'

'I don't think we should mess around with this if your dad doesn't want us to.'

'Will you relax, for Christ's sake?'

With an odd mixture of reluctance and pleasant anticipation, Colin sat on the second stool.

Roy carefully turned a dial on the board in front of him. It was connected to a rheostat, and the overhead garage lights slowly dimmed.

29

'It's like a theater,' Colin said.

'No,' Roy said. 'It's more like . . . I'm God.'

Colin laughed. 'Yeah. Because you can make it day or night any time you want.'

'And a whole lot more than that.'

'Show me.'

'In a minute. I won't make it completely dark. Not full night. Too hard to see. I'll make it early evening. Twilight.'

Next, Roy flipped four switches, and all over the miniature world, lights came on. In every village, street lamps threw down opalescent pools on the pavement beneath them. In most of the houses, a yellow, warm, and welcoming glow brought life to the windows. Some houses even had porch lights and little lamp-posts at the ends of their walks, as if guests were expected. Churches cast colorful stained-glass patterns on the ground around them. At a few major intersections traffic lights changed gradually from red to green to amber to green again. In one hamlet a movie marquee pulsed with a score of tiny lights.

'Fantastic!' Colin said.

As he stared at the layout, Roy's expression and posture were peculiar. His eyes were narrow slits; his lips were pressed tightly together. His shoulders were drawn up, and he was clearly tense.

'Eventually,' Roy said, 'the old man's going to put working headlights in the automobiles. And he's designing a pump and drainage system that'll let water flow through the rivers. There'll even be a waterfall.'

'Your dad sounds like an interesting guy.'

Roy did not respond. He stared at the small world in front of him.

30

At the far left corner of the platform, four trains waited for orders on the sidings in the railroad yard. Two were freight trains, and two were for passengers only.

Roy threw another switch, and one of the trains came to life. It buzzed softly; lights flickered in the cars.

Colin leaned forward in anticipation.

Roy manipulated switches, and the train chugged out of the yard. As it moved toward the nearest town, red warning lights flashed where a street intersected the tracks; black-and-white-striped crossing barriers lowered over the roadway. The train gathered speed, whistled noisily as it passed through the village, climbed a slight incline, vanished into a tunnel, reappeared around the far side of the mountains, accelerated, crossed a trestle, picked up more speed, entered a straightaway, really moving now, rounded a wide rise with a violent clatter, wheels whizzing, took a sharper curve with a dangerous tilt, and moved faster, faster, faster.

'For God's sake, don't wreck it,' Colin said nervously.

'That's exactly what I'm going to do.'

'Then your dad will know we've been here.'

'Nah. Don't worry about it.'

The train flashed through the Swiss station without slowing down, rocked wildly on the edge of disaster as it negotiated a switchback, roared through a tunnel, and entered a straightaway, picking up speed by the second.

'But if the train's broken, your dad—'

'I won't break it. Relax.'

A drawbridge began to go up directly in the path of the train.

31

Colin gritted his teeth.

The train reached the river, swept beneath the raised bridge, and plunged off the track. The miniature locomotive and two cars wound up in the channel, and all the other cars fell off the rails in a brief splash of sparks.

'Jeez,' Colin said.

Roy slid off his stool and went to the scene of the accident. He bent down and peered closely at the wreck.

Colin joined him. 'Is it ruined?'

Roy didn't answer. He squinted through the tiny windows in the train.

'What are you looking for?' Colin asked.

'Bodies.'

'What?'

'Dead people.'

Colin squinted into one of the fallen cars. There were no people in it — that is, there were no figurines. He looked at Roy. 'I don't understand.'

Roy didn't look up from the train. 'Understand what?'

'I don't see any "dead people." '

Moving slowly from car to car, staring into each of them, almost entranced, Roy said, 'If this was a *real* train full of people that went off the tracks, the passengers would have been thrown out of their seats. They'd have cracked their heads against the windows, and against the handrails. They'd have ended up in a big tangled pile on the floor. There'd be broken arms, broken legs, smashed teeth, slashed faces, eyes punched out, blood over everything . . . You'd be able to hear them screaming a mile away. Some of them would be dead, too.'

'So?'

'So I'm trying to imagine what it would look like in there if this was real.'

'Why?'

'It interests me.'

'What does?'

'The idea.'

'The idea of a real train wreck?'

'Yeah.'

'Isn't that kind of sick?'

Roy looked up at last. His eyes were flat and cold. 'Did you say "sick"?'

'Well,' Colin said uneasily, 'I mean . . . finding enjoyment in other people's pain . . .'

'You think that's unusual?'

Colin shrugged. He didn't want to argue.

'In other parts of the world,' Roy said, 'people go to bullfights, and deep down inside most of them hope they'll see a matador get gored. They *always* get to see the bull in pain. They love it. And a hell of a lot of people go to the auto races to see the bad crackups.'

'That's different,' Colin said.

Roy grinned. 'Oh, is it? How?'

Colin thought hard about it, trying to find words to express what he knew intuitively to be true. 'Well . . . for one thing the matador knows when he goes into the arena that he might get hurt. But people riding home on a train . . . not expecting anything . . . not asking for trouble . . . and then it happens . . . That's a tragedy.'

Roy laughed. 'You know what "hypocrite" means?'

'Sure.'

'Well, Colin, I hate to say this 'cause you're my good friend, my *real* good friend. I like you a lot. But as far as this thing goes, you're a hypocrite.

33

You think I'm sick because the idea of a train wreck interests me, but then you spend most of your spare time going to horror movies or watching them on television or reading books about zombies and werewolves and vampires and other monsters.'

'What's that got to do with anything?'

'Those stories are *filled* with murders!' Roy said. 'Death. Killing. That's practically all they're about. People get bitten and clawed and torn apart and chopped up with axes in those stories. And you love 'em!'

Colin winced at the mention of axes.

Roy leaned close. His breath carried the scent of Juicy Fruit chewing gum.

'That's why I like you, Colin. We're two of a kind. We got things in common. That's why I want to get you the job of team manager. So we could knock around together during football season. We're both smarter than other people. We both get straight-A averages in school without half trying. Each of us has been given IQ tests, and each of us has been told he's a genius or the next thing to it. We see deeper into things than most kids do and even deeper than a hell of a lot of grown-ups. We're special. Very special people.'

Roy put a hand on Colin's shoulder and locked eyes with him, seemed to be looking not just at him but also deep into him and ultimately through him. Colin could not look away.

'We're both interested in the things that count,' Roy said. 'Pain and death. That's what intrigues you and me. Most people think death is the end of life, but we know different, don't we? Death isn't the end. It's the center. It's the center of life. Everything else revolves round it. Death is the most important thing in life, the most interesting, the most mysterious, the most *exciting* thing in life.'

Colin cleared his throat nervously. 'I'm not sure I know what you're talking about.'

'If you aren't afraid of death,' Roy said, 'then you can't be afraid of anything. When you learn to conquer that biggest fear, you conquer all the smaller fears at the same time. Isn't that right?'

'I . . . I guess so.'

Roy spoke in a stage whisper for emphasis, spoke with amazing intensity, fervently. 'If I'm not afraid of death, then no one can do anything to hurt me. Nobody. Not my old man or the old woman. No one. Not ever again as long as I live.'

Colin didn't know that to say.

'Are you afraid of death?' Roy asked.

'Yes.'

'You've got to learn not to be.'

Colin nodded. His mouth went dry. His heart was racing, and he felt slightly dizzy.

'You know the first thing you've got to do to get over the fear of dying?' Roy asked.

'No.'

'Become familiar with death.'

'How?'

'By killing things,' Roy said.

'I can't do that.'

'Of course you can.'

'I'm a peaceable kid.'

'Deep down everyone's a killer.'

'Not me.'

'Shit.'

'Same to you.'

'I know myself,' Roy said. 'And I know you.'

'You know me better than *I* know me?'

'Yeah.' Roy grinned.

They stared at each other.

The garage was as quiet as an undisturbed Egyptian tomb.

At last Colin said, 'You mean . . . like we'd kill a cat?'

'For starters,' Roy said.

'For starters? Then what?'

Roy's hand tightened on Colin's shoulder. 'Then we'd move on to something bigger.'

Suddenly Colin realised what was happening, and he relaxed. 'You almost had me going again.'

'Almost?'

'I know what you're trying to do.'

'Do you?'

'You're testing me again.'

'Am I?'

'You're setting me up,' Colin said. 'You want to see if I'll make a fool of myself.'

'Wrong.'

'If I'd agreed to kill a cat to prove something to you, you'd have busted out laughing.'

'Try me.'

'No way. I know your game.'

Roy let go of his shoulder. 'It's not a game.'

'You don't have to test me. You can trust me.'

'To some extent,' Roy said.

'You can trust me completely,' Colin said earnestly. 'Jeez, you're the best friend I ever had. I wouldn't disappoint you. I'll do a good job as team manager. You won't be sorry you recommended me to the coach. You can trust me with that. You can trust me with anything. So what's the big secret?'

'Not yet,' Roy said.

36

'When?'
'When you're ready.'
'When will that be?'
'When I say you are.'
'Jeez.'

5

Colin's mother came home from work at five-thirty.

He was waiting in the cool living room. The furniture was all shades of brown, and the walls were papered in burlap. Wooden shades covered the windows. The lighting was indirect, soft, and easy on the eyes. It was a restful room. He was on the big sofa, reading the latest issue of his favorite comic book, *The Incredible Hulk.*

She smiled at him, ruffled his hair, and said, 'What kind of a day have you had, Skipper?'

'It was OK,' Colin said, aware that she didn't really want the details and would gently cut him off when he was halfway through the story. 'What about your day?' he asked.

'I'm pooped. Will you be a love and mix me a vodka martini the way I like?'

'Sure.'

'Twist of lemon.'

'I wouldn't forget it.'

'Of course you wouldn't.'

He got up and went into the family room, where there was a well-stocked wet bar. He couldn't stand the taste of hard liquor, but he mixed her drink quickly, with professional skill; he had done it hundreds of times.

When he returned to the living room, she was

sitting in a large chocolate-brown chair, her legs tucked under her, head laid back, eyes closed. She didn't hear him coming, so he stopped just inside the doorway and studied her for a moment.

Her name was Louise, but everyone called her Weezy, which was sort of a kid's name, but which suited her because she looked like a college girl. She was wearing jeans and a short-sleeved blue sweater. Her bare arms were tan and slender. Her hair was long, dark, shiny; and it framed a face that Colin suddenly thought was pretty, really quite beautiful, although some people might say the mouth was too wide. As he looked at her, he began to realise that thirty-three was not really old, as he'd always thought.

For the first time in his life, Colin was consciously aware of her body: full breasts, narrow waist, round hips, long legs. Roy was right; she had a terrific figure.

Why didn't I ever notice it before?

He answered himself at once: Because she's my own *mother*, for God's sake!

Heat blossomed in his face. He wondered if he was turning into some sort of pervert, and he forced himself to stop looking at her well-filled sweater.

He cleared his throat and went to her.

She opened her eyes, lifted her head, took the martini, and sipped it. 'Mmmmm. Perfect. You're a sweetheart.'

He sat on the sofa.

After a while she said, 'When I got into this thing with Paula, I didn't realise that the owner of a business has to work harder than the employees.'

'Was the gallery busy today?' Colin asked.

'We had more people in and out of there than you'd find in a bus station. This time of year you expect a lot of browsers, tourists who don't really intend to buy anything. They figure that because they're vacationing in Santa Leona they're entitled to a few free hours of each shopkeeper's time.'

'Sell many paintings?' Colin asked.

'Surprisingly, we sold quite a few. In fact, it's the best day on record.'

'That's great.'

'Of course, it's just one day. Considering what Paula and I paid for the gallery, we have to have a lot more days like this if we're going to keep our heads above water.'

Colin couldn't think of anything more to say.

She sipped her martini. Her throat rippled slightly when she swallowed. She looked so dainty and graceful.

'Skipper, can you make your own supper this evening?'

'Aren't you eating at home?' he asked.

'The shop's still very busy. I can't leave Paula alone this evening. I just came home to freshen up. Much as I dread the thought of it, I'll be going back to the grind in twenty minutes.'

'You've only been home for supper once in the past week,' he said.

'I know, Skipper, and I'm sorry about that. But I'm trying hard to build a future for us, for me *and* you. You understand that, don't you?'

'I guess so.'

'It's a tough world, baby.'

'I'm not hungry anyway,' Colin said. 'I can wait until you get home after the gallery closes.'

41

'Well, baby, I won't be coming straight home. Mark Thornberg asked me to share a late dinner with him.'

'Who's Mark Thornberg?'

'An artist,' she said. 'We opened a show of his work yesterday. In fact, about a third of what we're selling is his stuff. I want to persuade him to let us be his sole representatives.'

'Where's he taking you to dinner?'

'We're going to Little Italy, I think.'

'Boy, that's a neat place!' Colin said, leaning forward on the sofa. 'Can I come? I won't be any bother. You wouldn't even have to stop back here to pick me up. I can ride my bike and meet you there.'

She frowned and avoided his eyes. 'Sorry, Skipper. This is strictly for grown-ups. We'll be talking a lot of business.'

'I won't mind.'

'Perhaps not, but we would. Listen, why don't you go to Charlie's Cafe and have one of those big cheeseburgers you like so much? And one of those extra-thick milkshakes that you have to eat with a spoon.'

He settled back against the sofa as if he were a balloon that had rapidly deflated.

'Don't pout,' she said. 'It doesn't become you. Pouting's for little babies.'

'I'm not pouting,' he said. 'It's OK.'

'Charlie's Cafe?' she prompted.

'I guess so. Sure.'

She finished her martini and picked up her handbag. 'I'll give you some money.'

'I've got money.'

'So I'll give you some more. I'm now a successful businesswoman. I can afford it.'

She brought him a five-dollar bill, and he said, 'It's too much.'

'Blow the rest of it on comic books.'

She bent down, kissed his forehead, and left to freshen up and change clothes.

For several minutes he sat in silence, staring at the five-dollar bill. At last he sighed and stood and took out his wallet and put the money away.

6

Mr and Mrs Borden gave Roy permission to have
supper with Colin. The boys ate at the counter at
Charlie's Cafe, basking in the incomparably wonderful aroma of bubbling grease and onions.
Colin paid the check.

From the diner they went to the Pinball Pit, an
amusement arcade that was one of the chief
gathering places for young people in Santa Leona.
It was a Friday night, and the Pit was crowded
with kids feeding coins to pinball machines and a
wide variety of electronic games.

Half the customers knew Roy. They called to
him, and he called back. 'Ho, Roy!' 'Ho, Pete!' 'Hi
there, Roy!' 'What ya say, Walt?' 'Roy!' 'Roy!'
'Here, Roy!' They wanted to challenge him to
games or tell him jokes or just talk. He stopped
here and there for a minute or two at a time, but
he didn't want to play with anyone but Colin.

They competed in a two-player pinball game
that was decorated with paintings of big-breasted,
long-legged girls in skimpy bikinis. Roy chose
that machine rather than one with pirates, monsters, or spacemen; and Colin tried not to blush.

Colin usually disliked cheap thrill palaces like
the Pit and avoided them. The few times he'd
ever ventured into one, he'd found the din un-
bearable. The sounds of computer scorekeepers

45

and robot adversaries – *beep-beep-beep, pong-pong-pong, bomp-bompada-bomp, whoop-whoop-whoooooooooop* – mixed with laughter and girls' happy screams and half-shouted conversations. Assaulted by continuous, thunderous noise, he became claustrophobic. He always felt like an alien, a being from a distant world, trapped on a primitive planet, caught in a mob of hostile, screeching, gibbering, barbaric, loathsome natives.

But he didn't feel that way tonight. He was enjoying every minute, and he knew why. Because of Roy, he was no longer a frightened visitor from space; he was now one of the natives.

With his thick yellow hair, blue eyes, muscles, and quiet self-confidence, Roy drew the girls. Three of them – Kathy, Laurie, and Janet – gathered around to watch the game. They were all better than average-looking: taut, tan, vital teenage girls in halter tops and shorts, with shiny hair and California complexions and budding breasts and slender legs.

Roy clearly favored Laurie, while Kathy and Janet showed more than passing interest in Colin. He didn't think they were attracted to him for himself. In fact, he was certain they were not. He had no illusions. Before girls like them swooned over boys like him, the sun would rise in the west, tiny babies would grow beards, and an honest man would be elected President. They were flirting with him because he was Roy's friend, or because they were jealous of Laurie and wanted to make Roy jealous of them. Whatever their reasons, they were concentrating on Colin, asking questions, drawing him out, laughing at his jokes, cheering when he won a game. Until now, girls had never wasted time with him. He really didn't care what their motives were; he just reveled in all the attention and prayed it would never end. He knew he was blushing brightly, but the arcade's odd orange lighting provided him with cover.

Forty minutes after entering the Pit, they left to a chorus of good-byes: 'So long, Roy; take it easy, Roy; see ya around, Roy.' Roy seemed to want to be rid of all of them, including Kathy, Laurie, and Janet. Colin went reluctantly.

Outside, the evening air was mild. A light breeze carried the faint scent of the sea.

Complete darkness had not yet descended. Santa Leona lay in a smoky yellow twilight similar to that which Roy had created earlier in the day for the miniature world in the Borden garage.

Their bicycles were chained to a rack in the parking lot behind the Pit.

As he bent and unlocked his bike, Roy said, 'You like the Pit?'

'Yeah.'

'I thought you would.'

'You spend much time there?' Colin asked.

'Nah. Not much.'

'I thought you were a regular.'

Roy stood and pulled his bike from between the pipes. 'I hardly ever go.'

'Everybody knew you.'

'I know the kids who *are* regulars. But not me. I'm not a fan of games. At least not games as easy as the ones in the Pit.'

Colin finished unchaining his bicycle. 'If you don't like it, why'd we come?'

'I knew you'd enjoy it,' Roy said.

Colin frowned. 'But I don't want to do things that bore you.'

'I wasn't bored,' Roy said. 'I didn't mind playing a game or three. And I sure didn't mind having a chance to look at Laurie. She has a terrific little body, doesn't she?'

'I guess so.'

'You *guess*!'

'Well, sure . . . she has a nice body.'

'I'd like to settle down between her pretty legs for a few months.'

'You seemed anxious to get away from her.'

'After about fifteen minutes I get sick of talking to her,' Roy said.

'Then how could you stand her for a few months?'

'We wouldn't talk,' Roy said, grinning wickedly.

'Oh.'

'Kathy, Janet, Laurie . . . all those girls are just teasers.'

'What do you mean?'

'They never put out.'

'Put out what?'

'Ass, for Christ's sake! They never put out any ass, not ever, not for anyone.'

'Oh.'

'Laurie shakes it at me, but if I actually put a hand on her tits, she'd scream so loud the roof would fall in.'

Colin was blushing and sweating. 'Well, after all, she's only fourteen, isn't she?'

'Plenty old enough.'

Colin wasn't pleased with the direction the conversation had taken. He tried to get it back on course. 'Anyway, what I wanted to say was, from now on let's not do anything that bores you.'

Roy put a hand on his shoulder and squeezed gently. 'Listen, Colin, am I your friend or not?'

'Sure you are.'

'A good friend should be willing to keep you company even when you're doing things that you enjoy but maybe he doesn't care so much about. I mean, I can't expect to always do exactly what *I* like, and I can't expect that you and I will always want to do the same things.'

'We like the same things,' Colin said. 'We have the same interests.' He was afraid Roy would suddenly realise how different they were and would walk away, never to be seen again.

'You love horror films,' Roy said. 'I don't have any interest in that stuff.'

'Well, aside from that one thing—'

'We've got other differences. But the point is, if you're my buddy, you'll do things with me that *I* want to do but that *you* don't like at all. So it works both ways.'

'No, it doesn't,' Colin said, 'because I happen to like doing everything you suggest.'

'So far,' Roy said. 'But there'll come a time when you won't want to do something that's important to me, but you *will* do it because we're friends.'

'I can't imagine what,' Colin said.

'Just wait,' Roy said. 'You'll see. Sooner or later, good buddy, the time will come.'

The scarlet light of the Pit's neon sign was refracted in Roy's eyes, giving them a strange and somewhat frightening aspect. Colin thought they resembled a movie vampire's eyes: glassy, red, violet, two windows on a soul that had been corrupted by the repeated satisfaction of un-natural desires. (But then again, Colin thought the same thing every time he saw Mr Arkin's eyes, and Mr Arkin was just the man who owned

49

the corner grocery store; the closest thing Mr Arkin had to an unnatural desire was a taste for liquor, and his red eyes were nothing more than the most obvious sign of a nearly continuous hangover.)

'Just the same,' Colin said to Roy, 'I hate the idea that I'm boring you with—'

'I wasn't bored! Will you relax? I don't mind going to the Pit if that's what you want. Just remember what I said about those girls. They'll hang on you a little bit. Now and then they'll "accidentally" run their tight little asses against you or maybe "accidentally" rub their boobs against your arm. But you'll never have any real fun with them. Their idea of a big, big night is to sneak out to the parking lot, hide in the shadows, and steal kisses.'

That was also Colin's idea of a big, big night. In fact, it was his idea of heaven on earth, but he didn't tell Roy.

They walked their bicycles across the lot to the alley.

Before Roy could climb on his bike and pedal away, Colin got up the nerve to say: 'Why me?'

'Huh?'

'Why do you want to be friends with me?'

'Why shouldn't I be friends with you?'

'I mean with a nobody like me.'

'Who said you're a nobody?'

'I did.'

'What kind of a thing is that to say about yourself?'

'Anyway, I've been wondering for a month.'

'Wondering what? You aren't making sense.'

'I've been wondering why you want to be friends with someone like me?'

50

'What do you mean. What makes you different? You got leprosy or something?'

Colin wished he had never brought up the subject, but now that he had done so, he stumbled ahead with it. 'Well, you know, someone who's not normally very popular and, you know, not good at sports, you know, not really good at much of anything and . . . well, you know.'

'Stop saying, "you know," ' Roy said. 'I hate that. One of the reasons I want to be friends with you is that you can *talk*. Most kids around here chatter away all day and never use more than twenty words. Two of which are "you know." But you actually have a decent vocabulary. It's refreshing.'

Colin blinked. 'You want to be friends because of my vocabulary?'

'I want to be friends because you're as smart as I am. Most kids bore me.'

'But you could pal around with any guy in town, any guy your age, even some a year or two older than you. Most of those guys in the Pit—'

'They're assholes.'

'Be serious. They're some of the most popular guys in town.'

'Assholes, I tell you.'

'Not all of them.'

'Believe me, Colin, *all* of them. Half of them can't figure any way to have a good time except to smoke dope or pop pills or get stinking drunk and vomit all over themselves. The rest of them want to be either John Travolta or Donny Osmond. *Yech!*'

'But they like you.'

'Everyone likes me,' Roy said. 'I make sure of that.'

'I sure wish I knew how to make everyone like me.'

'It's easy. You just have to know how to manipulate them.'

'OK. How?'

'Stick around me long enough, and you'll learn.'

Instead of riding away from the Pit, they walked down the alley, side by side, pushing their bikes. They both knew there was more to be said.

They passed an oleander hedge. The flowers looked slightly phosphorescent in the growing gloom, and Colin took a deep whiff of them.

Oleander berries contained one of the deadliest substances known to man. Colin had seen an old movie in which a lunatic had murdered a dozen people with a poison extracted from the plant. He couldn't remember the title. It had been a really dumb film, even worse than *Godzilla Versus King Kong*, which meant it was one of the all-time most terrible works in cinematic history.

After they had gone nearly a block, Colin said, 'You ever used dope?'

'Once,' Roy said.

'What was it?'

'Hash. Through a waterpipe.'

'You like it?'

'Once was enough. What about you?'

'No,' Colin said. 'Drugs scare me.'

'You know why?'

'You can get killed.'

'Dying doesn't scare you.'

'It's doesn't?'

'Not much.'

'Dying scares me a lot.'

'No,' Roy insisted. 'You're like me, exactly like me. Drugs scare you because if you used them you wouldn't be in control. You can't bear the idea of losing control of yourself.'

'Well, sure, that's part of it.'

Roy lowered his voice, as if he was afraid someone would overhear, and he spoke rapidly, running the words together in his eagerness to get them out. 'You've got to stay sharp, on your toes, alert. Always look over your shoulder. Always protect yourself. Don't let your guard down for even a second. There are people who will take advantage of you the moment they see you're not in complete control. The world's filled with people like that. Nearly everyone you meet is like that. We're animals in a jungle, and we've got to be prepared to fight if we want to survive.' Roy walked his bike with his head thrust forward, shoulders hunched, muscles corded in his neck, as if he expected someone to strike him hard on the back of the head. Even in the fast-dwindling, purple-amber light of late evening, the sudden sprinkle of sweat on his forehead and upper lip was visible; darkly glistening jewels. 'You can't trust hardly anyone, hardly anyone at all. Even people who're supposed to like you can turn on you faster than you think. Even friends. People who say they love you are the worst, the most dangerous, the most untrustworthy of all.' He was breathing harder, talking faster by the moment. 'People who say they love you will pounce when they get the chance. You gotta always remember that they're just waiting for the opportunity to get you. Love's a trick. A cover. A way to catch you off guard. Never let down your guard. Never.' He glanced at Colin, and his eyes were wild.

53

'Do you think I'd turn on you, tell lies about you, snitch on you to your parents, things like that?'

'Would you?' Roy asked.

'Of course not.'

'Not even if your own neck was in the wringer, too, and the only way you could save yourself was to snitch on me?'

'Not even then.'

'What if I broke some law, some really serious law, and the cops were after me and came to you with a lot of questions?'

'I wouldn't snitch on you.'

'I hope you wouldn't.'

'You can trust me.'

'I hope so. I really hope so.'

'You don't have to hope. You should *know*.'

'I gotta be careful.'

'Should I be careful of you?'

Roy said nothing.

'Should I be careful of you?' Colin asked again.

'Maybe. Yeah, maybe you should. When I said we were all just animals, just a bunch of selfish animals, I meant me, too.'

There was such a haunted look in Roy's eyes, such a knowledge of pain that Colin had to look away.

He didn't know what had sparked Roy's diatribe, but he didn't want to pursue the subject. He was worried that it would lead to an argument and that Roy would never want to see him again; and he desperately wanted to be friends with Roy for the rest of their lives. If he blew apart this relationship, he would never get another chance to be best buddies with anyone as terrific as Roy.

He was positive of that. If he spoiled this, he would have to go back to being a loner; and now that he had experienced acceptance, companionship, and involvement, he didn't think he *could* go back.

For a while they walked in silence. They crossed a busy side street under a canopy of oak trees and entered another block of the alleyway.

Gradually the extraordinary tension that had given Roy the appearance of an angry snake began to seep out of him, much to Colin's relief. Roy lifted his head and let his shoulders down and stopped breathing like a horse at the end of an eight-furlong race.

Colin knew a bit about race horses. His father had taken him to the track half a dozen times, expecting him to be impressed with the amount of money wagered and with the sweaty manliness of the sport. Instead, Colin had been delighted by the grace of the horses and had spoken of them as if they were dancers. His father hadn't liked that and had thereafter gone to the races alone.

He and Roy reached another corner, turned left, out of the alley, and pushed their bicycles along an ivy-framed sidewalk.

Look-alike stucco houses lay on both sides of the street, sheltering under a variety of palm trees, skirted by oleander and jade plants and dracaena and schefflera and roses and cacti and holly and ferns and poinsettia bushes – ugly houses made elegant by California's lush natural beauty.

Finally Roy spoke. 'Colin, you remember what I said about how a guy sometimes has to do things his buddy wants to do even if he himself maybe really doesn't like it?'

'I remember.'

'That's one of the true tests of friendship. Don't you agree?'

'I guess so.'

'For Christ's sake, can't you at least once in a while have a firm opinion about something? You never say a flat yes or no. You're always "guessing." '

Stung, Colin said, 'All right. I think it's a true test of friendship. I agree with you.'

'Well, what if I said I wanted to kill something just for fun and I wanted you to help me.'

'You mean like a cat?'

'I've already killed a cat.'

'Yeah. It was in all the newspapers.'

'I *did*. In a cage. Like I said.'

'I just can't believe it.'

'Why would I lie?'

'OK, OK,' Colin said. 'Let's not go through the whole argument again. Let's pretend I swallowed your story – hook line, and sinker. You killed a cat in a birdcage. So what next – a dog?'

'If I wanted to kill a dog, would you help?'

'Why would you want to?'

'It might be a popper.'

'Jeez.'

'Would you help kill it?'

'Where would you get the dog? You think the humane society gives them out to people who want to torture them?'

'I'd just steal the first pooch I saw,' Roy said.

'Someone's pet?'

'Sure.'

'How would you kill it?'

'Shoot it. Blow its head off.'

'And the neighbors wouldn't hear?'

'We'd take it out in the hills first.'

'You expect it to just pose and smile while we plug it?'

'We'd tie it up and shoot it a dozen times.'

'Where do you expect to get the gun?'

'What about your mother?' Roy asked.

'You think my mother sells illegal guns out of the kitchen or something?'

'Doesn't she have a gun of her own?'

'Sure. A million of 'em. And a tank and a bazooka and a nuclear missile.'

'Just answer the question.'

'Why would she have a gun?'

'A sexy woman living alone usually has a gun for protection.'

'But she doesn't live alone,' Colin said. 'Did you forget about me?'

'If some crazy rapist wanted to get his hands on your mom, he'd walk right over you.'

'I'm tougher than I look.'

'Be serious. Does your mother have a gun?'

Colin didn't want to admit there was a gun in the house. He had a hunch that he would save himself a lot of trouble if he lied. But at last he said, 'Yeah. She has a pistol.'

'You're sure?'

'Yeah. But I don't think she keeps it loaded. She could never shoot anyone. My father loves guns; *ergo*, my mother hates them. And so do I. I'm not going to borrow her gun to do something crazy like shooting your neighbors' dog.'

'Well, we could kill it some other way.'

'What would we do – bite it?'

A night bird sang in the branches above them.

The sea breeze was cooler than it had been ten minutes ago.

Colin was tired of pushing the bike, but he sensed that Roy still had a lot to say and wanted to say it quietly, which he couldn't do if they were riding.

Roy said, 'We could tie the dog up and kill it with a pitchfork.'

'Jeez.'

'*That* would be a popper!'

'You're making me sick.'

'Would you help me?'

'You don't need my help.'

'But it would prove you're not just a fair-weather friend.'

After a long while Colin said, 'I suppose if it was really important to you, if you just had to do it or die, I could be there when you did it.'

'What do you mean by "be there"?'

'I mean . . . I guess I could watch.'

'What if I wanted you to do more than watch?'

'Like what?'

'What if I wanted you to take the pitchfork and stab the dog a few times yourself?'

'Sometimes you can be really weird, Roy.'

'Could you stab it?' Roy persisted.

'No.'

'I'll bet you could.'

'I couldn't ever kill anything.'

'But you could watch?'

'Well, if it would prove to you once and for all that I'm your friend and that I can be trusted . . .'

They entered the circle of light under a street lamp, and Roy stopped. He was grinning. 'You're getting better every day.'

'Oh?'

'You're developing nicely,' Roy said.

'Am I?'

'Yesterday, you'd have said you couldn't even watch a dog being killed. Today, you say you could watch but you couldn't participate. Tomorrow or the day after tomorrow, you'll tell me you could find it within yourself to pick up that pitchfork and make mincemeat of that damned dog.'

'No. Never.'

'And a week from now, you'll finally admit that you'd *enjoy* killing something.'

'No. You're wrong. This is stupid.'

'I'm right. You're just like me.'

'And you're no killer.'

'I am.'

'Not in a million years.'

'You don't know me.'

'You're Roy Borden.'

'I mean what's inside me. You don't know, but you'll learn.'

'There's no cat-and-dog killer inside you.'

'I've killed things bigger than a cat.'

'Like what?'

'Like people.'

'And then I suppose you moved on to even bigger things – like elephants.'

'No elephants. Just people.'

'I guess with an elephant there's problems disposing of the corpse.'

'Just people.'

Another night bird cried hollowly from its perch in a nearby tree, and in the distance two lonely dogs howled to each other.

'This is ridiculous,' Colin said.

'No, it's true.'

'You're trying to tell me you've *killed* people?'

'Twice.'

'Why not a hundred times?'

'Because it was only twice.'

'Next you'll be saying you're really an eight-legged, six-eyed creature from Mars disguised as a human being.'

'I was born in Santa Leona,' Roy said soberly. 'We've always lived here, all my life. I've never been to Mars.'

'Roy, this is getting boring.'

'Oh, it'll be anything *but* boring. Before the summer's through, you and me together, we're going to kill someone.'

Colin pretended to think about it. 'The President of the United States maybe?'

'Just someone here in Santa Leona. It'll be a real popper.'

'Roy, you might as well give up. I don't believe a word of this, and I'm never going to believe it.'

'You will. Eventually you will.'

'No. It's just a fairy tale, a game, a test of some sort that you're putting me through. And I wish you'd tell me what I'm being tested *for*.'

Roy said nothing.

'Well, so far as I can see,' Colin said, 'I've passed the test, whatever it is. I've proven to you that I can't be fooled. I won't fall for this dumb story of yours. You understand?'

Roy smiled and nodded. He glanced at his watch. 'Hey, what do you want to do now? Want to go to the Fairmont and see a movie?'

Colin was disconcerted by the sudden change of subject and Roy's abruptly transformed attitude. 'What's the Fairmont?'

'The Fairmont Drive-in, of course. If we ride

way the hell out on Ranch Road and then double back through the hills, we'll come out on the slope above the Fairmont. We can sit up there and watch the movie for nothing.'

'But can you hear it?'

'No, but you don't need to hear the kind of movies they play at the Fairmont.'

'What the hell do they play – silent films?'

Roy was amazed. 'You mean you've lived here a whole month and you don't know what the Fairmont is?'

'You're making me feel retarded.'

'You really don't *know*?'

'You said it was a drive-in.'

'It's more than that,' Roy said. 'Boy, are you in for a surprise!'

'I don't like surprises.'

'Come on. Let's go.'

Roy climbed onto his bike and pedaled away. Colin followed, off the sidewalk and into the street, from lamp-post to lamp-post, through alternating patches of shadow and light, pumping his legs hard to keep up.

When they reached Ranch Road and headed southeast, away from town, there were no more street lamps, and they switched on their headlights. The last traces of the sun had disappeared from the westward edges of the high-flying clouds: Night had arrived. Chains of gentle, treeless, pitchblack hills rose on both sides, silhouetted against a gray-black sky. Now and then a car passed them, but most of the time they had the road to themselves.

Colin was not on good terms with darkness. He had never lost his childish fear of being alone at night, a weakness that sometimes dismayed his mother and never failed to infuriate his father. He always slept with a light on. And right now he stayed close to Roy, genuinely afraid that if he fell behind he would be in extreme danger; something hideous, something unhuman, something hiding in the impenetrable shadows of the roadside would reach out for him, seize him in ghastly claws as big as sickles, tear him from his seat, and devour him alive with a noisy crunching of bones and splattering of blood. Or worse. He was a devoted fan of horror movies and novels, not because they dealt with colorful myths and were crammed full of movement and excitement, but because to his way of thinking, they explored a sobering reality that most adults refused to take seriously. Werewolves, vampires, zombies, decaying corpses that would not rest peacefully in their coffins, and a hundred other hellish creatures *did* exist. Intellectually he could dismiss them as mere beasts of fantasy, denizens of the imagination, but in his heart he knew the truth. They were out there. The undead. Lurking. Waiting. Concealed. Hungry. The night was a vast, dank cellar, home to that which crept and crawled and slithered. The night had ears and eyes. It had a horrible, scratchy old voice. If you listened closely, tuning out your doubt and keeping an open mind, you could hear the dreadful voice of the night. It whispered about graves and rotting flesh and demons and ghosts and swamp monsters. It spoke of unspeakable things.

I have absolutely got to stop this, he told himself. Why do I do this to myself all the time? Jeez.

He rose slightly from the bicycle seat to gain

better leverage and jammed his thin legs down hard on the pedals, determined to stay close to Roy.

His arms had broken out in gooseflesh.

7

From Ranch Road they turned onto a dirt track that was barely visible in the moonlight. Roy led the way. Over the crown of the first hill, the track became a narrow footpath. A quarter of a mile farther on, the footpath turned north, and they continued west, pushing their bicycles through coarse grass and sandy soil.

Less than a minute after they left the path, Roy's bike light went out.

Colin stopped at once, heart leaping wildly like a startled rabbit in a cage. 'Roy? Where are you? What's wrong? What's happened, Roy?'

Roy walked out of the darkness, into the pale fan of light that spread in front of Colin's bicycle. 'We've got two more hills to cross before we reach the drive-in. No sense struggling with the bikes any further than this. We'll leave them here and pick them up on the way back.'

'What if somebody steals them?'

'Who?'

'How should I know? But what if somebody does?'

'An international ring of bicycle thieves with undercover operatives in every town?' Roy shook his head, making no effort to conceal his exasperation. 'You worry about more goddamned things than anyone I've ever known.'

'If somebody stole them, we'd have to walk all the way home – five or six miles, maybe more.'

'For Christ's sake, Colin, no one even knows the bikes are here! No one's going to see them, let alone steal them.'

'Well, what if we come back and can't find them in the dark?' Colin asked.

Roy grimaced, and he looked not just disgusted but demonic. It was a trick of light; the head-lamp's glow illuminated only the sharp edges of his features, leaving most of his face in darkness, so that he looked distorted, less than human.

'I know this place,' Roy said impatiently. 'I come here all the time. Trust me. Now will you come on? We're missing the movie.'

He turned and walked away.

Colin hesitated until he realised that if he didn't leave the bike, Roy would leave him. He didn't want to be alone in the middle of nowhere. He put the bike on its side and switched off the lamp.

The darkness enfolded him. He was suddenly acutely aware of a thousand eerie songs: the incessant croaking of toads. Just toads? Perhaps something much more dangerous than that. The many strange voices of the night rose in a screeching chorus.

Fear washed through him like bile spreading from a pierced gut. The muscles in his throat grew tight. He had difficulty swallowing. If Roy had spoken to him, he could not have replied. In spite of the cool breeze, he began to sweat.

You're no longer a child, he told himself. Don't act like a baby.

He desperately wanted to bend down and switch on the bike light again, but he didn't want Roy to discover that he was afraid of the dark. He wanted to be like Roy, and Roy wasn't afraid of anything.

Fortunately Colin was not entirely blind. The bike light was not terribly powerful, and his eyes adapted quickly to a world without it. Milky moonlight spilled across the rolling land. He could see Roy loping swiftly up the hillside ahead.

Colin tried to move; he couldn't. His legs seemed to weigh a thousand pounds each.

Something hissed.

Colin tilted his head. Listened.

The hissing again. Louder. Closer.

Something rustled through the grass a few inches from his foot, and Colin bolted. It might have been only a harmless toad, but it gave him the motivation he needed to get moving.

He caught up with Roy, and a few minutes later they reached the slope behind and above the Fairmont. They descended halfway down the hill and sat on the ground, side by side in the dark.

Below them, the parked cars in the bowl of the drive-in pointed westward. The movie screen faced them, and beyond lay the main highway to Santa Leona.

On the giant screen a man and a woman were walking on a beach at sunset. Although there was no speaker on the hillside and therefore no sound, Colin could see from the close-ups that the actors were talking animatedly, and he wished he could read lips.

After a while Colin said, 'I'm beginning to think this was a dumb idea – coming all the way out here to see a movie we can't even hear.'

'You don't need to hear this one,' Roy said.

'If we can't hear it, how can we follow the plot?'

'People don't go to the Fairmont for plot. All they want to see here is tits and ass.'

Colin gaped at Roy. 'What are you talking about?'

'The Fairmont's got a good location. No houses nearby. You can't see the screen from the highway. So they play soft-core porn.'

'They play what?' Colin asked.

'Soft-core porn. Don't you know what that is?'

'No.'

'You got a lot to learn, good buddy. Fortunately, you have a good teacher. Namely, me. It's pornography. Dirty movies.'

'Y-you mean we're going to see people . . . *doing it*?'

Roy grinned. His teeth and eyes caught the moonlight. 'That's what we'd see if this was hardcore,' Roy said. 'But it's only soft stuff.'

'Oh,' Colin said. He didn't have the slightest idea what Roy meant.

'So all we get to see,' Roy explained, 'is naked people *pretending* to do it.'

'They're . . . really naked?'

'Sure.'

'Not completely naked.'

'Completely.'

'Not the girls.'

'Especially the girls,' Roy said. 'Pay attention to the movie, dummy.'

Colin looked at the screen, afraid of what he might see.

The couple on the beach was kissing. Then the man stepped back, and the woman smiled, and she caressed herself, teasing him, and then she reached behind her back and unhooked the bikini top she was wearing and let it slide slowly down her arms, and suddenly her bare breasts bobbled into view, large and firm and upswept, jiggling deliciously, and the man touched them—

'Yeah, get her. Get her good,' Roy said.

— and the man stroked the breasts, squeezed them, and the woman closed her eyes and seemed to be sighing, and the man gently thumbed the swollen nipples.

Colin had never been so embarrassed in his life.

'What a set she's got,' Roy said enthusiastically.

Colin wished he were somewhere else. Anywhere else. Even back with the bicycles, in the dark, alone.

'Doesn't she have a terrific set?'

Colin wanted to crawl into a hole and hide.

'You like that set?'

Colin couldn't speak.

'Like to suck on those?'

He wished Roy would shut up.

On the screen, the man bent down and sucked on the woman's breasts.

'Like to smother yourself in those?'

Although the movie both shocked and embarrassed Colin, he couldn't look away from it.

'Colin? Hey, Colin!'

'Huh?'

'What do you think?'

'Of what?'

'Her set.'

On the screen the man and the woman were running up the beach toward a grassy spot where they could lie down. Her breasts bounced and swung.

'Colin? You forget how to talk?'

'Why do you want to talk about it?'

'It's more fun if we do. We don't have any

69

sound up here, so we can't hear *them* talking about it.'

The couple had stretched out on the grass, and the man was kissing her breasts again.

'You like her knockers?'

'Jesus, Roy.'

'Do you?'

'I guess.'

'You *guess*?'

'Well, sure. They're nice.'

'What kind of guy wouldn't like that set?'

Colin didn't respond.

'Maybe a queer wouldn't like them,' Roy said.

'I like them.' Colin said thinly.

'What do you like?'

'Did you forget what we're talking about?'

'I want to hear you say it.'

'I said it already. I like them.'

'What do you like?' Roy persisted.

On the screen: erect nipples.

'What's wrong with you?' Colin said.

'Nothing's wrong with *me*.'

'You're weird, Roy.'

'*You're* the one who's afraid to say it.'

'Say what?'

'What do you call them?'

'Jeez.'

'What do you call them?'

'OK, OK. If it'll make you shut up, I'll say it.'

'So say it.'

'I like her set,' Colin said. 'There. Happy now?'

Colin was blushing like crazy. He was glad it was dark.

'Give me another word,' Roy said.

'Huh?'

'Something besides "set." '

'Will you buzz off?'

On the screen: breasts wet with saliva.

Roy put a hand on his arm and squeezed, hurting him a little. 'Another word.'

'*You* say it. You seem to know all the words.'

'And you've got to learn them.'

'What's such a big deal about talking dirty?'

'Is little Colin afraid his mommy will hear him and wash out his mouth with soap?'

'Don't be absurd,' Colin said, struggling to hold on to his dignity.

'So if you aren't afraid of Mommy, give me another word. Look up there at that screen and tell me what you see that you like.'

Colin nervously cleared his throat. 'Well . . . I like her breasts.'

'Breasts? Jesus, Colin! Breasts are what you find on a chicken!'

'Well, a woman's are called that, too,' Colin said defensively.

'By doctors maybe.'

'By everyone.'

Roy tightened his grip on Colin's arm, dug his sharp fingernails into the flesh.

'Damnit, let go!' Colin said. 'You're hurting me.'

He tried to pull away but couldn't free himself. Roy was very strong.

Roy's face was only partly visible in the frosty moonlight, but Colin didn't like what little he was able to see. The eyes were wide, piercing, fevered; Colin imagined he could feel heat radiating from them. Roy's lips were drawn back in a mirthless grin, as if he were going to snarl like an attack dog.

Because of something extraordinary in those

eyes, something eerie and powerful but indefinable, and because of the intensity with which the other boy spoke. Colin realised that this bizarre conversation held tremendous importance for Roy. He was not just teasing Colin; he was challenging him. This was a battle of wills, and in some way that Colin could not grasp, the outcome would determine their future together. He also sensed, without truly understanding why, that if he didn't win this contest he would live to regret it with all his heart.

Roy squeezed harder.

Colin said, 'Ahhhh, Jeez. Please let go.'

'Give me another word.'

'What's the point?'

'Give me another word.'

'Roy, you're hurting me.'

'Give me another word and I'll let go.'

'I thought you were my friend.'

'I'm the best friend you'll ever have.'

'If you were my friend you wouldn't hurt me,' Colin said between clenched teeth.

'If you were *my* friend, you'd say the word. What the hell does it cost you to say it?'

'And what does it cost you if I don't say it?'

'I thought you said I could trust you, that you'd do anything I wanted, like a friend should do. Now you won't even talk with me about this lousy movie.'

'OK, OK,' Colin said. And he actually felt a little guilty because it *was* such a small thing that Roy wanted from him.

'Say "tits" for me.'

'Tits,' Colin said thickly.

'Say "knockers" for me.'

'Knockers.'

'Say "boobs." '

'Boobs.'

'Tell me you like her tits.'

'I like her tits.'

Roy let go. 'Was that so difficult?'

Colin gingerly massaged his arm.

'Hey,' Roy said, 'wouldn't you like to wear her tits for earmuffs?'

'You're gross.'

Roy laughed. 'Thank you.'

'I think you drew blood.'

'Don't be a baby. I just squeezed a little. Wow! Look at the screen!'

The man had pulled off the bottom half of the girl's bikini. He was caressing her bare buttocks, which were very white against her tan back and thighs, so white that they looked like the plump halves of a pale nut surrounded by soft brown shell.

'I could eat ten pounds of that ass for breakfast,' Roy said.

The man on the screen was naked, too. He stretched out on his back, and the girl straddled him.

'They won't show us the good part,' Roy said. 'Not at the Fairmont. They won't show her getting it.'

The camera concentrated on her bouncing breasts and on her gorgeous face, which was contorted with feigned ecstasy.

'Does that make you stiff?' Roy asked.

'Huh?'

'Does it give you a hard-on?'

'You're weird.'

'You afraid of that word, too?'

'I'm not afraid of any words.'

'So say it.'

'Jeez.'

'Say it.'

'Hard-on.'

'You got one?'

Colin was almost sick with embarrassment.

'You got a hard-on, good buddy?'

'Yeah.'

'Know what it's called?'

'Marvin.'

Roy laughed. 'That's funny. Real quick. I like that.'

The other boy's approval was a palliative. Colin's fear subsided just a bit.

'Do you really know what it's called?' Roy asked.

'A penis.'

'That's as bad as "breast." '

Colin said nothing.

'Say "cock" for me.'

Colin said it.

'Very good,' Roy said. 'Excellent. Before this movie's over, you'll know all the words, and you'll feel comfortable with them just like I do. Stick with me, kid, and I'll bring you up right. Hey, look! Look what he's doing to her now! Look, Colin! What a popper! Look!'

Colin felt as if he were on a skateboard, rocketing down a long, steep hill, totally out of control. But he looked.

8

They got back to Santa Leona at ten forty-five and stopped at a service station on Broadway. The place was closed for the night; the only light was in the soft-drink machine.

Roy fished in his pocket for change. 'What do you want? I'm buying.'

'I have some money,' Colin said.

'You bought supper.'

'Well . . . OK. I'll have grape.'

They were silent for a while, chugging their drinks.

Finally Roy said, 'This is a great night, isn't it?'

'Yeah.'

'You having fun?'

'Sure.'

'I'm having one hell of a good time, and you know why?'

'Why?'

'Because you're here,' Roy said.

'Yeah,' Colin said, heavy on the self-deprecation, 'I'm always the life of the party.'

'I mean it,' Roy said. 'A guy couldn't ask for a better friend than you.'

This time, the cause of Colin's blush was as much pride as embarrassment.

'In fact,' Roy said, 'you're the only friend I have, and the only friend I need.'

'You've got hundreds of friends.'

'They're just acquaintances. There's a big difference between friends and acquaintances. Until you moved to town, I'd been a long time between friends.'

Colin didn't know if Roy was telling the truth or making fun of him. He had no experience by which to judge, for no one else had ever talked to him as Roy had just done.

Roy put down his half-finished bottle of cola and took a penknife out of his pocket. 'I think it's time for this.'

'For what?'

Standing in the soft light from the soda machine, Roy opened the knife, put the sharp point against the meaty part of his palm, and pressed hard enough to draw blood: a single thick drop like a crimson pearl. He squeezed the tiny wound until more blood oozed from it and trickled down his hand.

Colin was aghast. 'Why'd you do that?'

'Hold out your hand.'

'Are you crazy?'

'We'll do it just like the Indians.'

'Do what?'

'We'll be blood brothers.'

'We're already friends.'

'Being blood brothers is a whole lot better.'

'Oh yeah? Why?'

'When our blood has mingled, we'll be like one person. In the future, any friends I make will automatically become your friends. And your friends will be mine. We'll always stand together, never apart. The enemies of one will be the enemies of the other, so we'll be twice as strong and twice as smart as anyone else. We'll never

76

fight alone. It'll be you and me against the whole damned world. And the world better look out.'

'All of that just because of a bloody handshake?' Colin asked.

'The important thing is what the handshake symbolises. It stands for friendship and love and trust.'

Colin was unable to take his eyes from the scarlet thread that crossed Roy's palm and wrist.

'Give me your hand,' Roy said.

Colin was excited about being blood brothers with Roy, but he was also squeamish. 'That knife doesn't look clean.'

'It is.'

'You can get blood poisoning from a dirty cut.'

'If there was any chance of that, would I have cut myself first?'

Colin hesitated.

'For Christ's sake,' Roy said, 'the hole won't be any bigger than a pinprick. Now give me your hand.'

Reluctantly Colin held out his right hand, palm up. He was trembling.

Roy grasped him firmly and put the point of the blade to his skin.

'It'll just sting for a second,' Roy assured him.

Colin didn't dare speak for fear his voice would quaver badly.

The pain was sudden, sharp, but not long-lasting. Colin bit his lip, determined not to cry out.

Roy folded the knife and put it away.

With shaky fingers Colin pressed the wound until it was bleeding freely.

Roy slipped his bloody hand into Colin's. His grip was firm.

Colin squeezed back with all his strength. Their wet flesh made a barely audible squishing sound as they shook hands.

They stood in front of the deserted service station, in cool night air scented with gasoline, staring into each other's eyes, breathing each other's breath, feeling strong and special and wild.

'My brother,' Roy said.

'My brother.'

'Forever,' Roy said.

'Forever.'

Colin concentrated hard on the pinprick in his hand, trying to sense that moment when Roy's blood first began to creep into his own veins.

9

After the impromptu ceremony, Roy wiped his sticky hands on his jeans and picked up his unfinished Pepsi. 'What do you want to do next?'

'It's after eleven,' Colin said.

'An hour from now, do you turn into a pumpkin?'

'I'd better go home.'

'It's early.'

'If my mother gets back and I'm not there, she'll worry.'

'From what you've told me, she doesn't sound like the kind of mother who'd worry about a kid too much.'

'I don't want to get into trouble.'

'I thought she went to dinner with this Thornberg guy.'

'That was around nine o'clock,' Colin said. 'She might be getting home soon.'

'Boy, are you naïve.'

Colin looked at him warily. What's that supposed to mean?'

'She won't be home for hours.'

'How do you know?'

'About now,' Roy said, 'they've had dinner and brandy, and old Thornberg's just getting her into bed at his place.'

'You don't know what you're talking about,'

Colin said uneasily. But he remembered how his mother had looked when she'd gone out: fresh, crisp, and beautiful in a clinging, low-cut dress.

Roy leered at him, winked. 'You think your mother's a virgin?'

'Of course not.'

'So did she suddenly become a nun or something?'

'Jeez.'

'Face it, good buddy, your mother screws around like everyone else.'

'I don't want to talk about it.'

'*I'd* sure as hell like to screw her.'

'Stop it!'

'Touchy, touchy.'

'Are we blood brothers or not?' Colin asked.

Roy swallowed the last of his soft drink. 'What's that got to do with it?'

'If you're my blood brother, you've got to show some respect for my mother, just as if she were your mother.'

Roy put his empty bottle in the rack beside the soda machine. He cleared his throat and spat on the pavement. 'Hell, I don't even respect my own mother. The bitch. She's a real bitch. And why should I treat your old lady like some sort of goddess when *you* don't have any respect for her?'

'Who says I don't?'

'*I* say you don't.'

'You think you can read minds or something?'

'Didn't you tell me that your old lady always spent more time with her girlfriends than she did with you? Was she ever around when you needed her?'

'Everyone has friends,' Colin said weakly.

'Did you have friends before you met me?'

Colin shrugged. 'I've always had my hobbies.'

'And didn't you tell me that when she was married to your old man, she left him once a month—'

'Not that often.'

'— just walked out for a few days at a time, even for a week or more?'

'That was because he beat her,' Colin said.

'Did she take you with her when she left?'

Colin finished his grape soda.

'Did she take you with her?' Roy asked again.

'Not usually.'

'She left you there with *him*.'

'He's my father, after all.'

'He sounds dangerous to me,' Roy said.

'He never touched me. Just her.'

'But he might have hurt you.'

'But he didn't.'

'She couldn't know for sure what he'd do when she left you with him.'

'It worked out OK. That's all that matters.'

'And now all her time's taken up with this art gallery,' Roy said. 'She works every day and most evenings.'

'She's building a future for herself and me.'

Roy made a sour face. 'Is that her excuse? Is that what she tells you?'

'It's true, I guess.'

'How touching. Building a future. Poor, hard-working Weezy Jacobs. It breaks my heart, Colin. It really does. Shit. More nights than not, she's out with someone like Thornberg—'

'That's business.'

'— and she *still* doesn't have time for you.'

'So what?'

'So you should stop worrying about getting home,' Roy said. 'Nobody gives a damn if you're home or not. Nobody cares. So let's have some fun.'

Colin put his empty bottle in the rack. 'What'll we do?'

'Let's see ... I know. The Kingman place. You'll like the Kingman place. You been there yet?'

'What's the Kingman place?' Colin asked.

'It's one of the oldest houses in town.'

'I'm not much interested in landmarks.'

'It's that big house at the end of Hawk Drive.'

'The spooky old place on top of the hill?'

'Yeah. Nobody's lived there for twenty years.'

'What's so interesting about an abandoned house?'

Roy leaned close and cackled like a fiend, twisted his face grotesquely, rolled his eyes, and whispered dramatically: '*It's haunted!*'

'What's the joke?'

'No joke. They say it's haunted.'

'Who says?'

'Everyone.' Roy rolled his eyes and again tried to imitate Boris Karloff. 'People have seen exceedingly strange things at the Kingman place.'

'Such as?'

'Not now,' Roy said, dropping the Karloff voice. 'I'll tell you all about it when we get there.'

As Roy lifted his bicycle away from the wall, Colin said, 'Wait a minute. I think you're serious. You mean this house is really haunted?'

'I guess it depends on whether or not you believe in that sort of thing.'

'People have seen ghosts there?'

'People *say* they've seen and heard all kinds of

crazy things at that house ever since the Kingman
family died up there.'

'Died?'

'They were killed.'

'The whole family?'

'All seven of them.'

'When was this?'

'Twenty years ago.'

'Who did it?'

'The father.'

'Mr Kingman?'

'He went crazy one night and chopped up
everyone while they were sleeping.'

Colin swallowed hard. 'Chopped them up?'

'With an ax.'

Axes again! Colin thought.

For a moment his stomach seemed to be not a
part of him but a separate entity alive within him,
for it slipped and slid and twisted wetly back and
forth, as if trying to crawl out of him.

'I'll tell you all about it when we get there,' Roy
said. 'Come on.'

'Wait a minute,' Colin said nervously, stalling
for time. 'My glasses are dirty.'

He took off his glasses, pulled a handkerchief
from his pocket, and carefully polished the thick
lenses. He could still see Roy fairly well, but
everything farther than five feet was blurry.

'Hurry up, Colin.'

'Maybe we should wait for tomorrow.'

'Is it going to take you that long to clean your
goddamned glasses?'

'I mean, in daylight we'll be able to see more of
the Kingman place.'

'Seems to me it's more fun to look at a haunted
house at night.'

'But you can't see much at night.'

Roy regarded him silently for a few seconds. Then: 'Are you scared?'

'Of what?'

'Ghosts.'

'Of course not.'

'Sounds like it.'

'Well . . . it *does* seem kind of foolish to go poking around a place like that in the dark, in the dead of night, you know.'

'No. I don't know.'

'I'm not talking about ghosts. I mean, one of us is bound to get hurt if we mess around in an old broken-down house in the middle of the night.'

'You *are* scared.'

'Like hell.'

'Prove you're not.'

'Why should I prove anything?'

'Want your blood brother to think you're a coward?'

Colin was silent. He fidgeted.

'Come *on*!' Roy said.

Roy mounted his bike and pedaled out of the deserted service station, heading north on Broadway. He did not glance back.

Colin stood at the soda machine. Alone. He didn't like being alone. Especially at night.

Roy was a block away and still moving.

'Damn!' Colin said. He shouted, 'Wait for me,' and clambered on to his bicycle.

10

They walked the bikes up the last steep block toward the dilapidated house that crouched above them. With each step, Colin's trepidation grew.

It sure *looks* haunted, he thought.

The Kingman place was well within the Santa Leona city limits, yet it was separated from the rest of the town, as if everyone were afraid to build nearby. It stood on top of a hill and held dominion over five or six acres. At least half of that land had once been well-tended, formal gardens, but long ago it had gone sadly to seed. The north leg of Hawk Drive dead-ended in a wide turnaround in front of the Kingman property; and the lamp-posts did not go all the way to the end of the street, so that the old mansion and its weed-choked grounds were shrouded in blackest shadows, high-lighted only by the moon. On the lower two thirds of the hill, on both sides of the road, modern California-style ranch houses clung precariously to the slopes, waiting with amazing patience for a mudslide or the next shock wave from the San Andreas Fault. Only the Kingman place occupied the upper third of the hill, and it appeared to be waiting for something far more terrifying, something a great deal more malevolent than an earthquake.

The house faced the center of town, which lay below it, and the sea, which was not visible at night, except in the negative as a vast expanse of lightlessness. The house was a huge, rambling wreck, ersatz Victorian, with too many fancy chimneys and too many gables, and with twice as much gingerbread around the eaves and windows and railings as true Victorian demanded. Storms had ripped shingles from the roof. Some of the ornate trim was broken, and in a few spots it had fallen down altogether. Where shutters still survived, they often hung at a slant, by a single mounting. The white paint had been weathered away. The boards were silver-gray, bleached by the sun and the constant sea wind, water-stained. The front-porch steps sagged, and there were gaps in the railing. Half of the windows were haphazardly boarded shut, but the others were without protection, thus shattered; moonlight revealed jagged shards of glass like transparent teeth biting at the empty blackness where stones had been pitched through. In spite of its shabby condition, however, the Kingman place did not have the air of a ruin; it did not give rise to sadness in the hearts of those who looked upon it, as did many once-noble but now decrepit buildings; somehow it seemed vital, alive . . . even frighteningly alive. If a house could be said to have a human attitude, an emotional aspect, then this house was angry, very angry. *Furious.*

They parked their bicycles by the front gate. It was a big, rusted iron grill with a sunburst design in the center.

'Some place, huh?' Roy said.

'Yeah.'

'Let's go.'

'Inside?'

'Sure.'

'We don't have a flashlight.'

'Well, at least let's go up on the porch.'

'Why?' Colin asked shakily.

'We can look in the windows.'

Roy walked through the open gate and started up the broken flagstone walk, through the tangled weeds, toward the house.

Colin followed him for a few steps, then stopped and said, 'Wait. Roy, wait a sec.'

Roy turned back. 'What is it?'

'You been here before?'

'Of course.'

'You been inside?'

'Once.'

'Did you see any ghosts?'

'Nah. I don't believe in 'em.'

'But you said people see things here.'

'Other people. Not me.'

'You said it was haunted.'

'I told you other people said it was haunted. I think they're full of shit. But I knew you'd enjoy the place, what with you being such a big horror-movie fan and everything.'

Roy began to walk along the path again.

After several more steps, Colin said, 'Wait.'

Roy looked back and grinned. 'Scared?'

'No.'

'Ha!'

'I just have some questions.'

'So hurry up and ask them.'

'You said a lot of people were killed here.'

'Seven,' Roy said. 'Six murders, one suicide.'

'Tell me about it.'

During the past twenty years, the very real

tragedy of the Kingman murders had evolved into a highly embellished tale, a grisly Santa Leona legend, recalled most often at Halloween, composed of myth and truth, perhaps more of the former than the latter, depending on who was telling it. But the basic facts of the case were simple, and Roy stuck close to them when he told the story.

The Kingmans had been wealthy. Robert Kingman was the only child of Judith and Big Jim Kingman; but Robert's mother died of massive hemorrhaging while delivering him. Big Jim was even then a rich man, and he grew continually richer over the years. He made millions from California real estate, farming, oil, and water rights. He was a tall, barrel-chested man, as was his son, and Big Jim liked to boast that there was no one west of the Mississippi who could eat more steak, drink more whiskey, or make more money than he could. Shortly before Robert's twenty-second birthday, he inherited the entire estate when Big Jim, having drunk too much whiskey, choked to death on a large, inadequately chewed chunk of filet mignon. He lost that eating contest to a man who had yet to make a million dollars in plumbing supplies, but who could at least boast at having lived through the feast. Robert had not developed his father's competitive attitude toward food and beverage, but he had acquired the old man's business sense, and although he was quite young, he made even more money with the funds that had been left to him.

When he was twenty-five, Robert married a woman named Alana Lee, built the Victorian house on Hawk Hill, just for her, and began fathering a new generation of Kingmans. Alana was not from a wealthy family, but she was said to be the most beautiful girl in the county, with the sweetest temper in the state. The children came fast, five of them in eight years – three boys and two girls. Theirs was the most respected family in town, envied, but also liked and admired. The Kingmans were churchgoers, friendly, graced with the common touch in spite of their high station, charitable, involved in their community. Robert obviously loved Alana, and everyone could see that she adored him; and the children returned the affection their parents lavished upon them.

On a night in August, a few days before the Kingmans' twelfth wedding anniversary, Robert secretly ground up two dozen sleeping tablets that a physician had prescribed for Alana's periodic insomnia, and sprinkled the powder in drink and food that his family shared for a bedtime snack, as well as in various items consumed by the live-in maid, cook, and butler. He neither ate nor drank anything he had contaminated. When his wife, children, and servants were soundly asleep, he went out to the garage and fetched an ax that was used to chop wood for the mansion's nine fireplaces. He spared the maid, cook, and butler, but no one else. He killed Alana first, then his two young daughters, then his three sons. Every member of the family was dispatched in the same hideously brutal, gory fashion: with two sharp and powerful blows of the ax blade, one vertical and one horizontal, in the form of a cross, either on the back or on the chest, depending on the position in which each was sleeping when attacked. That done, Robert visited his victims a second time and crudely decapitated all of them. He carried their dripping heads downstairs and lined them up on the long mantel above the fireplace in the drawing room. It was a shockingly gruesome tableau: six lifeless, blood-splashed faces observing him as if they were a jury of judges in the court of Hell. With his beloved dead watching him, Robert Kingman wrote a brief note to those who would find him and his maniacal handiwork the following morning: 'My father always said that I entered the world in a river of blood, my dying mother's blood. And now I will shortly leave on another such river.' When he had written that curious good-bye, he loaded a .38-caliber Colt revolver, put the barrel in his mouth, turned toward the death-shocked faces of his family, and blew his brains out.

As Roy finished the story, Colin grew cold all the way through to his bones. He hugged himself and shivered violently.

'The cook was the first to wake up,' Roy said. 'She found blood all over the hallway and stairs, followed the trail to the drawing room, and saw the heads on the mantel. She ran out of the house, down the hill, screaming at the top of her lungs. Went almost a mile before anyone stopped her. They say she nearly lost her mind over it.'

The night seemed darker than it had been when Roy had begun the story. The moon appeared to be smaller, farther away than it had been earlier.

On a distant highway a big truck shifted gears and accelerated. It sounded like the cry of a prehistoric animal.

Colin's mouth was as dry as ashes. He worked

up enough saliva to speak, but his voice was thin. 'For God's sake, *why*? Why did he kill them?'

Roy shrugged. 'No reason.'

'There *had* to be a reason.'

'If there was, nobody ever figured it out.'

'Maybe he made some bad investments and lost all of his money.'

'Nah. He left a fortune.'

'Maybe his wife was going to leave him.'

'All of her friends said she was very happy with her marriage.'

A dog barking.

A train whistling.

Wind whispering in the trees.

The stealthy movement of unseen things.

The night was speaking all around him.

'A brain tumor,' Colin said.

'A lot of people thought the same thing.'

'I'll bet that's it. I'll bet Kingman had a brain tumor, something like that, something that made him act crazy.'

'At the time it was the most popular theory. But the autopsy didn't turn up any signs of a brain disease.'

Colin frowned. 'You seem to have filed away every single fact about the case.'

'I know it almost as well as if it had happened to me.'

'But how do you know what the autopsy uncovered?'

'I read about it.'

'Where?'

'The library has all the back issues of the Santa Leona *News Register* on microfilm,' Roy said.

'You researched the case?'

'Yeah. It's exactly the kind of thing that interests me. Remember? Death. I'm fascinated by death. As soon as I heard the Kingman story, I wanted to know more. A whole lot more. I wanted to know every last bit and piece of it. You understand? I mean, wouldn't it have been terrific to be in that house on that night, the night it happened, just sort of observing, just hiding in a corner, on *that* night, hiding and watching him do it, watching him do it to all of them and then to himself? Think of it! Blood everywhere. You've never seen so much goddamned blood in your life! Blood on the walls, soaked and clotted in the bedclothes, slick puddles of blood on the floor, blood on the stairs, and blood splashed over the furniture . . . And those six heads on the mantel! Jesus, what a popper! What a terrific popper!'

'You're being weird again,' Colin said.

'Would you like to have been there?'

'No thanks. And neither would you.'

'I sure as hell would!'

'If you saw all that blood, you'd puke.'

'Not me.'

'You're trying to gross me out.'

'Wrong again.'

Roy started toward the house.

'Wait a minute,' Colin said.

Roy didn't turn back this time. He climbed the sagging steps and walked onto the porch.

Rather than stand alone, Colin joined him. 'Tell me about the ghosts.'

'Some nights there are strange lights in the house. And people who live farther down the hill say that sometimes they hear the Kingman children screaming in terror and crying for help.'

'They hear the *dead kids*?'

'Moaning and carrying on something fierce.'

Colin suddenly realised he had his back to one of the broken first-floor windows. He shifted away from it.

Roy continued somberly: 'Some people say they've seen spirits that glow in the dark, crazy things, headless children who come out on this porch and run back and forth as if they're being chased by someone . . . or something.'

'*Wow!*'

Roy laughed. 'What they've probably seen is a bunch of kids trying to hoax everybody.'

'Maybe not.'

'What else?'

'Maybe they've seen just what they say they have.'

'You really *do* believe in ghosts.'

'I keep an open mind,' Colin said.

'Yeah? Well, you better be more careful about what kind of junk falls into it, or you'll wind up with an open sewer.'

'Aren't you clever.'

'Everyone says so.'

'And modest.'

'Everyone says that, too.'

'Jeez.'

Roy went to the shattered window and peered inside.

'What do you see?' Colin asked.

'Come look.'

Colin moved beside him and stared into the house.

A stale, extremely unpleasant odor wafted through the broken window.

'It's the drawing room,' Roy said.

'I can't see anything.'

'It's the room where he lined up their heads on the mantel.'

'What mantel? It's pitch dark in there.'

'In a couple of minutes our eyes will adjust.'

In the drawing room something moved. There was a soft rustling, a sudden clatter, and the sound of something rushing toward the window.

Colin leaped back. He stumbled over his own feet and fell with a crash.

Roy looked at him and burst out laughing.

'Roy, there's something in there!'

'Rats.'

'Huh?'

'Just rats.'

'The house has rats?'

'Of course it does, a rotten old place like this. Or maybe we heard a stray cat. Probably both – a cat chasing a rat. One thing I guarantee: It wasn't any ghoul or ghost. Will you relax, for God's sake?'

Roy faced the widow again, leaned into it, head cocked, listening, watching.

Having sustained much greater injury to his pride than to his flesh, Colin got up quickly and nimbly, but he didn't return to the window. He stood at the rickety railing and looked west toward town, then south along Hawk Drive.

After a while he said, 'Why haven't they torn this place down? Why haven't they built new houses up here? This must be valuable land.'

Without looking away from the window, Roy said, 'The entire Kingman fortune, including the land, went to the state.'

'Why?'

'There weren't any living relatives on either side of the family, nobody to inherit.'

'What's the state going to do with the place?'

'In twenty years they've managed to do absolutely zilch, nothing at all, big zero,' Roy said. 'For a while there was talk of selling the land and the house at public auction. Then they said they were going to make a pocket park out of it. You still hear the park rumor every once in a while, but nothing ever gets done. Now will you please shut up for a minute? I think my eyes are finally beginning to adjust. I have to concentrate on this.'

'Why? What's so important in there?'

'I'm trying to see the mantel.'

'You've been here before,' Colin said. 'You've already seen it.'

'I'm trying to pretend it's *that* night. The night Kingman went berserk. I'm trying to imagine what it must have been like. The sound of the ax . . . I can almost hear it . . . *whooooosh-chunk, whooooosh-chunk* . . . and maybe a couple of short screams . . . his footsteps coming down the stairs . . . heavy footsteps . . . the blood . . . all that blood . . .'

Roy's voice gradually trailed away as if he had mesmerised himself.

Colin walked to the far end of the porch. The boards squeaked underfoot. He leaned against the shaky railing and craned his neck so that he could look around the side of the house. He could see only the overgrown garden in shades of gray and black and moonlight-silver; knee-high grass; shaggy hedges; orange and lemon trees pulled to the ground by the weight of their own untrimmed boughs; sprawling rose bushes, some with pale flowers, white or yellow, that looked like puffs of smoke in the darkness; and a hundred other plants that were woven into a single, tangled entity by the loom of the night.

He had the feeling something was watching him from the deeps of the garden. Something less than human.

Don't be childish, he thought. There's nothing out there. This isn't a horror movie. This is *life*.

He tried to stand his ground, but the possibility that he was being observed became a certainty, at least in his own mind. He knew that if he stood there much longer, he would surely be seized by a creature with huge claws and dragged into the dense shrubbery, there to be gnawed upon at the beast's leisure. He turned away from the garden and went back to Roy.

'You ready to go?' Colin asked.

'I can see the whole room.'

'In the dark?'

'I can see a lot of it.'

'Yeah?'

'I can see the mantel.'

'Yeah?'

'Where he lined up the heads.'

As if he were drawn by a magnet stronger than his will, Colin stepped up beside Roy and bent forward and peered into the Kingman house. It was extremely dark in there, but he could see a bit more than he had seen a while ago; strange shapes, perhaps piles of broken furniture and other rubble; shadows that seemed to be moving but, of course, were not; and the white-marble mantel above the enormous fireplace, the sacrificial altar upon which Robert Kingman had offered up his family.

Suddenly Colin felt that this was a place he must get away from at once, a place he must stay away from forever. He knew it instinctively, on a deep animal level, and as if he were an animal, the hairs rose on the back of his neck, and he hissed softly, involuntarily, through bared teeth.

Roy said, '*Whooooosh-chunk!*'

11

Midnight.

They cycled down Hawk Drive to Broadway and followed Broadway until it ended at Palisades Lane. They stopped at the head of the wooden steps that led down to the public beach. On the other side of the narrow street, elegant old Spanish houses faced the sea. The night was still. There was no traffic. The only sound was the steady pounding of the surf fifty feet below them. From here they would go separate ways: Roy's house was several blocks north, and Colin's lay to the south.

'What time will we get together?' Roy asked.

'We won't. I mean, we can't,' Colin said unhappily. 'My dad's coming up from L.A. to take me fishing with a bunch of his friends.'

'You like to fish?'

'Hate it.'

'Can't you get out of it?'

'No way. He spends two Saturdays a month with me, and he makes a big production out of it every time. I don't know why, but I guess it's important to him. If I tried to back out, he'd raise hell.'

'When you lived with him, did he even spend two days a month with you?'

'No.'

99

'So tell him to take his fishing pole and shove it up his ass. Tell him you won't go.'

Colin shook his head. 'No. It's not possible, Roy. I just can't. He'd think my mom put me up to it, and then there'd be real trouble between them.'

'What do you care?'

'I'm in the middle.'

'So let's get together tomorrow evening.'

'That's out, too. I won't be home until ten o'clock.'

'I really think you should tell him to shove it.'

'We'll get together Sunday,' Colin said. 'Come over about eleven. We'll swim for an hour before lunch.'

'OK.'

'Then we can do whatever you want.'

'Sounds good.'

'Well . . . see ya then.'

'Wait a minute.'

'Huh?'

'Someday soon, if I can manage it for us, you want to get a piece?'

'A piece of what?'

'A piece of *ass.*'

'Oh.'

'Do you?'

Colin was embarrassed. 'Where? I mean, who?'

'You remember those girls we saw tonight?'

'At the Pinball Pit?'

'Nah. They're just kids. Teasers. I told you that. I'm talking about *real* girls, the ones in that movie.'

'What about them?'

'I think I know where I can get something that good for us, a girl just like one of those.'

'You been drinking?'

'I'm serious.'

'I'm Colin.'

'She's got a beautiful face.'

'Who?'

'The girl I think we can get.'

'Jeez.'

'And really big boobs.'

'Really big?'

'Really.'

'Big as Raquel Welch?'

'Bigger.'

'Big as weather balloons?'

'I'm serious. And she has a pair of *gorgeous* legs.'

'Good,' Colin said. 'One-legged girls never turn me on.'

'Will you stop it? I told you I'm serious. She's hot stuff.'

'I'll bet.'

'She really is.'

'How old is she?'

'Twenty-five or twenty-six.'

'First of all,' Colin said, 'you'll have to put on a false moustache. Then you can stand on my shoulders, and we can dress up in one suit, just one suit to cover us both, so she won't realise we're only a couple of kids. She'll think we're a tall, dark, handsome man.'

Roy scowled. 'I'm serious.'

'You keep saying that, but you sure don't sound very serious to me.'

'Her name's Sarah.'

'A beautiful, twenty-five-year-old girl won't be interested in you and me.'

'Maybe not at first.'

'Not in a million years.'

'She'll just need some persuading.'

'Persuading?'

'You and me together should be able to handle her.'

Colin gaped at him.

'You willing to try?' Roy asked.

'Are you talking about – *rape*?'

'What if I am.'

'You want to wind up in prison?'

'She's hot stuff. She's worth taking the chance.'

'Nobody's worth going to prison for.'

'You haven't see her.'

'Besides, it's wrong.'

'You sound like a preacher.'

'It's a terrible thing to do.'

'Not if it feels good.'

'It won't feel good to *her*.'

'She'll love me by the time I'm done with her.'

Blushing fiercely, Colin said, 'You're weird.'

'Wait'll you see Sarah.'

'I don't want to see her.'

'You'll want her when you see her.'

'This is all jive.'

'Think about it.'

A cream-colored van went by on Palisades Lane. A desert scene, framed in grinning skulls, was painted on the side of it.

They heard loud rock music and the high, sweet laughter of a girl.

'Think about it,' Roy said again.

'I don't need to think about it.'

'Beautiful big boobs.'

'Jeez.'

'Think about it.'

'This is just like that story about the cat,' Colin said. 'You wouldn't ever kill a cat, and you wouldn't rape anyone, either.'

'If I knew I could get away with it, I'd sure as hell get me a piece or two of that Sarah, and you'd better believe it, good buddy.'

'I don't.'

'Two of us working together *could* get away with it. Easy. Real easy. Will you at least think about it for a couple of days?'

'Give up, Roy. I know you're putting me on.'

'I'm serious.'

Colin sighed, shook his head, glanced at his watch. 'I can't waste time listening to this baloney. It's late.'

'Think about it.'

'*Jeez!*'

Roy smiled. The odd, metallic light played a trick on him, transformed his teeth into fangs; the cold glow of the mercury-vapor street lamp tinted his teeth blue-white, darkened and emphasised the narrow spaces between them, made them look ragged and pointy. At least to Colin's eyes, Roy appeared to be wearing a set of costume-party teeth, the ugly wax dentures you could buy in a novelty shop.

'I've got to get home,' Colin said. 'See you Sunday at eleven?'

'Sure.'

'Don't forget to bring your swimsuit.'

'Have fun on your fishing trip.'

'Fat chance.'

Colin rose on his bike, jammed his feet on the pedals, and pumped south on Palisades Lane. As the wind *shushed* over him, as the relentless crash of the surf echoed off to his right, and as his fear of being alone at night returned, he heard Roy shouting behind him:

'*Think about it!*'

12

When Colin arrived home at twelve-thirty, his mother had not yet returned from her date with Mark Thornberg. Her car was not in the garage. The house was dark and forbidding.

He did not want to go inside by himself. He stared at the blank windows, at the pulsing darkness beyond the glass, and he suspected that something was waiting for him in there, some nightmare creature that intended to chew him up alive.

Stop it, stop it, stop it! he told himself angrily. There's nothing waiting for you in there. Nothing. Don't be so damned silly. Grow up! You want to be like Roy, so do exactly what Roy would do if he was here. Waltz right into the house, just like Roy would. Do it. Now. Go!

He fished the key out of a redwood planter that stood beside the walk. His hand shook. He thrust the key into the lock, hesitated, then found sufficient strength to open the door. He reached inside and switched on the light but didn't step across the threshold.

The front room was deserted.

No monsters.

He went to the corner of the house, stepped behind a screen of bushs, and urinated. He didn't want to have to use the bathroom when he got in

105

the house. Something might be waiting there for him, waiting behind the door, behind the shower-curtain, perhaps even in the clothes hamper, something dark and fast with wild eyes and lots of teeth and razor-sharp claws.

Got to stop thinking like this! he told himself. It's crazy. Got to stop it. Grown-ups aren't afraid of the dark. If I don't get over this fear soon, I'm going to wind up in an asylum. Jeez.

He replaced the key in the planter and entered the house. He tried to swagger as Roy would have done; however, as if he were a giant marionette, he needed ropes of courage to hold him in a hero's stance, but all that he could find within himself was one thin thread of bravery. He closed the door and put his back against it. He stood quite still, holding his breath, listening.

Ticking. An antique mantel clock.

Moaning. Wind pressing the windows.

Nothing else.

He locked the door behind him.

Paused.

Listened.

Silence.

Suddenly he dashed across the living room, dodging furniture, burst into the downstairs hall-way, slapped the light switch there, saw nothing out of the ordinary, thundered up the stairs, turned on the second-floor hall lights, ran into his bedroom, hit the lights there, too, felt a tiny bit better when he saw he was still alone, jerked open the closet door, found no werewolves or vampires lurking among the clothes, shut the bedroom door, locked it, braced it with a straight-backed chair, drew the drapes over both windows so that nothing could look in at him, and collapsed on to the mattress, gasping. He didn't have to look under the bed: it was a platform job, built right on the floor.

He would be safe until morning – unless, of course, something broke down the door in spite of the chair that was wedged under the knob.

Stop it!

He got up, undressed, put on a pair of blue pajamas, set the clock for six-thirty so he'd be ready when his dad arrived, slipped under the sheet, and fluffed his pillow. When he took off his glasses, the room turned fuzzy at the edges, but he had secured the territory and didn't have to be 100 per cent watchful. He stretched out on his back, and for a long time he lay listening to the house.

Click! Creeeeaaak . . . A soft groan, a brief rattle, a barely audible squeak. Just the normal sounds of a house. Settling noises. Nothing more than that.

Even when his mother was home, Colin slept with a night light. But tonight, unless she returned before he fell asleep, he would leave *all* the lamps burning. The room was as bright as an operating theater that had been prepared for surgery.

The sight of his possessions provided him with a little comfort. Five hundred paperbacks filled two tall shelves. The walls were decorated with posters: Bela Lugosi in *Dracula*; Christopher Lee in *The Horror of Dracula*; the monster in *The Creature from the Black Lagoon*; Lon Chaney Jr, as the Wolfman; the monster from Ridley Scott's *Alien*; and the spooky night-highway poster from *Close Encounters of the Third Kind*. His monster models, which he had built himself from kits, were arranged on a table beside his desk. A

107

plastic ghoul lurched forever through a hand-painted graveyard. Frankenstein's creation stood with plastic arms outstretched, face frozen in a snarl of pure hatred. There were a dozen models in all. The many hours he had spent building them had been hours during which he'd been able to suppress his fear of the night and his awareness of its sinister voice; for so long as he had held those plastic symbols of evil in his hands, he had felt in control of them, master of them, and, curiously, he had felt superior to the very real monsters they represented.

Click!

Creeeeeaaak . . .

After a while he became accustomed to the noises made by the house and almost ceased to hear them. He heard, instead, the voice of the night, the voice that no one else seemed able to hear. It was there from sundown to sunrise, a constant evil presence, a supernatural phenomenon, the voice of the dead who wanted to come back from their graves, the voice of the Devil. It jabbered insanely, cackled, chuckled, wheezed, hissed, murmured about blood and death. In sepulchral tones, it spoke of the dank and airless crypt, of the dead who still walked, of flesh riddled with worms. To most of the world, it was a subliminal voice and spoke only to the subconscious mind; but Colin was *very* aware of it. A steady whisper. Sometimes a shout. Sometimes even a loud scream.

One o'clock.

Where in the hell was his mother?

Tap-tap-tap!

Something at the window.

Tap. Tap-tap. Tap-tap-tap-tap. Tap.

Just a big moth bumping against the glass. That was it. That *had* to be it. Just a moth.

One-thirty.

He had been spending nearly every night alone. He didn't mind eating supper by himself. She had to work a lot, and she had every right to date men now that she was single again. But did she have to leave him alone every night at bedtime?

Tap-tap.

The moth again.

Tap-tap-tap.

He tried to tune out the moth and think about Roy. What a guy Roy was. What a great friend. What a truly terrific buddy. Blood brothers. He could still feel the shallow puncture in the palm of his hand; it throbbed faintly. Roy was on his side, there to help, now and forever, always and always, or at least until one of them died. That's what it meant to be blood brothers. Roy would protect him.

He thought about his best friend, papered over the visions of monsters with images of Roy Borden, blocked out the voice of the night with memories of Roy's voice, and shortly before two o'clock he drifted into sleep. But there were nightmares.

13

The alarm clock woke him at six-thirty.

He got out of bed and pulled open the drapes. For a minute or two he basked in the wan early-morning sunshine, which had no voice and presented no threat.

Twenty minutes later he was showered and dressed.

He walked down the hall to his mother's room and found the door ajar. He rapped lightly, but there was no response. He pushed the door open a few inches and saw her. She was out cold, lying on her belly, her face turned toward him; the knuckles of her left hand were pressed against her slack mouth. Her eyelids fluttered as if she was dreaming; she breathed shallowly and rhythmically. The sheet had pulled halfway down her body during the night. She appeared to be nude beneath the flimsy covers. Her back was bare, and he could see just a hint of her left breast, an exciting suggestion of fullness where it was squashed against the mattress. He stared at the smooth flesh, hoping she would roll over in her sleep and reveal the entire, soft, white globe.

– She's your own *mother!*
But she's built.
– Close the door.
Maybe she'll roll over.

– You don't want to see.
Like hell I don't. Roll over!
– Close the door.
I want to see her breasts.
– This is disgusting.
Her tits.
– Jeez.
I'd sure like to touch them.
– Are you crazy?
Sneak in and touch 'em without waking her.
– You're turning into a pervert. A regular goddamned pervert. You ought to be ashamed.

Blushing, he quietly closed the door. His hands were cold and damp with sweat.

He went downstairs and ate breakfast: two cookies and a glass of orange juice.

Although he tried to clear his mind of it, he could think of nothing except Weezy's bare back and the plump outline of her breasts.

'What's happening to me?' he said aloud.

14

His father arrived in a white Cadillac at 7:05, and
Colin was waiting for him at the curb in front of
the house.

The old man slapped him on the shoulder and
said, 'How ya doin', Junior?'

'OK,' Colin said.

'Ready to catch some big ones?'

'I guess.'

'They're going to be biting today.'

'They are?'

'That's the word.'

'From who?'

'From those who know.'

'The fish?'

His father glanced at him. 'What?'

'Who are those who know?'

'Charlie and Irv.'

'Who're they?'

'The guys who run the charter service.'

'Oh.'

Sometimes Colin had difficulty believing that
Frank Jacobs was really his father. They were not
at all alike. Frank was a big, rangy, rugged man,
six-foot-two, a hundred and eighty pounds, with
long arms and large, leathery hands. He was an
excellent fisherman, a hunter with many trophies,
and a highly skilled archer. He was a poker

113

player, a partygoer, a hard drinker but not a drunk, an extrovert, a man's man. Colin admired some of his father's qualities; however, there was a great deal that he merely tolerated, and a few things that aroused anger, fear, and even hatred. For one thing, Frank routinely refused to admit to his mistakes, even when proof of them was before his eyes. On those rare occasions when he realised he could not avoid an owning up, he sulked like a spoiled child, as if it were grossly unfair for him to be held responsible for the results of his own errors. He never read books or any magazines other than those published for sportsmen, yet he had an unshakable opinion about everything from the Arab-Israeli situation to the American ballet; and he stubbornly, vociferously defended his uninformed views without ever realising that he was making a fool of himself. Worst of all, he lost his temper at the slightest provocation but regained his composure only with enormous effort. When he was very angry he behaved like a raging madman: shouting paranoid accusations, screaming, punching, breaking things. He had been in more than a few fist fights. And he was a wife beater.

He also drove too fast and recklessly. During the forty-minute ride south to Ventura, Colin sat straight and stiff, hands fisted at his sides, afraid to look at the road but also afraid *not* to look. He was amazed when they made it to the marina alive.

The boat was the *Erica Lynn*. She was large and white and well maintained, but there was an unpleasant odor about her that only Colin seemed to notice – a blend of gasoline fumes and the stench of dead fish.

The charter group was composed of Colin, his father, and nine of his father's friends. They were all tall, tan, rugged-looking men, just as Frank was, with names like Jack and Rex and Pete and Mike.

As the *Erica Lynn* cast off, maneuvered out of the harbor, and motored toward the open sea, a breakfast of sorts was served on the deck aft of the pilot's cabin. They had several thermos bottles filled with bloody marys, two kinds of smoked fish, chopped green onions, slices of melon, and soft rolls.

Colin ate nothing because, as usual, mild seasickness took hold of him the moment the boat moved away from the dock. From experience he knew that he would be all right in an hour or so, but until he got his sea legs, he wasn't taking any chances with food. He even regretted having eaten the two cookies and orange juice, although that had been an hour ago.

At noon the men ate sausage and chugged beer. Colin nibbled at a roll, drank a Pepsi, and tried to stay out of everyone's way.

By then it was clear to all of them that Charlie and Irv had been wrong. The fish were not biting.

They had begun the day in pursuit of shallow-water game only a couple of miles from shore, but the shoals had seemed deserted, as if every aquatic citizen in the neighborhood had gone away on vacation. At ten-thirty they had moved farther out, into deeper water, where they rigged for bigger game. But the fish were having none of it.

The combination of high energy, boredom, frustration, and too much liquor created an explosive mood. Colin sensed trouble coming

115

long before the men decided to play their dangerous, violent, and bloody games.

After lunch they trolled in a zigzag pattern – northwest, south, northwest, south – starting ten miles off shore, moving steadily farther out. They cursed the fish that weren't there and the heat that was. They stripped out of their shirts and trousers, put on swimsuits they'd brought along; the sun darkened their already brown bodies. They told dirty jokes and talked about women as if they were discussing the relative merits of sports cars. Gradually they began to spend more time drinking than watching their lines, chasing shots of whiskey with cold cans of Coors.

The cobalt-blue ocean was unusually calm. The swells seemed to have been tamed with oil; they rolled smoothly, almost sluggishly, beneath the *Erica Lynn*.

The boat's engine produced a monotonous noise – *chuga-chuga-chuga-chuga-chuga* – that you could eventually *feel* as well as hear.

The cloudless summer sky was as blue as a gas flame.

Whiskey and beer. Whiskey and beer.

Colin smiled a lot, spoke when spoken to, but mostly just tried to be invisible.

At five o'clock the sharks showed up, and the day got ugly after that.

Ten minutes earlier, Irv had started chumming again, dumping bucketsful of stinking, chopped bait into their wake, trying to attract big fish. He had done the same thing half a dozen times before, always without effect; but even under the gimlet-eyed stares of his disillusioned clients, he continued to express confidence in his methods.

Charlie was the first to spot the action from his

place on the bridge. He called to them through the loudspeakers: 'Sharks off the stern, gentlemen. Approximately one hundred and fifty yards.'

The men crowded along the railing. Colin found a spot between his father and Mike, wedged himself into it.

'One hundred yards out,' Charlie said.

Colin squinted, concentrated hard on the fluid landscape, but he could not find the sharks. The sun shimmered on the water. There appeared to be millions upon millions of living things wriggling across the surface of the sea, but most of them were only slivers of light dancing from point to point on the waves.

'Eighty yards!'

A shout went up as several of the men spotted the sharks at the same instant.

A moment later Colin saw a fin. Then another. Two more. At least a dozen.

Suddenly line sang out of one of the reels.

'A bite!' Pete said.

Rex jumped into the deck-mounted chair behind the bent and jerking rod. As Irv strapped him down, Rex slipped the deep-sea rig out of the steel brace that had been holding it.

'Hell, sharks are just junk fish,' Jack said disdainfully.

'You're not going to get a trophy for a shark, no matter how damned big it is,' Pete said.

'I know,' Rex said. 'And I'm not about to eat the damned thing either. But I sure as hell won't let the bastard get away!'

Something took the bait on the second line and ran with it, Mike claimed that chair.

At the start it was one of the most exciting things Colin had ever seen. Although this wasn't his first time on a charter boat, he watched in awe as the men battled their catches. They shouted and swore, and the others urged them on. Muscles bulged in their thick arms. Veins popped out in their necks and at their temples. They goaded and thrashed and held on, pulling and reeling, pulling and reeling. Perspiration streamed from them, and Irv patted their faces with a white rag to keep the sweat from getting in their eyes.

'Keep the line taut!'

'Don't let him throw the hook!'

'Run him some more.'

'Tire him out.'

'He's already tired out.'

'Be careful they don't tangle the lines.'

'It's been fifteen minutes.'

'Jesus, Mike, a little old lady would've landed him by now.'

'My *mother* would've landed him by now.'

'Your mother's built like Arnold Schwarzenegger.'

'He's breaking water!'

'You got him now, Rex!'

'Big! Six foot or more!'

'And the other one. There!'

'Keep fighting!'

'What the hell will we do with two sharks?'

'Have to cut 'em loose.'

'Kill 'em first,' Colin's father said. 'You never let a shark go back alive. Isn't that right, Irv?'

'Right, Frank.'

Colin's father said, 'Irv, you better get the gun.'

Irv nodded and hurried away.

'What gun?' Colin asked uneasily. He was uncomfortable around firearms.

118

'They keep a .38 revolver aboard just for killing sharks,' his father said.

Irv returned with the gun. 'It's loaded.'

Frank took it and stood by the railing.

Colin wanted to put his fingers in his ears, but he didn't dare, the men would laugh at him, and his father would be angry.

'Can't see either of the critters yet,' Frank said.

The fishermen's hard bodies glistened with sweat.

Each rod appeared to be bent far beyond its breaking point, as if it were held together by nothing more than the indomitable will of the man who controlled it.

Suddenly Frank said, 'You've almost got yours, Rex! I can see him.'

'He's an ugly son-of-a-bitch,' Pete said.

Someone else said, 'He looks like Pete.'

'He's right on the surface,' Frank said. 'He doesn't have enough line to run deep again. He looks beat.'

'So am I,' Rex said. 'So will you for God's sake shoot the bastard?'

'Bring him a bit closer.'

'What the hell do you want? You want me to make him stand up against a wall and wear a blindfold?'

Everyone laughed.

Colin saw the slick, gray, torpedolike creature only twenty or thirty feet from the stern. It was riding just under the waves, dark fin protruding into the air. For a moment it was very still; then it began to pitch and toss and twist wildly, trying to free itself from the hook.

'Jesus!' Rex said. 'It'll tear my arms right out of their sockets.'

As the fish was drawn nearer in spite of its violent struggle, it rolled from side to side, writhing on the hook, willing to tear its own mouth to shreds in hope of getting loose, but succeeding only in setting the barbed hook even deeper. Its flat, malevolent head rose from the sea as it rolled, and for an instant Colin was staring into a bright and very alien eye that shone with a fierce inner light and seemed to radiate pure fury.

Frank Jacobs fired the .38 revolver.

Colin saw the hole open a few inches behind the shark's head. Blood and flesh sprayed across the water.

Everyone cheered.

Frank fired again. The second shot entered a couple of inches back of the first.

The shark should have been dead, but instead it seemed to take new life from the bullets.

'Look at the bastard kick!'

'He doesn't like that lead.'

'Shoot him again, Frank.'

'Get him square in the head.'

'Shoot him in the head.'

'You got to get a shark in the head.'

'Between the eyes, Frank!'

'Kill it, Frank!'

'Kill it!'

The foam that sloshed around the fish had once been white. Now it was pink.

Colin's father squeezed the trigger twice. The big gun bucked in his hands. One shot missed, but the other took the prey squarely in the head.

The shark leaped convulsively, as if trying to heave itself aboard the boat, and everyone on the *Erica Lynn* cried out in surprise; but then it fell back into the water and was absolutely still.

A second later Mike brought his catch to the surface, within striking distance, and Frank fired at it. This time his aim was perfect, and he finished the shark with the first shot.

The sea foam was crimson.

Irv rushed forward with a tackle knife and severed both lines.

Rex and Mike collapsed in their chairs, relieved and surely aching from head to foot.

Colin watched the dead fish drifting belly-up on the waves.

Without warning the sea began to boil as if a great flame had been applied beneath it. Fins appeared everywhere, converging on a small area immediately aft of the *Erica Lynn*: a dozen . . . two dozen . . . fifty sharks or more. They slashed viciously at their dead comrades, ripped and tore at meat like their very own meat, smashed into one another, fought over every morsel, soaring and diving and striking in a mindless, savage feeding frenzy.

Frank emptied the revolver into the turmoil. He must have hit at least one of the monsters, for the commotion grew considerably worse than it had been.

Colin wished he could look away from the slaughter. But he couldn't. Something held him.

'They're cannibals,' one of the men said.

'Sharks will eat anything.'

'They're worse than goats.'

'Fishermen have found some pretty strange things in sharks' stomachs.'

'Yeah. I know a guy who found a wrist-watch.'

'I heard of someone finding a wedding ring.'

'A cigar case full of water-logged stogies.'

'False teeth.'

'A rare coin worth a small fortune.'

'Anything indigestible that the victim was wearing or carrying, it stays right there in the shark's gut.'

'Why don't we haul in one of these mothers and see what it's keeping in its belly!'

'Hey, that might be interesting.'

'Cut it open right here on the deck.'

'Might find a rare coin and get rich.'

'Probably just find a lot of freshly eaten shark meat.'

'Maybe, maybe not.'

'At least it's something to do.'

'You're right. It's been one hell of a day.'

'Irv, better rig one of those rods again.'

They started drinking whiskey and beer again. Colin watched.

Jack took the chair, and two minutes later he had a bite. By the time he'd brought the shark alongside, the feeding frenzy had ended; the pack had moved away. But the frenzy aboard the *Erica Lynn* had just begun.

Colin's father reloaded the .38. He leaned over the railing and pumped two bullets into the huge fish.

'Right in the head.'

'Scrambled his fuckin' brains a little.'

'Shark's got a brain like a pea.'

'Same as yours?'

'That thing dead?'

'Ain't movin'.'

'Bring it up.'

'Let's have a look inside.'

'Find that rare coin.'

'Or the false teeth.'

122

Whiskey and beer.

Jack reeled in as much line as he could. The dead shark was bumping against the side of the boat.

'Damn thing's ten feet long.'

'Nobody's going to haul that baby up with just a gaff.'

'They have a winch.'

'It's going to be a messy job.'

'Might be worth it if we find that rare coin.'

'We're more likely to find a coin in *your* stomach.'

With five men, two ropes, three gaffs, and a power winch, they managed to hoist the shark out of the sea and over the stern railing, and then lost control of it a second before it was down, so that it crashed on to the deck, whereupon it came back to life unexpectedly, or half life anyway, for the bullets had hurt it and stunned it, but they had not killed it, and the beast thrashed on the deck, and everyone jumped back, and Pete grabbed a gaff and swung and slammed the hook into the shark's head, spraying blood on several people, and the mighty jaws snapped, trying to get at Pete, and another man rushed forward with another gaff and embedded the long point in one of the shark's eyes, and a third gaff found its way into one of the bullet wounds, and there was blood everywhere, so that Colin thought of the Kingman killings, and all the men in their swimsuits were spotted and streaked with blood, and Colin's father yelled for everyone to stand back, and athough Irv told him not to fire toward the deck, Colin's father put one more round in the shark's brain, and finally it stopped moving, and every-one was *very* excited, talking and shouting at once, and they got down in the blood and rolled the shark over and tore at its belly with the gutting knife, and the white flesh resisted for a moment but then gave, and out of the long rent spilled a putrid, slimy mass of guts and half-digested fish, and those still standing cheered while those on their knees pawed through the disgusting muck, looking for the mythical rare coin, the wedding ring, the cigar case, or the false teeth, laughing and joking, even tossing handfuls of gore at one another.

Suddenly Colin found the strength to move. He bolted toward the front of the boat, slipped in blood, stumbled, almost fell, regained his balance. When he had gone as far from the revelers and as far forward as he could, he leaned through the railing and vomited over the side.

By the time Colin finished, his father was there, towering over him, the very image of savagery, skin painted with blood, hair matted with blood, eyes wild. His voice was soft but intense. 'What's wrong with you?'

'I was sick,' Colin said weakly. 'Just sick. It's over now.'

'What the hell is *wrong* with you?'

'I'm OK now.'

'Do you *try* to embarrass me?'

'Huh?'

'In front of my friends like this?'

Colin stared, unable to comprehend.

'They're making jokes about you.'

'Well . . .'

'They're making fun of you.'

Colin was dizzy.

'Sometimes I wonder about you,' his father said.

124

'I couldn't help it. I threw up. There wasn't anything I could do to stop it.'

'Sometimes I wonder if you *are* my son.'

'I am. Of course I am.'

His father leaned close and studied him, as if searching for the telltale features of an old friend or milkman. His breath was foul.

Whiskey and beer.

And blood.

'Sometimes you don't act like a boy at all. Sometimes you don't look like you'll ever make a man,' his father said quietly but urgently.

'I'm trying.'

'Are you?'

'I really am,' Colin said despairingly.

'Sometimes you act like a pansy.'

'I'm sorry.'

'Sometimes you act like a goddamned queer.'

'I didn't mean to embarrass you.'

'Do you want to pull yourself together?'

'Yeah.'

'*Can* you pull yourself together?'

'Yeah.'

'Can you?'

'Sure I can.'

'Will you?'

'Sure.'

'Do it.'

'I need a couple of minutes—'

'Now! Do it now!'

'OK.'

'Pull yourself together.'

'OK. I'm OK.'

'You're shaking.'

'No I'm not.'

'You going to come back with me?'

'All right.'

'Show those guys whose son you are.'

'I'm your son.'

'You've got to prove it, Junior.'

'I will.'

'You've got to show me proof.'

'Can I have a beer?'

'What?'

'I think maybe it would help.'

'Help what?'

'It might make me feel better.'

'You want a beer?'

'Yeah.'

'Now, that's more like it!'

Frank Jacobs grinned and mussed his son's hair with one bloody hand.

15

Colin sat on a bench by the cabin wall, sipped his cold beer, and wondered what would happen next.

Having found nothing of interest in the shark's stomach, they heaved the dead beast over the side. It floated for a moment, then suddenly sank or was dragged under by something with a big appetite.

The blood-drenched men lined up along the starboard rail while Irv hosed them down with sea water. They stripped out of their swimsuits, which had to be thrown away, and they lathered up with bars of grainy, yellow soap, all the while making jokes about one another's genitalia. Each received one bucket of fresh water with which to rinse. While they went below to dry off and change into their street clothes, Irv sluiced the deck, washing the last traces of blood into the scuppers.

Later, the men did some skeet shooting. Charlie and Irv always carried two shotguns and a target launcher aboard the *Erica Lynn*, to entertain customers when the fish weren't biting. The men drank whiskey and beer, blasted away at the whirling discs, and forgot all about fishing.

At first Colin winced each time the guns boomed, but after a while the explosions didn't bother him.

Later still, when the men became bored with shooting clay pigeons, they opened up on the seagulls that were diving for small fish not far from the *Erica Lynn*. The birds did not react to the roar of the shotguns; they continued to feed and to issue strange shrill cries, apparently unaware that they were being cut down one by one.

The slaughter did not sicken Colin, as it once would have done, nor did it appeal to him. He felt nothing at all as he watched the birds being blown away, and he wondered about his inability to respond. He felt cool and perfectly still inside.

The guns fired, and the gulls burst apart in the sky. Thousands of tiny droplets of blood sprayed up like beads of molten copper in the golden air.

At seven-thirty they said good-bye to Charlie and Irv, and they went to a harbor restaurant for a steak-and-lobster dinner. Colin was starved. He greedily devoured everything on his plate, without a thought about the disemboweled shark or the gulls.

Well after the late, summer sunset, his father took him home. As always, Frank drove too fast and with no regard at all for other motorists.

Ten minutes from Santa Leona, Frank Jacobs turned the conversation away from the events of the day to more personal matters. 'Are you happy living with your mother?'

The question put Colin on the spot. He didn't want to spark an argument. He shrugged and said, 'I guess.'

'That's no answer.'

'I mean, I guess I'm happy.'

'You don't know?'

'I'm happy enough.'

'Is she taking good care of you?'

128

'Sure.'

'Are you eating well?'

'Yeah.'

'You're still so skinny.'

'I eat real well.'

'She's not much of a cook.'

'She does OK.'

'Does she give you enough spending money?'

'Oh yeah.'

'I could send you something every week.'

'I don't need it.'

'How about if I sent ten dollars every week?'

'You don't have to do that. I have plenty. I'd just waste it.'

'You like Santa Leona.'

'It's OK.'

'Just OK?'

'It's really nice.'

'You miss your friends from Westwood?'

'I didn't have any friends there.'

'Of course you did. I saw them once. That red-headed boy and—'

'Those were just guys from school. Acquaintances.'

'You don't have to keep a stiff upper lip for me.'

'I'm not.'

'Know you miss them.'

'I really don't.'

They swerved left, passed a truck that was already exceeding the speed limit, and pulled back into the right lane much too quickly.

Behind them the trucker angrily blew his horn.

'What the hell's eating him? I left plenty of room, didn't I?'

Colin said nothing.

Frank let up on the accelerator. The car slowed from sixty-five to fifty-five miles an hour.

The truck tooted again.

Frank pounded hard on the Cadillac's horn, trumpeted for at least a minute to show the other driver that he wasn't intimidated.

Colin glanced back anxiously. The big truck was no more than four feet from their bumper. Its headlights flashed.

'Bastard,' Frank said. 'Who the hell does he think he is?' He slowed down to forty miles an hour.

The truck swung into the passing lane.

Frank whipped the Cadillac to the left, in front of the truck, blocking it and holding it at forty.

'Hah! That'll piss the son-of-a-bitch! That'll burn his ass, won't it?'

The trucker used his horn again.

Colin was sweating.

His father was hunched forward, hands like talons on the wheel. His teeth were bared; his eyes were wide as they moved rapidly back and forth from the road to the mirror. He was breathing heavily, almost snorting.

The truck shifted to the right-hand lane.

Frank quickly cut it off again.

At last the trucker seemed to realise that he was dealing with either a drunk or a nut, and that extreme caution was the best course of action. He slowed to about thirty and fell steadily behind.

'That'll teach the asshole. Did he think he owned the goddamned road?'

Having won the battle, Frank put the Cadillac back up to seventy, and they rocketed away into the night.

Colin closed his eyes.

They rode in silence for a few miles, and then Frank said, 'What with your friends all down there in Westwood, how'd you like to come back and live with me?'

'You mean all the time?'

'Why not?'

'Well . . . I guess that would be OK,' Colin said, only because he knew it was impossible.

'I'll see what I can do, Junior.'

Colin glanced at him with alarm. 'But the judge gave Mom custody. You've just got visiting rights.'

'Maybe we can change that.'

'How?'

'There's several things we'd have to do, and a couple of them wouldn't be exactly pleasant.'

'Like what?'

'For one thing, you'd have to be willing to stand up in court and say you're not happy living with her.'

'I'd have to do that before they'd make a change?'

'I'm pretty sure you would.'

'I suppose you're right,' Colin said noncommittally. He relaxed a little because he didn't intend to tell the court any such thing.

'You've got the guts to do it, don't you?'

'Oh sure,' Colin said. Because it might help to know the enemy's strategy, he said, 'What else would we have to do?'

'Well, we'd have to show that she's an unfit mother.'

'But she's not.'

'Oh, I don't know. I have a hunch we could prove a loose-morals charge to the satisfaction of any judge.'

'Huh?'

'That art crowd,' Frank said sullenly. 'Those people she hangs around with.'

'What about them?'

'Those artists have different values from most people. They pride themselves on it.'

'I don't understand.'

'Well ... weird politics, atheism, drugs ... orgies. They sleep around a lot.'

'You think Mom—'

'I hate to say it.'

'Then don't.'

'For your sake, I've got to consider the possibility.'

'She doesn't ... live like that,' Colin said, although he wasn't sure if she did or not.

'You've got to face the facts of life, Junior.'

'She doesn't.'

'She's human. She might surprise you. She's sure as hell no saint.'

'I can't believe we're talking about this.'

'It's worth considering, worth looking into if it'll get you back with me. A boy needs to have his father around when he's growing up. He needs a man there to show him how to become a man himself.'

'But how would you ever prove that she ... did things like that?'

'Private detectives.'

'You'd really hire a bunch of private eyes to snoop on her everywhere she goes?'

'I don't want to have to do that! But it might be necessary. It would be the quickest and easiest way to find out about her.'

'Don't do it.'

'I'd only be doing it for you.'

132

'Then don't.'

'I want you to be happy.'

'I am.'

'You'd be happier in Westwood.'

'Please, Dad, I wouldn't be happy if you put a pack of dogs on her.'

His father scowled. 'Dogs? Who's talking about dogs? Look, these detectives are professionals. They aren't goons. They wouldn't hurt her. She wouldn't even know they were watching.'

'Please, don't do it.'

All his father would say was, 'I hope it isn't necessary.'

Colin thought about going back to Westwood, about living with his father, and it was like having a nightmare without being asleep.

16

At eleven o'clock Sunday morning, Roy arrived
with his swimsuit wrapped in a towel. 'Where's
your mother?'

'She's at the gallery.'

'On Sunday?'

'Seven days a week.'

'I thought I'd get to see her in a bikini.'

''Fraid not.'

The house was what the real-estate people
called 'prime lease property.' Among other
things, it had a sunken living room with a huge
stone fireplace, three large bathrooms, a gourmet
kitchen, and a forty-foot pool. Since they'd moved
in, they'd used the living room less than two
hours a week, for they'd had no company; they
hadn't entertained over-night guests and had no
reason to use the third bath; and of all the fancy
equipment in the kitchen, they'd used nothing but
the refrigerator and two burners on the stove.
Only the pool was worth the rent.

Colin and Roy raced the length of the pool,
played with inner tubes and inflated plastic rafts,
made a game of retrieving coins from the bottom,
splashed, splattered, and finally dragged themselves out onto the concrete apron to bake in the
sun.

It was the first time Colin had been swimming

with Roy, and the first time he had gotten a look at him without a shirt – and the first time that he had seen the horrible marks that disfigured Roy's back. Jagged bands of scar tissue slanted from the boy's right shoulder to his left hip. Colin tried to count them – six, seven, eight, perhaps as many as ten. It was difficult to be sure, for they melted together at a couple of points. Where there was healthy skin between the ugly lines, it was well tanned, but the raised scars did not take the sun; they were pale and shiny-smooth in some places, pale and puckered in others.

'What happened to you?' Colin asked.

'Huh?'

'What happened to your back?'

'Nothing.'

'What about those scars?'

'It's nothing.'

'You weren't *born* that way.'

'Just an accident.'

'What kind of accident?'

'It was a long time ago.'

'Were you in a car wreck or something?'

'I don't want to talk about it.'

'Why not?'

Roy glared at him. 'I said I don't want to fucking talk about the fucking scars!'

'OK. Sure. Forget it.'

'I don't have to give you any reason either.'

'I didn't mean to pry.'

'Well, you did.'

'I'm sorry.'

'Yeah.' Roy sighed. 'So am I.'

Roy got up and walked to the far end of the pool. He stood there for a while, his back to Colin, staring at the ground.

Feeling stupid and awkward, Colin quickly slid into the pool, as if he wanted to hide in the cool water. He swam hard, trying to work off a sudden overcharge of nervous energy.

Five minutes later, when Colin climbed out of the pool again, Roy was still at the corner of the concrete apron, but now he was hunkered down. He was poking at something in the grass.

'What'd you find?' Colin asked.

Roy was so intent on whatever he was doing that he did not hear the question.

Colin went to him and squatted beside him.

'Ants,' Roy said.

At the edge of the concrete lay a teacup-size mound of powdery earth. Tiny red ants were scurrying around and over it.

Grinning broadly, Roy mashed the insects into the concrete. A dozen. Two dozen. As he killed them other ants came out of the hill and raced into his shadow, as if they had abruptly realised that their destiny was not mindless labor in the hive but sacrificial death under the hands of a monster god a million times their size.

Roy paused now and then to look at the greasy, rust-coloured remains that stained his fingers. 'No bones,' he said. 'They squash into nothing, into just a little drop of juice, 'cause they don't have any bones.'

Colin watched.

17

After Roy had smashed a great many ants and had kicked apart their hill, he and Colin played water polo with a blue-and-green beach ball. Roy won.

By three o'clock they were tired of the pool. They changed out of their swimsuits and sat in the kitchen, eating chocolate-chip cookies and drinking lemonade.

Colin drained his glass, chewed on a sliver of ice, and said, 'Do you trust me?'

'Sure.'

'Did I pass the test?'

'We're blood brothers, aren't we?'

'Then tell me.'

'Tell you what?'

'You know. The big secret.'

'I already told you,' Roy said.

'You did?'

'I told you Friday night, after we left the Pit, before we went out to the Fairmont to see that porno flick.'

Colin shook his head. 'If you told me, I didn't hear.'

'You heard, but you didn't want to.'

'What kind of double-talk is that?'

Roy shrugged. He rattled the ice in his glass.

'Tell me again,' Colin said. 'This time I want to hear.'

'I kill people.'

'Jeez. That's *really* your big secret?'

'Seemed like a hell of a secret to me.'

'But it's not true.'

'Am I your blood brother?'

'Yeah.'

'Do blood brothers lie to each other?'

'They're not supposed to,' Colin admitted. 'OK. If you killed people, they must have had names. What were their names?'

'Stephen Rose and Philip Pacino.'

'Who were they?'

'Just two kids.'

'Friends?'

'They could have been if they'd wanted.'

'Why'd you kill 'em?'

'They refused to be blood brothers with me. After that I couldn't trust them.'

'You mean you'd have killed me if I hadn't wanted to be blood brothers?'

'Maybe.'

'Bullshit.'

'If it makes you happy to think so.'

'Where'd you kill them?'

'Right here in Santa Leona.'

'When?'

'I got Phil last summer, the first day of August, the day after his birthday, and I nailed Steve Rose the summer before that.'

'How?'

Roy smiled dreamily and closed his eyes, as if he were reliving it in his mind. 'I pushed Steve off the cliff at Sandman's Cove. He hit the rocks at the bottom. You should have seen him bounce. When they brought him up the next day, he was such a mess that even his old man couldn't make a positive ID.'

140

'What about the other one – Phil Pacino?'

'We were at his house, building a model airplane,' Roy said. 'His parents weren't home. He didn't have any brothers or sisters. Nobody knew I'd gone there. It was a perfect opportunity, so I squirted lighter fluid on his head and lit him.'

'Jeez.'

'As soon as I could see for sure that he was dead, I got the hell out of there. The whole house burned down. It was a real popper. A couple of days later, the fire marshal decided that Phil had started it by playing with matches.'

'You sure tell a good story,' Colin said.

Roy opened his eyes but didn't speak.

Colin took their plates and glasses to the sink, washed them, and stacked them in the rack. As he worked he said, 'You know, Roy, with your imagination, maybe you ought to write horror stories when you grow up. You'd make a bundle at it.'

Roy made no move to help with the clean-up. 'You mean you still think I'm playing some sort of game with you?'

'Well, you make up a couple of names—'

'Steve Rose and Phil Pacino were real people. You can check on that easy enough. Just go to the library and look through the back issues of the *News Register.* You can read all about how they died.'

'Maybe I'll do that.'

'Maybe you should.'

'But even if this Steve Rose did fall off the cliff at Sandman's Cove, and even if Phil Pacino burned to death in his own home – it wouldn't prove anything. Not a thing. Both of them could have been accidents.'

'Then why would I try to take credit for them?'

141

'To make your story about being a killer seem more realistic. To make me believe it. To set me up for some kind of joke.'

'You sure can be stubborn,' Roy said.

'So can you.'

'What will it take to make you face the truth?'

'I already know the truth,' Colin said. He finished the dishes and dried his hands on a red-and-white-checked dish towel.

Roy got up and went to the window. He stared at the sun-dappled swimming pool. 'I guess the only way I'm ever going to convince you is to kill someone.'

'Yeah,' Colin said. 'Why don't you do that?'

'You think I won't.'

'I *know* you won't.'

Roy turned to him. Sunlight streamed through the window, painted one side of Roy's face, left one side in shadow, and made one of his eyes even more fiercely blue than the other. 'Are you daring me to kill someone?'

'Yeah.'

'Then if I do it,' Roy said, 'half the responsibility will be yours.'

'OK.'

'Just like that?'

'Just like that.'

'Doesn't it bother you that you might wind up in jail?' Roy asked.

'No. Because you won't do it.'

'Is there anyone special you'd like me to take care of, anyone you'd like to see dead?'

Colin grinned because he was now certain that it was just a game. 'Nobody particular. Anyone you want. Why don't you pick a name out of the phone book?'

142

Roy turned to the window again.

Colin leaned against the counter and waited.

After a while Roy looked at his watch and said, 'I've got to be getting home. My parents are going to dinner at my Uncle Marlon's place. He's a genuine asshole. But I have to go with them.'

'Wait a minute, wait a minute!' Colin said. 'You can't change the subject that easily. You can't slip out of it. We were talking about who you're going to kill.'

'I wasn't trying to slip out of it.'

'Well?'

'I've got to think about it for a while.'

'Yeah,' Colin said. 'Like for fifty years.'

'No. By tomorrow I'll tell you who it'll be.'

'I won't let you forget.'

Roy nodded somberly. 'And once I'm rolling, I won't let you stop me.'

18

Weezy Jacobs had an important dinner engagement Sunday evening. She gave Colin money to eat at Charlie's Cafe, and she also gave him a short lecture about the importance of ordering something more nutritious than a greasy cheese-burger and french fries.

On his way to dinner, Colin stopped at Rhinehart's, a big drugstore one block from the cafe. Rhinehart's had a large paperback-book section. Colin browsed through the titles in the wire pockets, searching for interesting science fiction and novels about the supernatural.

After a while he realised that a pretty girl, about his own age, had walked up to the racks a few feet away. There were two shelves of books above the wire pockets, and those titles were shelved sideways instead of with their covers showing; she was looking at these, her head tilted to one side so that she could read the spines. She was wearing shorts, and for a moment he stared at her lovely slender legs. She had a graceful neck. Her hair was golden.

She became aware that he was staring at her, and she looked up, smiled. 'Hi.'

He smiled, too. 'Hi.'

'You're a friend of Roy Borden's, aren't you?'

'How'd you know that?'

She cocked her head to one side again, as if he were another book on the shelf and she was reading his title. She said, 'The two of you are almost like Siamese twins. I hardly ever see one without the other.'

'You see me now,' he said.

'You're new in town.'

'Yeah. Since the first of June.'

'What's your name?'

'Colin Jacobs. What's yours?'

'Heather.'

'That's pretty.'

'Thank you.'

'Heather what?'

'Promise you won't laugh.'

'Huh?'

'Promise you won't laugh at my name.'

'Why would I laugh at your name?'

'It's Heather Lipshitz.'

'No,' he said.

'Yes. It would be bad enough if it were Zelda Lipshitz. Or Sadie Lipshitz. But Heather Lipshitz is worse because the two don't go together, and the first name just calls attention to the last. You didn't laugh.'

'Of course not.'

'Most kids do.'

'Most kids are stupid.'

'You like to read?' Heather asked.

'Yeah.'

'What do you read?'

'Science fiction. You?'

'I'll read almost anything. I've read some science fiction. *Stranger in a Strange Land.*'

'That's a great book.'

'You see *Star Wars*?' she asked.

146

'Four times. And *Close Encounters* six times.'

'Have you seen *Alien*?'

'Yeah. You enjoy stuff like that?'

'Sure. When there's an old Christopher Lee movie on TV, you can't pull me away from the set,' she said.

He was amazed. 'You actually like horror movies?'

'The scarier the better.' She looked at her wristwatch. 'Well, I've got to get home for dinner. It's been real nice talking to you, Colin.'

As she started to turn away, he said, 'Uh . . . wait a sec.' She looked back at him, and he shifted awkwardly from one foot to the other. 'Uh . . . there's a new horror flick coming to the Baronet this week.'

'I saw the previews.'

'Did it look good to you?'

'Might be,' she said.

'Would you . . . well . . . I mean . . . do you think . . .'

She smiled. 'I'd like to.'

'You would?'

'Sure.'

'Well . . . should I call you or what?'

'Call me.'

'What's your number?'

'It's in the book. Believe it or not, we're the only Lipshitz family in town.'

He grinned. 'I'll call you tomorrow.'

'OK.'

'If that's all right.'

'That's fine.'

'Bye.'

'Goodbye, Colin.'

147

He watched her walk out of the store. His heart was racing.

Jeez.

Something strange was happening to him. For sure, for sure. He never before had been able to talk like that with a girl – or with a girl like that. He usually got tongue-tied right at the start, and the whole conversation went into the toilet. But not this time. He'd been smooth. For God's sake, he'd even made a date with her! His first date. Something sure was happening to him.

But what?

And why?

Several hours later, as he lay in bed, listening to a Los Angeles radio station, unable to sleep, Colin thought about all of the wonderful new developments in his life. With a terrific friend like Roy, with an important position like team manager, and with a girl as pretty and nice as Heather – what more could he possibly ask?

He had never been so content.

Roy was the most important part of his new life, of course. Without Roy, he would never have been brought to the attention of Coach Molinoff and would never have gotten the job as junior-varsity team manager. And without Roy's liberating influence, he would very likely never have had the nerve to ask Heather for a date. More than that – she probably wouldn't even have said hello to him if he hadn't been Roy's friend. Wasn't that the first thing she had said to him? *You're a friend of Roy Borden's, aren't you*? If he hadn't been a friend of Roy's, she probably wouldn't even have looked at him twice.

But she *had* looked twice.

And she had agreed to date him.

Life was good.

He thought about Roy's strange stories. The cat in the birdcage. The boy burned with lighter fluid. He knew those were just tall tales. Tests. Roy was testing him for something. He put the cat and the burned boy out of his mind. He wasn't going to let those silly stories destroy his lovely mood.

He closed his eyes and pictured himself dancing with Heather in a magnificent ballroom. He was wearing a tuxedo. She was in a red gown. There was a crystal chandelier. They danced so well together that they seemed to be floating.

19

Early Monday afternoon, Colin was at the work-table in his bedroom, putting together a plastic model of Lon Chaney as the Phantom of the Opera. When the telephone rang, he had to run into his mother's room to answer it, for he had no extension of his own.

It was Roy. 'Colin, you've got to come right away.'

'Come where?'

'My house.'

Colin looked at the digital read-out clock on the nightstand: 1:05. He said, 'We were supposed to meet at two o'clock.'

'I know. But you've got to come now.'

'Why?'

'My folks aren't home, and there's something here that you absolutely have to see. I can't talk about it on the phone. You've got to come now, right away, just as quick as you can. Hurry!'

Roy hung up.

The game continues, Colin thought.

Ten minutes later, Colin rang the bell at the Borden house.

Roy answered the door. He was flushed and excited.

'What's up?' Colin asked.

Roy pulled him inside and slammed the door.

They stood in the foyer. The immaculate living room lay beyond; the emerald-green drapes filtered the sun and filled the place with cold light that gave Colin the feeling they were deep beneath the sea.

'I want you to get a good look at Sarah,' Roy said.

'Who?'

'I told you about her Friday night, when we were at the beach steps on the palisades, just before we split up. She's the girl, the one who looks good enough to be in a porn movie, the one I think we can find a way to screw.'

Colin blinked. 'You've got her *here*?'

'Not exactly. Come on upstairs. You'll see.'

Colin had never been in Roy's bedroom before, and it surprised him. It didn't look like a kid's room; in fact, it didn't look like a place where anyone, either child or adult, really lived. The nap on the carpet stood up as if it had been vacuumed only minutes ago. The dark pine furniture was highly polished; Colin couldn't see a nick or a scratch in it, but he could see his reflection. No dust. No grime. No fingerprints around the light switch. The bed was neatly made, the lines as straight and the corners as tightly tucked as those on a bunk in an Army barracks. In addition to the furniture, there was a big red dictionary and the uniform volumes of an encyclopedia. But nothing else. Nothing else at all. There were no knick-knacks, no model airplanes, no comic books, no sports equipment, nothing to show that Roy had any hobbies or even any normal human interests. Quite clearly, the room was a mirror of Mrs Borden's personality and not her son's.

To Colin's eye, the oddest thing about the place

was the total absence of decoration on the walls. No paintings. No photographs. No posters. In the downstairs foyer, in the living room, and on the wall along the stairs, there were a couple of oils, a watercolor, and a few inexpensive prints, but here the walls were bare and white. Colin felt as if he were in a monk's cell.

Roy led him to a window.

Not more than fifty feet away, in the backyard of the house next door, a woman was sunbathing. She was wearing a white bikini and was lying on a red beach towel that was draped across a cot. Small cotton pads shielded her eyes from the sun.

'She's really a terrific piece of ass,' Roy said.

Her arms were at her sides, palms turned up as if in supplication. She was tan and lean and shapely.

'That's Sarah?' Colin asked.

'Sarah Callahan. She lives next door.' Roy picked up a pair of binoculars that had been on the floor beneath the window. 'Here. Take a closer look.'

'What if she sees me?'

'She won't.'

He put the glasses to his eyes, focused them, and found the woman. If she actually had been as close as she suddenly appeared to be, she would have felt his breath on her skin.

Sarah was beautiful. Even in repose, her features held great sensual promise. Her lips were full, ripe; she licked them once while he watched.

A peculiar sense of power overcame Colin. In his mind he touched and caressed Sarah Callahan, but in reality she was unaware of it. The binoculars were his lips and tongue and fingers, feeling

153

and tasting her, exploring her, surreptitiously violating the sanctity of her body. He experienced mild synesthesia: Magically, his eyes seemed to possess senses other than sight. With his eyes he smelled her fresh, thick, yellow hair. With his eyes he felt the texture of her skin, the pliancy of her flesh, the soft roundness of her breasts, and the moist warmth in the musky junction of her thighs. With his eyes he kissed her concave belly and tasted the salty beads of perspiration that ringed her like a jeweled belt. For a moment Colin felt that he could do anything to her that he wished; he had complete immunity. He was the invisible man.

'How'd you like to get in her pants?' Roy asked.

Finally Colin lowered the binoculars.

'You want her?' Roy asked.

'Who wouldn't?'

'We can have her.'

'You're living in a dream.'

'Her husband's at work all day.'

'So?'

'She's pretty much alone over there.'

'What do you mean — "pretty much"?'

'She has a five-year-old kid.'

'Then she's not alone at all.'

'The kid won't give us any trouble.'

Colin knew that Roy was playing the game again, but this time he decided to play along. 'What's your plan?'

'We just go over and knock on the door. She knows me. She'll open up.'

'And then?'

'You and me can handle her. We'll push inside, knock her down. I'll put a knife at her throat.'

'She'll scream.'

'Not with a knife at her throat.'

'She'll think you're bluffing.'

'If she does,' Roy said, 'I'll cut her a little to show we mean business.'

'What about the kid?'

'I'll have Sarah under control, so you'll be free to catch the brat and tie him up.'

'What'll I tie him with?'

'We'll take along some clothesline.'

'After I've gotten him out of the way, what happens?'

Roy grinned. 'Then we'll strip her, tie her to the bed, and use her.'

'And you think she's not going to tell anybody what we've done?'

'Oh, of course, when we're finished with her, we'll have to kill her.'

'And the kid, too?' Colin asked.

'He's a rotten little brat. I'd like to snuff him most of all.'

'It's a bad idea. Forget it.'

'Yesterday, you dared me to kill someone,' Roy said. 'And now the idea scares you.'

'Look who's talking.'

'What do you mean?'

Colin sighed. 'You've protected yourself by coming up with a plan that can't possibly work. You figured I'd shoot it down, and then you could say, "Well, I wanted to prove I could kill someone, but Colin chickened out on me."'

'What's wrong with my plan?' Roy demanded.

'First of all, you live next door to her.'

'So what?'

'The cops would suspect you right off.'

'Me? I'm just a fourteen-year-old kid.'

'Old enough to be a suspect.'

'You really think so?'

'Sure.'

'Well . . . you could give me an alibi. You could swear I was at your house when she was murdered.'

'Then they'd suspect both of us.'

For a long time Roy stared down at Sarah Callahan. Finally he turned away from the window and began to pace. 'What we'd have to do is leave clues that pointed away from us. We'd have to mislead them.'

'You realise the kind of lab equipment they've got? They can trace you by a single hair, a thread, almost anything.'

'But if we could snuff her in such a way that they'd never in a million years think it was just kids that did it . . .'

'How?'

Roy continued to pace. 'We'd make it look like some raving lunatic killed her, some sex maniac. We'd stab her a hundred times. We'd cut off her ears. We'd slice up the brat pretty good, too, and we'd use blood to write a lot of crazy things on the walls.'

'You're really gross.'

Roy stopped pacing and stared hard at him. 'What's the matter? Are you a sissy about blood?'

Colin felt queasy but tried not to show it. 'Even if you could mislead the cops that way, there's too many other things wrong with your plan.'

'Like what?'

'Someone will see us going into the Callahan place.'

'Who?'

'Maybe somebody taking out the garbage. Or

156

somebody washing windows. Or just somebody going by in a car.'

'So we'll use the Callahans' back door.'

Colin glanced out the window. 'Looks to me like that wall goes all around the property. We'd have to enter by the front walk and go around the house to get to the back door.'

'Nah. We could climb over the wall in a minute.'

'If anyone saw us, they'd be sure to remember. Besides, what about fingerprints when we get into the house?'

'We'll wear gloves, of course.'

'You mean we'll walk up to the door wearing gloves in ninety-degree heat, carrying a lot of rope and a knife – and she'll let us in without a second thought?'

Roy was becoming impatient. 'When she opens the door, we'll move so fast she won't have time to realise anything's wrong.'

'What if she does? What if she's faster than we are?'

'She won't be.'

'We've at least got to consider the possibility,' Colin insisted.

'OK. I've considered it, and I've decided it's nothing to worry about.'

'Another thing. What if she opens the inner door but not the storm door?'

'Then we'll open the storm door,' Roy said. 'What's the problem?'

'What if it's locked?'

'Christ!'

'Well, we have to expect the worst.'

'OK, OK. It's a bad idea.'

'That's what I said.'

'But I'm not giving up.'

'I don't want you to give up,' Colin said. 'I'm enjoying the game.'

'Soon or later, I'll find the right setup. I'll find someone for us to kill. You better believe it.'

For a while they took turns watching Sarah Callahan through the binoculars.

Earlier, Colin had been eager to tell Roy about Heather. But now, for reasons he couldn't quite define, he felt the time wasn't right. For the moment Heather would be his little secret.

When Sarah Callahan finished sunning herself, Colin and Roy went down to the garage and passed Monday afternoon with the trains. Roy engineered elaborate wrecks and laughed excitedly each time the cars plunged off the tracks.

That night Colin telephoned Heather, and she accepted a movie date for Wednesday. They talked almost fifteen minutes. When Colin finally hung up, he felt that his happiness was a visible light, that it was radiating from him in a golden nimbus; he was glowing.

20

Colin and Roy spent part of Tuesday at the beach, getting tanned and watching the girls. Roy seemed to have lost interest in his macabre game; he didn't say a single word about killing anyone.

At two-thirty Roy stood up and brushed sand from his bare legs and his cut-off jeans. He had decided it was time to go back into town. 'I want to stop by your mother's gallery.'

Colin blinked. 'What for?'

'To look at the paintings, of course.'

'Why?'

''Cause I'm interested in paintings, dummy.'

'Since when?'

'Since always.'

'You never mentioned it before.'

'You never asked,' Roy said.

They rode their bicycles back to town and parked on the sidewalk in front of the gallery.

A few browsers were in the shop. They moved slowly from painting to painting.

Weezy's business partner, Paula, was sitting at the big antique desk in the far right corner of the room, where sales were written. She was a wispy, freckled woman with lustrous auburn hair and large glasses.

Weezy was circulating among the browsers,

offering to answer any questions they might have about the paintings. When she saw Colin and Roy, she headed straight for them, smiling stiffly. It was clear to Colin that she thought a pair of sandy, sweaty, bare-chested boys in cut-off jeans were definitely not conducive to business.

Before Weezy could ask them what they wanted, Roy pointed to a large painting by Mark Thornberg and said, 'Mrs Jacobs, this artist is terrific. He really is. His work has a lot more depth than the two-dimensional stuff that most current painters are turning out. The detail is really something. Wow. I mean, it almost looks like he's trying to adapt the style of the old Flemish masters to a more modern sort of viewpoint.'

Weezy was surprised by Roy's observations.

Colin was surprised, too. More than surprised. Stunned. Depth? Two-dimensional? Flemish masters? He gaped at Roy, amazed.

'Are you interested in art?' Weezy asked.

'Oh yes,' Roy said. 'I'm thinking of majoring in art when I go to college. But that's still a few years away.'

'Do you paint?'

'A little. Mostly watercolors. I'm not really very good.'

'I'll bet you're being modest,' Weezy said. 'After all, you apparently have quite an understanding of art – and a very good eye. You went right to the heart of what Mark Thornberg is trying to achieve.'

'I did?'

'Yes. That's astounding. Especially for someone your age. Mark *is* attempting to take the meticulous detail and the three-dimensional techniques of the Flemish masters and combine those qualities with a modern sensibility and modern subject matter.'

Roy looked at other Thornberg canvases on the same wall as the first, and he said, 'I think I detect a trace of . . . Jacob DeWitt.'

'Exactly!' Weezy said, astonished. 'Mark is a great admirer of DeWitt. You really *do* have a knowledge of art. You're quite remarkable.'

Roy and Weezy moved from one Thornberg painting to another, spending a few minutes in front of each, discussing the artist's merits. Colin tagged along behind them, left out, embarrassed by his ignorance – and baffled by Roy's unexpected expertise and brilliant perception.

The very first time that Weezy had met Roy, she had been favorably impressed by him. She had told Colin as much, and she had suggested that a fine boy like Roy Borden was a much better influence than the few bookworms and social rejects with whom he had previously established tenuous relationships. She had seemed unaware that he, too, was a bookworm and a social reject and that her words stung him. Now she was intrigued by Roy's interest in fine arts. Colin could see the delight in her eyes. Roy knew how to be charming without ever seeming phony, insincere. He could win the approval of virtually any adult – even those he secretly despised.

In a flash of jealousy, Colin thought: *She approves of him more than she does of me. The way she's looking at him! Has she ever looked at me like that? Hell, no. The bitch!*

The intensity of his sudden anger surprised and disconcerted him. As Weezy and Roy looked at the last of the Thornberg paintings, Colin struggled to regain control of himself.

A few minutes later, outside the gallery, as he and Roy were climbing on their bicycles, Colin said, 'Why didn't you ever tell me you were interested in art?'

Roy grinned. 'Because I'm *not* interested in art. It's a bunch of crap. It's too damned boring.'

'But all that stuff you said in there—'

'I knew your old lady was dating this Thornberg and handling his paintings at the gallery. I went to the library to see if I could find out anything about him. They subscribe to several art magazines at the library. *California Artist* ran an article about Thornberg almost a year ago. I just read it for background.'

'Why?' Colin asked, perplexed.

'To impress your mother.'

'Why?'

''Cause I want her to like me.'

'You went to all that trouble just to make my mother like you? It's that important to you?'

'Sure,' Roy said. 'We don't want her getting the idea I'm a bad influence on you. She might forbid you to see me any more.'

'Why would she think you're a bad influence?'

'Grown-ups can get funny ideas sometimes,' Roy said.

'Well, she'd never tell me not to hang around with you. She thinks you're a *good* influence.'

'Yeah?'

'Yeah.'

'Well then, my little act was just more insurance.'

Roy pedaled away fast.

Colin hesitated, then followed him. He was

162

certain there was more behind Roy's 'little act' than the boy was willing to talk about. But what? What had Roy really been up to?

21

Weezy couldn't come home Tuesday evening; she had dinner with a business associate. She gave Colin money to eat at Charlie's Cafe again, and Colin took Roy with him.

After cheeseburgers and milkshakes, Colin said, 'Want to see a movie?'

'Where?'

'There's a good one on television.'

'What is it?'

'*The Shadow of Dracula*.'

'Why do you want to see junk like that?'

'It's not junk. It's gotten good reviews.'

'There's no such thing as vampires,' Roy said.

'Maybe. Maybe not.'

'No maybes. Positively not. Vampires . . . that's bunk.'

'But they make for scary movies.'

'Boring,' Roy said.

'Why don't you give it a chance?'

Roy sighed and shook his head. 'How can you be scared of something that doesn't exist?'

'You just have to use your imagination a little.'

'Why should I *imagine* scary things when there are so many *real* things to be afraid of?'

Colin shrugged. 'OK. So you don't want to see the movie.'

'Besides, I have something planned for later.'

'What?' Colin asked.

Roy gave him a sly look. 'You'll see.'

'Don't be mysterious. Tell me.'

'In good time.'

'When?'

'Oh . . . eight o'clock,' Roy said.

'What'll we do till then?'

They rode down Central Avenue to the small craft harbor, chained their bicycles in a parking lot, and explored the maze of waterfront shops and amusements. They strolled through swarms of buzzing tourists, looking for pretty girls in shorts or bikinis.

Over the bay, seagulls soared and swooped. With piercing, melancholy cries, they darted up and down, back and forth, sewing together the sky, the earth, and the water.

Colin thought the harbor was beautiful. The westering sun streamed between scattered white clouds and appeared to lie in shimmering bronze puddles on the water. Seven small boats were sailing in formation, snaking across the sheltered water toward the open sea. The evening was drenched in that peculiar California light that is perfectly clear but that seems at the same time to have considerable substance, as if you were looking at the world through countless sheets of expensive, highly polished crystal.

At that moment the harbor seemed to be the safest and most welcoming place on earth, but Colin was cursed with the ability to see how it would change for the worse in just an hour or two. In his mind he could picture it at night – the crowds gone, the shops closed, and no light but that from a few wharf lamps. In the late hours the only sound would be the voice of the night: the

166

continuous lapping of the sea at the dark pilings, the creaking of moored boats, the sinister rustling of wings as the gulls settled down to sleep, and that ever-present undercurrent of demonic whispers that most people could not hear. He knew that evil would creep in with the dying of the light. In the lonely shadows, something hideous would rise out of the water and snatch away the unwary passerby; something slimy and scaly; something with awful, insatiable hungers; something with razor teeth and powerful jaws that could tear a man apart.

Unable to shake that horror-movie image, Colin suddenly found that he could no longer enjoy the beauty around him. It was as if he were looking at a pretty girl and, against his will, seeing within her the rotting corpse that she would eventually become.

Sometimes he wondered if he were crazy.

Sometimes he hated himself.

'It's eight o'clock,' Roy said.

'Where we going?'

'Just follow me.'

With Roy in the lead, they cycled all the way to the eastern end of Central Avenue, then continued east on Santa Leona Road. In the hills beyond town, they turned on to a narrow dirt lane, followed it down one flank of a shallow glen and up the other. On both sides of the dusty track, wildflowers shone like blue-and-red flames in the tall, dry grass.

Sunset was nearly upon them; and this close to the sea, the twilight hour was more like fifteen minutes. Night would swiftly lay claim to the land. Wherever they were going, they would have to come back in the dark. And Colin didn't like that.

167

On high ground again, they rounded a curve that lay in shadows cast by several eucalyptus trees. The lane ended fifty yards beyond the curve, in the middle of an automobile grave-yard.

'Hermit Hobson's place,' Roy said.

'Who's he?'

'Used to live here.'

A one-story clapboard building, more shack than house, overlooked two hundred or more decaying automobiles that were strewn across a few acres of the grassy hilltop.

They parked their bicycles in front of the shack.

'Why's he called "Hermit"?' Colin asked.

'Because that's what he was. He lived all alone out here, and he didn't like people.'

A four-inch, blue-green lizard slithered on to a sagging porch step and halfway across the breadth of it, then froze, rolling one milky eye at the boys.

'What're all these cars for?' Colin asked.

'When he first moved in, that's how he sup-ported himself. He bought up cars that had been in real bad accidents and sold spare parts.'

'You can make a living that way?'

'Well, he didn't want much.'

'I can see that.'

The lizard came off the step, on to a patch of hard, dry earth. It was still watchful.

'Later on,' Roy said, 'old Hermit Hobson in-herited some money.'

'He was rich?'

'No. He got just enough so he could keep on living here without the spare-parts business. After that he saw other people just once a month, when he came to town for supplies.'

168

The lizard skittered back toward the step, froze again, this time facing away from them.

Roy moved fast. The lizard's eyes looked backward as well as sideways and forward, so it saw him coming. Nevertheless, he caught it by the tail, held it, and brought his foot down hard on its head.

Colin turned away in disgust. 'Why the hell did you have to do that?'

'Did you hear it crunch?'

'What was the point?'

'It was a popper.'

'Jeez.'

Roy wiped his shoe in the grass.

Colin cleared his throat and said, 'Where's Hermit Hobson now?'

'Dead.'

Colin looked suspiciously at Roy. 'I guess you're going to try to make me believe you killed him, too.'

'Nope. Natural causes. Four months ago.'

'Then why're we here?'

'For the train wreck.'

'Huh?'

'Come see what I've done.'

Roy walked toward the rusting automobiles.

After a moment, Colin followed him. 'It'll be dark before long.'

'That's good. It'll cover our escape.'

'Escape from what?'

'The scene of the crime.'

'What crime?'

'I told you. The train wreck.'

'What're you talking about?'

Roy didn't answer.

They walked through knee-high grass. Close to

169

the abandoned junkers, where a mower couldn't reach and where Hermit Hobson had never trimmed, the grass was much higher and thicker than it was elsewhere.

The hilltop ended in a rounded point somewhat like the prow of a ship.

Roy stood on the edge of the slope and looked down. 'That's where it'll happen.'

Eighty feet below, railroad tracks curved around the prow of the hill.

'We'll derail it on the curve,' Roy said. He pointed to two parallel ribbons of heavy corrugated sheet metal that led from the tracks, up the slope, and over the brow of the hill. 'Hobson was a real packrat. I found fifty of those six-foot-long sheets in big piles of junk behind his shack. That was a hell of a piece of luck. Without them, I wouldn't have been able to set this up.'

'What're they for?' Colin asked.

'The truck.'

'What truck?'

'Over there.'

A four-year-old, battered Ford pickup stood about thirty feet back from the slope. The corrugated strips led to it, then under it. The Ford had no tires; its rust-filmed wheels rested on the sheet metal.

Colin hunkered down beside the truck. 'How'd you get the corrugated panels under there?'

'I lifted one wheel at a time with a jack I found in one of these wrecks.'

'Why go to all that trouble?'

'Because we can't just push the truck across bare ground,' Roy said. 'The wheels would dig into the earth and stop it.'

Colin looked from the truck to the brow of the

hill. 'Let me get this straight. Let me see if I understand. You want to push the truck along this track you've made, let it roll down the slope, into the side of the train.'

'Yeah.'

Colin sighed.

'What's wrong?' Roy asked.

'Another damned game.'

'No game.'

'I guess I'm supposed to do what I did with the Sarah Callahan scheme. You want me to show you the holes in it so you'll have an excuse to chicken out.'

'What holes?' Roy challenged.

'For one thing, a train is too damned big and heavy to be derailed by a little truck like this.'

'Not if we do it right,' Roy said. 'If it's perfectly timed, if the truck's coming down the slope just as the train's rounding the bend, the engineer will hit the brakes. When he tries to stop the train on a sharp curve like that, it'll start rocking like crazy. And then when the truck hits it, it'll roll right off the tracks.'

'I don't think so.'

'You're wrong,' Roy said. 'There's a pretty good chance it'll happen just like I say.'

'No.'

'It's worth a try. Even if it doesn't derail the train, it'll scare the hell out of them. Either way, it'll be a popper.'

'There's something else you haven't thought of. This truck's been sitting out here for a couple of years. The wheels are rusted. No matter how hard we push, they aren't going to turn.'

'You're wrong again,' Roy said happily. 'I thought of that. There hasn't been that much rain

171

the past few years. They weren't rusted really bad. I had to spend a few days working on the truck, but now the wheels will turn for us.'

For the first time, Colin noticed dark, oily stains on the wheel beside him. He reached behind it and found that it had been freshly, excessively lubricated. His hand came away with gobs of grease on it.

Roy grinned. 'You see any other flaws in the plan?'

Colin wiped his hand in the grass and stood up.

Roy stood, too. 'Well?'

The sun had just set. The western sky was golden.

'When do you figure to do it?' Colin asked.

Roy looked at his wristwatch. 'About six or seven minutes from now.'

'There'll be a train then?'

'Six nights a week at this time, a passenger train comes through here. I've done some checking. It starts in San Diego, stops in L.A., goes on to San Francisco and then Seattle before starting back. I've sat on the hill and watched it a lot of nights. It really moves. It's an express.'

'You said the timing has to be perfect.'

'It will be. Or near enough.'

'But no matter how carefully you've planned it, you can't expect the railroad to co-operate. I mean, trains don't always run on time.'

'This one usually does,' Roy said confidently. 'Besides, that's not too important. All we have to do is push the truck closer to the edge, then wait until the train is almost here. When we see the locomotive coming, we'll give the truck a little shove, tip it over the brink, and away it'll go.'

172

Colin bit his lip, frowned. 'I know you set this up so it can't be done.'

'Wrong. I want to do it.'

'It's a game. There's a big hole in the plan, and you expect me to find it.'

'No holes.'

'I must be missing something.'

'You haven't missed anything.'

Each of the ruined pickup's front wheels was jammed against a wooden chock. Roy removed these braces and threw them aside.

'What's the joke?' Colin asked.

'We've got to get moving.'

'There must be a joke.'

'We don't have much time.'

Both of the truck's doors had been removed, either by the collision or by Hermit Hobson. Roy went to the open driver's side, reached in, and put his right hand on the steering wheel. He put his left hand on the door frame, ready to push.

'Roy, why don't you give up? I *know* there's got to be a catch.'

'Get around on the other side and help.'

Still trying to find the hole, still wondering what he had overlooked, still certain that Roy was playing an elaborate trick on him, Colin walked around the truck and stationed himself at the open passenger side.

Roy looked through the truck at him. 'Put both hands on the front of the door frame and push.'

Colin did as he was told, and Roy pushed from the other side.

The truck didn't move.

What's the joke?

'It's been sitting here awhile,' Roy said. 'It's made a sort of depression for itself.'

173

'Ahhh,' Colin said. 'And of course we're not strong enough to push it out.'

'Sure we are,' Roy said. 'Put your back into it.'

Colin strained.

'Harder!' Roy said.

It won't come up out of its little depression, Colin thought. He knows it. That's the way he planned it.

'Push!'

The land was not flat. It graded down toward the edge of the hill.

'Harder!'

The firm, sun-baked earth helped them, and the corrugated metal tracks helped them.

'Harder!'

The recent grease job helped them.

'Harder!'

But most of all, the gently sloping land and gravity helped them.

The truck moved.

22

When he felt the pickup moving, Colin jumped back, astonished.

The truck stopped with a sharp squeak.

'What'd you do that for?' Roy demanded. 'We had it going, for Christ's sake! Why'd you stop?'

Colin looked at him through the open cab of the truck. 'OK. Tell me. What's the joke?'

Roy was angry. His voice was hard and cold, and he emphasised each word. 'Get . . . it . . . through . . . your . . . head. There . . . is . . . no . . . joke!'

They stared at each other in the fast-fading, smoky light of dusk.

'Are you my blood brother?' Roy asked.

'Sure.'

'Isn't it you and me against the world?'

'Yeah.'

'Won't blood brothers do anything for each other?'

'Almost anything.'

'Anything! It has to be anything! No ifs, ands, or buts. Not with blood brothers. Are you my blood brother?'

'I said I was, didn't I?'

'Then push, damnit!'

'Roy, this has gone far enough.'

'It won't have gone far enough until it's gone over the edge of the hill.'

'Fooling around like this could be dangerous.'

'Have you got concrete for brains?'

'We might accidentally wreck the train.'

'It won't be an accident. Push!'

'You win. I give up. I won't push the truck or you any further. You win the game, Roy.'

'What the hell are you doing to me?'

'I just want to get out of here.'

Roy's voice was strained now, almost hysterical. His eyes were wild. He glared at Colin through the truck. 'Are you turning your back on me?'

'Of course not.'

'Betraying me?'

'Look, I—'

'Are you a phony, too? Are you just like all the other goddamned cheats and back-stabbers and liars?'

'Roy—'

'Didn't you mean one word you said to me?'

In the distance a train whistle pierced the twilight.

'That's it!' Roy said frantically. 'The engineer always blows the whistle when he crosses Ranch Road. We've only got three minutes. Help me.'

Even in the dimming, orange-purple light, Colin could clearly see the rage in Roy's face, the madness in his blue, blue eyes. Colin was shocked. He took another step back, away from the truck.

'Bastard!' Roy said.

He tried to push the Ford by himself.

Colin remembered how Roy acted in the garage when they played with Mr Borden's trains. How he wrecked them with such fierce glee. How he peered through the windows of the derailed toy cars. How he imagined that he was seeing real bodies, real blood, real tragedy – and somehow found pleasure in those sick fantasies.

This was not a game.

It had never been a game.

Pushing, then relaxing, pushing, then relaxing, keeping a hard, fast rhythm, Roy rocked the truck until suddenly he overcame inertia. The pickup moved.

'No!' Colin said.

Gravity helped again. The truck's wheels turned slowly, reluctantly. They squealed and squeaked. The metal rims ground harshly against the heavy corrugated tracks. But they *turned*.

Colin raced around the pickup, grabbed Roy, and pulled him away from the truck.

'You little creep!'

'Roy, you can't!'

'Let me alone!'

Roy wrenched loose, shoved Colin backward, and returned to the truck.

The pickup had ceased all movement the instant Roy had been dragged from it. The slope was not steep enough to encourage the Ford to run away.

Roy rocked it again.

'You can't kill all those people.'

'Just watch me.'

The truck needed considerably less coaxing this time than it had the last. Or perhaps Roy had found even greater strength in his madness. In a few seconds the Ford began to roll.

Colin leaped at him and wrestled him away from the truck.

Furious, cursing, Roy turned and punched him twice in the stomach.

Colin collapsed around the blows. He let go of Roy, gagged, bent forward, caved in, staggered back, and fell. The pain was terrible. He felt as if Roy's fists had gone all the way through him, leaving two big holes. He couldn't get his breath.

His glasses had been knocked off. He could see only blurry outlines of the junkyard. Coughing, gagging, still struggling to breathe, he felt the grass around him, anxious to regain his sight.

Roy grunted and mumbled to himself as he tried to move the pickup.

Suddenly Colin was aware of another sound: a steady *chuka-chuka-chuka-chuka-chuka-chuka*.

The train.

In the distance. But not too far.

Coming closer.

Colin found his glasses and put them on. Through tears, he saw that the truck was still more than twenty feet from the brink, and that Roy had only just begun to get it moving again.

Colin attempted to stand. He got as far as his knees when a wave of excruciating pain washed through his guts, immobilising him.

The truck was no more than twenty feet from the edge of the hill, gaining inches slowly, slowly but relentlessly.

By the sound of it, the train had reached the curve in the glen below.

The truck was eighteen feet from the brink.

Sixteen.

Fourteen.

Twelve.

Then it ran off the corrugated track; its wheels bit into the dry earth; and it would not move. If

178

they had been pushing from both sides, if the force had been applied evenly, the truck would not have deviated from the twin ribbons of metal. But because all the effort was being exerted on the left side, the Ford turned inexorably to the right, and Roy didn't use the steering wheel fast enough to correct the truck's course.

Colin clutched the door handle of a dilapidated Dodge beside him and drew himself to his feet. His legs were shaky.

The thunderous clatter of the rails filled the night: a cacophonous roar like an orchestra of machinery tuning itself.

Roy ran to the edge of the hill. He looked down at the train that Colin couldn't see.

In less than a minute, the sound of the passenger express diminished. The last car was around the curve; it was speeding away, toward San Francisco.

The small noises of the oncoming night crept back across the hilltop. For a while, Colin was too stunned to hear anything at all. Gradually, he began once more to perceive the crickets, the toads, the breeze in the trees, and the pounding of his own heart.

Roy screamed. He looked down at the tracks that were now empty, and he raised his fists toward the sky, and he cried out like an animal in agony. He turned and started toward Colin.

Only thirty feet of open ground separated them.

'Roy, I had to do it.'

'I hate you.'

'You don't really.'

'You're like all the rest.'

'Roy, you'd have gone to jail.'

'I'll kill you.'

179

'But Roy—'
'You fucking traitor!'
Colin ran.

23

As Colin ran for his life, he was acutely aware that he had never won a race. His legs were thin; Roy's legs were muscular. His reserves of strength were pathetically shallow; Roy's energy and power were awesome. Colin did not dare look back.

The automobile graveyard was an elaborate maze. He ran in a crouch through the twisting, crisscrossing passages, taking full advantage of the cover provided by the junkers. He turned right, between the gutted shells of two Buicks. He ran past huge stacks of tires, past bent and rusted Plymouths, past smashed and corroded Fords, Dodges, Toyotas, Oldsmobiles, and Volkswagens. He jumped over a disconnected transmission, did broken-field running through scattered tires, darted east toward Hermit Hobson's shack, which lay impossibly far away, at least six hundred feet, and then he swung sharply south through a narrow alley dotted with mufflers and headlamp assemblies that were like land mines in the tall grass. Ten yards farther along, he turned west, expecting to be tackled from behind at any second, but nevertheless determined to put walls of wreckage between himself and Roy.

After what seemed like an hour but was probably no more than two minutes, Colin realised that he could not keep running forever, and that he might quickly become confused about directions and dash headlong into Roy at a turn or an intersection. In fact, Colin was no longer certain whether he was rushing toward or away from the point at which the chase had begun. He risked a glance over his shoulder and saw that he was miraculously alone. He stopped at a crumpled Cadillac and huddled in the darkness along its ruined flank.

The last few minutes of murky copper-colored sunlight did little to illuminate the open spaces between the cars. Purple-black velvet shadows lay everywhere; and as he watched they grew with incredible speed, like a nightmare fungus intent upon blanketing the entire planet. Colin was terrified of being trapped in the dark with Roy. But he was equally frightened of the threatening creatures that might lurk in the junkyard at night: strange beasts; monsters; bloodsucking things; perhaps even the ghosts of people who had died in these broken cars.

Stop it! he thought angrily. That's stupid. It's childish.

He had to concentrate on the danger he *knew* was out there. Roy. He had to save himself from Roy. *Then* he could worry about the other things.

Think, damnit!

He became aware of his noisy breathing. His panting would carry quite a distance in the crisp night air, and Roy would be able to home in on it. In view of his precarious position, Colin could not be calm, but with a bit of effort he managed to breathe quietly.

He listened for Roy.

Nothing.

Colin began to notice the minutiae of the little

world in which he cowered. The Cadillac was hard and warm against his back. The grass was dry and stiff and smelled like hay. Heat radiated upward as the earth gave off its stored sun to the cooler night. As the final light seeped out of the sky, the shadows on the land appeared to sway and shiver like dark masses of kelp at the bottom of the sea. There were noises, too: the shrill cry of a bird; the furtive scampering of a field mouse; the omnipresent toads; and the wind soughing through the eucalyptus trees that lined three sides of the property.

But Roy didn't make a sound.

Was he still out there?

Had he gone home in a rage?

Too nervous to keep still for long, Colin rose up far enough to look through the Cadillac's dirty windows, at the wreckage-strewn field beyond. There was not much to be seen. The cars were fading rapidly into the spreading stain of night.

Suddenly his attention was diverted as he sensed rather than heard movement behind him. He whirled, heart pounding. Roy loomed over him, grinning, demonic. He was holding a tire iron as if it were a baseball bat.

For a moment neither of them moved. They were totally immobilised by a web of memories, by pleasant recollections that were like countless strands of spider silk. They had been friends, but now they were enemies. The change had been too abrupt, the motivation too bizarre for either of them to puzzle out the meaning of it. At least that's what Colin felt. And as they stared at each other, he began to hope Roy would see how crazy this was and would regain his senses.

'I'm your blood brother,' Colin said softly.

Roy swung the tire iron. Colin fell to avoid the blow, and the iron smashed through the side window of the Cadillac.

In one swift graceful movement, screaming all the while like a banshee, Roy pulled the tire iron out of the window, raised it high, as if he were chopping wood, and brought it down with all his strength. Colin rolled away from the Cadillac, tumbled over and over, through the crackling grass, as the club descended. He heard it strike the earth with incredible force where he had been just a second ago, and he knew it would have shattered his skull if he had not gotten out from under it.

'Son-of-a-bitch!' Roy said.

Colin rolled five or six yards and scrambled to his feet. As he got up, Roy rushed him and struck with the tire iron again. It cut the air – *whoosh!* – and missed him by only a few inches. Gasping, Colin stumbled backward, trying to stay out of Roy's reach, and he came up against another car.

'Trapped,' Roy said. 'Got you trapped, you little bastard.'

Roy swung the club so fast that Colin almost didn't see it coming. He ducked at the last possible instant, and the iron bar whistled over his head; it rang off the automobile behind him. The loud, sharp sound was like a rifle shot striking a huge unmelodious bell, and it echoed through the junkyard. The iron hit the car so hard that it leaped from Roy's grasp, spun up into the night, and fell back to the grass a few yards from him.

Roy cried out in agony. The shock of the impact had been transmitted through the tire iron, into his flesh. He gripped one stinging hand with the other and swore at the top of his voice.

Colin took advantage of Roy's brief incapacitation and got the hell out of there.

24

The interior of the Chevrolet stank. There were quite a few distinctly different, unpleasant odors, and Colin was able to imagine the source of some of them, although not all. Old grease alive with mold. Damp upholstery laced with mildew. Rotting carpet. But one of the smells that he could not identify was the strongest of them all: an odd fragrance like cooking ham, sweet one moment but rancid the next. It made him wonder if there was a dead animal in the car, a decaying squirrel or mouse or rat, festooned with writhing maggots, just inches away in the impenetrable dark. At times the image of an oozing corpse became so vivid in his mind that he gagged with revulsion, even though he knew the noise he made, small as it was, might draw Roy's attention.

Colin was stretched out on the Chevrolet's musty back seat, on his right side, facing front, knees drawn up a bit, arms against his chest, fetal, afraid, sweating yet shivering, seeking safety in the deep shadows but uncomfortably aware that there was no real security to be found in this place. The car's rear window and two rear side windows were intact, but all the glass in front was gone. Now and again, a breeze eddied into the car, but it didn't freshen the air; it only stirred the odors until they became thicker, even more pungent than they had been. He listened intently for any sound of Roy that the breeze might bring, but for a long time the junkyard was silent.

Night had come at last. On the western horizon, every trace of the sun had been blacked over. A fragment of the moon hung low in the east, but its light did not penetrate the interior of the automobile.

Lying in the darkness, Colin had nothing to do but think, and he could think of nothing but Roy. Colin could no longer resist the truth: This was not a game; Roy was really a killer. Roy would have pushed the truck down the hill. No doubt about it. He would have wrecked the train. He would have raped and killed Sarah Callahan if Colin hadn't found holes in his plan. And, Colin thought, he would have cracked my head open with that tire iron if I hadn't gotten away from him. There was not the slightest doubt about that either. The blood-brother oath no longer meant anything. Perhaps it never had. He supposed it was even possible that Roy had killed those two boys, just as he claimed he had: one pushed off the cliff at Sandman's Cove, the other drenched with lighter fluid and set afire.

But why?

The truth was clear, but its origins were not. The truth made no sense to him, and that was frightening. The facts were all in plain sight; but the facts were the end product of a long manufacturing process, and the machinery that had made them could not be seen.

Questions tumbled through Colin's mind. Why does Roy want to kill people? Does he get pleasure from it? What kind of pleasure, for God's sake? Is he a lunatic? Why doesn't he look like a lunatic if that's what he is? Why does he look so normal? He asked himself those questions and a hundred others, but he had no answers.

Colin expected the world to be simple and straightforward. He liked to be able to divide it into two camps: forces for good and forces for evil. In that way every event and a problem and solution clearly had a black side and a white side, and you always knew exactly where you stood. He pretty much believed that the real world was like the land in *The Lord of the Rings*, with the blessed and the damned marshaled into two distinct armies. But no matter how hard he probed at it, regardless of the angle from which he considered it, Roy's behavior over the past month could be labeled neither saintly nor entirely wicked. Roy had many qualities that Colin envied, admired, and wished to acquire; but Roy was also a cold-blooded murderer. Roy was not black. He was not white. He wasn't even gray. He was a hundred, no, a *thousand* shades of gray, all whirling and blending and shifting together like a thousand columns of smoke. Colin could not reconcile his view of life with the sudden discovery of a creature like Roy. The endless ramifications of Roy's quicksilver morality were frightening. It meant that Colin would have to reconsider everything in his cosy philosophy. All the people in his life would have to be taken out of the pigeonholes into which he had stuffed them. He would have to judge each of them again, more carefully than he had done before, and then he would have to put them . . . Put them where? If there was no black-and-white system, there were no pigeonholes either. If there was not always a clear division between right and wrong, people

189

could not safely be labeled, slotted, and forgotten; and life would be unbearably difficult to manage.

Of course, Roy might be possessed.

As soon as that thought crossed Colin's mind, he knew it was the answer, and he eagerly seized it. If Roy was possessed by an evil spirit, he was not responsible for the monstrous acts he committed. Roy himself was good, but the demon within him was evil. Yes! That was it! That explained the apparent contradiction. Possessed. Like the girl in *The Exorcist*. Or the little boy in *The Omen*. Or perhaps Roy was possessed by an alien, a thing from another planet, an entity that had traveled to earth from the far stars. Sure. That must be it. That was a better, more scientific, less superstitious explanation than the first. Not a demon, but an evil, alien being. Maybe it was similar to the villains in the old Don Siegel movie, *Invasion of the Body Snatchers*. Or even more likely, maybe the thing that had Roy under its power was a parasite from another galaxy like in that great Heinlein novel, *The Puppet Masters*. If that were the case, there were steps he must take at once, without a moment's delay, while there was still a chance, however slim, to save the world. First of all, he had to find irrefutable proof of the invasion. Then he had to use that proof to convince other people that there was a clear and present danger. And finally he had to—

'Colin!'

He jerked, sat up, terrified, shaking. For a moment he was too shocked to get his breath.

'Hey, Colin!'

The sound of Roy calling his name snapped him back to reality.

'Colin, can you hear me?'

Roy was not close. At least a hundred yards away. Shouting.

Colin leaned toward the front seat, peered through the empty windshield frame, but he could not see anything.

'Colin, I made a mistake.'

Colin waited.

'Do you hear me?' Roy asked.

Colin didn't respond.

'I did a very stupid thing,' Roy said.

Colin shook his head. He knew what was coming, and he was amazed that Roy would try anything so obvious.

'I carried the game too far,' Roy said.

It won't work, Colin thought. You won't convince me. Not now. Not any more.

'I guess I scared you more than I meant to,' Roy said. 'I'm sorry. I really am.'

'Jeez,' Colin said softly, to himself.

'I didn't really want to wreck the train.'

Colin stretched out on the seat once more, on his side, knees drawn up, down in the shadows that smelled of decay.

For a few minutes, Roy went through other verses of his siren song, but eventually he realised that Colin was not going to be entranced by it. Roy was unable to conceal his frustration. With each patently insincere exhortation, his voice grew increasingly strained. Finally he exploded: 'You rotten little creep! I'll find you. I'll get my hands on you. I'm going to beat your fuckin' head in, you little son-of-a-bitch! You traitor!'

Then silence.

The wind, of course.

And crickets, toads.

But not a peep from Roy.

The quiet was unnerving. Colin would have preferred to hear Roy cursing, bellowing, and crashing about the junkyard in search of him, for then he would have known where the enemy was.

As he listened for Roy, the sometimes sweet and sometimes rancid hamlike odor grew stronger than ever, and he developed a macabre explanation for it. The Chevy had been in a terrible accident; the front end was squashed and twisted; the windshield was gone; both front doors were buckled – one in, one out; the steering wheel was broken in half, a semicircle that ended in jagged points. Perhaps (Colin theorised) the driver had lost a hand in the crash. Perhaps the severed hand had fallen to the floor. Perhaps it had somehow gotten under the seat, into a recess where it could not be reached or even seen. Perhaps the ambulance crew had looked for the amputated member but had been unable to find it. The car had been towed to Hermit Hobson's place, and the hand had begun to wither and rot. And then . . . then . . . Oh God, and then it was just like that O'Henry story in which a blood-spotted rag had fallen behind a radiator and, due to unique chemical and temperature conditions, had acquired a life of its own. Colin shuddered. That's what had happened to the hand. He felt it. He knew it. The hand had started to decompose, but then a combination of intense summer heat and the chemical composition of the dirt under the seat had caused an incredible, evil change in the dead flesh. The process of decay had been arrested, though not reversed, and the hand had been infused with an eerie sort of life, a malevolent half life. And now, right this minute, he

192

was in the car, in the dark, alone with the damned thing. It knew he was here. It could not see or hear or smell, but it *knew*. Mottled brown and green and black, slimy, riddled with weeping pustules, the hand must even now be dragging itself out from beneath the front seat and across the floorboards. If he reached down to the floor, he would find it, and it would seize him. Its cold fingers would grip like steel pincers, and it would—

No, no, no! I've got to stop this, Colin told himself. What the hell's the matter with me?

Roy was out there, hunting him. He had to listen for Roy and be prepared. He had to concentrate. Roy was the real danger, not some imaginary disembodied hand.

As if to confirm the advice that Colin had given himself, Roy began to make noises again. A car door slammed not far away. A moment later there was the sound of another rusted door being wrenched open; it screeched as the seal that time had put upon it was broken. After a few seconds, that door, too, slammed shut.

Roy was searching the cars.

Colin sat up, cocked his head.

Another corroded door opened with noisy protest.

Colin could not see anything important through the missing windshield.

He felt caged.

Trapped.

The third door slammed.

Panicky, Colin slid to the left, got off the back seat, leaned over the front seat as far as he could, and stuck his head out the front driver's side window. The fresh air that hit his face was cool and smelled of the sea even this far inland. His eyes had adjusted to the night, and the partial moon cast just enough light for him to see eighty or a hundred feet into the junkyard.

Roy was a shadow among shadows, barely visible, four cars in front of the Chevrolet in which Colin was hiding. Roy opened the door of another junker, leaned into it, came out a moment later, and threw the door shut. He moved toward the next car, closer to the Chevy.

Colin returned to the rear seat and slid quickly over to the door on the right. He had come in on the left side, but that's where Roy was now.

Another door crashed shut: *ka-chunk!*

Roy was only two cars away.

Colin took hold of the handle, then realised that he didn't know if the right-hand door worked. He had used only the one on the left. What if this one was jammed and made a lot of noise but wouldn't open? Roy would come on the double and trap him in here.

Colin hesitated, licked his lips.

He felt as if he had to pee.

He clamped his legs together.

The sensation was still there, and in fact it was getting worse: a warm pain in his loins.

Please, God, he thought, don't make me have to pee. Not here. Not now. It's the wrong damned place for that!'

Ka-chunk!

Roy was one car away.

There was no time to worry whether the right-hand door would work or not. He had no choice but to try it and take his chances. He tugged on the handle. It moved. He took a deep breath, nearly choked on the rank air, and pushed the door all the way open with one violent shove. He

194

winced at the loud scraping sound it made but thanked God that it functioned at all.

Frantically, gracelessly, he clambered out of the Chevy, making no effort to be quiet now that the door had betrayed him. He took two steps, tripped over a muffler, dropped to his knees, popped up again as if he were on springs, and bolted into the darkness.

'Hey!' Roy said from the far side of the car. The sudden explosive movement had caught him by surprise. 'Hey, wait a minute.'

25

Running at his top speed, Colin saw the tire a split second before it would have tripped him. He jumped over it, side-stepped a pile of fenders, and ran on through the high grass. He turned left and rounded a battered Dodge delivery van that was up on blocks. After a brief hesitation and a quick glance behind him, he sank to the ground and wriggled under the truck.

As Colin slipped out of sight, Roy came around the front of the van and stopped, looked both ways. When he saw that that avenue of the maze was deserted, he spat on the ground. 'Damn.'

The night was very dark, but from his hiding place beneath the Dodge, Colin could see Roy's white sneakers. Colin was lying on his belly, his head turned to the left, right cheek pressed against the earth; and Roy was standing no more than a yard away. He could have grabbed the other boy's ankle and toppled him. But then what?

After a moment of indecision, Roy opened the door on the driver's side of the van. When he saw that no one was in there, he slammed the door and stalked to the rear of the Dodge.

Colin drew shallow breaths through his mouth and wished he could soften the pounding beat of his heart. If he made any sound at all that Roy could hear, he would die for it.

At the back of the delivery van, Roy opened one of the double doors. When he peered into the rear compartment, he apparently could not see every corner of it to his satisfaction, for he opened the second door as well, then climbed into the cargo hold.

Colin listened to him poking at the shadows in the metal box overhead. He considered squeezing out from under the truck and creeping swiftly to another shelter, but he didn't think he would have sufficient time to get away undetected.

Even as Colin was assessing his chances, Roy came out of the truck and closed the doors. The opportunity, if there ever had been one, was lost.

Colin twisted around a bit and looked over his shoulder. He saw the white tennis shoes, and he prayed that Roy wouldn't think to investigate the narrow space beneath the Dodge.

Incredibly, his prayers were answered. Roy stepped to the front of the truck, paused, seemed to be looking at the junkyard on all sides, and said, 'Where the hell . . . ?' He stood there for a while, drumming his fingers on the van, and then he walked northward until Colin could no longer see his shoes or hear his footsteps.

For a long time Colin lay motionless. He found the courage to breathe normally once more, but he still thought it wise to be as silent as possible.

His situation had improved in at least one respect: The air circulating under the van was not as stale and disgusting as that in the Chevrolet had been. He could smell wildflowers, the teasing scent of goldenrod, and the dusty aroma of the parched grass.

His nose itched. Tickled.

To his horror, he realised he was going to sneeze. He clamped one hand to his face, pinched his nose, but found he couldn't stop the inevitable. He muffled the noise as best he could and waited with dread to be discovered.

But Roy didn't come. He evidently hadn't been close enough to hear.

Colin passed another couple of minutes under the truck, just to be safe, then slithered out. Roy was not in sight, but he could be hunkered down in any of a thousand pockets of darkness, waiting to strike.

Cautiously, Colin stole eastward through the cemetery of dead machinery. He ran in a crouch across the open spaces, lingered in the wreckage between until he was fairly certain that the next unprotected patch of ground was safe, then dashed on. When he was fifty or sixty yards from the delivery van where he had last seen Roy, he turned north, toward Hermit Hobson's shack.

If only he could get to the bicycles while Roy was searching for him elsewhere, he would be able to escape. He would damage Roy's bike – bend a wheel or something – and then leave on his own, confident that there could be no effective pursuit.

He reached the edge of the junkyard and huddled next to a demolished station wagon while he surveyed the deep pools of blackness that lay around Hobson's shack. He saw the bicycles at the foot of the sagging porch steps, lying side by side where the grass was stunted and still a bit green, but he didn't go straight to them. Roy might expect him to come back to this place; he might be concealed already in those shadows, tense, waiting to pounce. Colin stared hard at each trouble spot, looking for movement or the glint of an errant moonbeam on a shape that did not belong there. In time he was able to see through most of the dark pockets and to determine that they were uninhabited. But in a few small areas the night seemed to back up like river sludge; and in those puddles it was far too thick for the eye to penetrate it.

At last Colin decided that the possibility of escape outweighed the risk of going to the bicycles and making a target of himself. He stood, wiped sweat from his brow, and walked into the twenty-yard-wide band of open ground between the junkyard and the shack. Nothing moved in the darkness. He advanced slowly at first, then more boldly, and finally sprinted the last ten yards.

Roy had locked their bikes together. He had used his security parking chain and padlock to bind one wheel of his bicycle to one wheel of Colin's.

Colin pulled on the chain and tugged angrily at the gate of the lock, but his efforts were wasted; the device was heavy and sturdy. He could see no way to get the bikes apart without the combination to Roy's lock. And he certainly couldn't use them in tandem, even if the chain had been loose enough to permit them to be stood on their wheels and moved simultaneously – which it was not.

Crestfallen, he scurried back to the station wagon to consider his options. He really had only two. He could try to get home on foot – or he could continue to play cat-and-mouse with Roy in the endless passageways of the junkyard.

He preferred to stick where he was. The chief recommendation for it was that he had survived thus far. If he held out long enough, his mother would report him missing. She might not get home until one or two o'clock in the morning, but it must be past midnight now. He pushed the button on his digital watch and was stunned to see how early it was: a quarter till ten. He could have sworn that he had been playing this dangerous game of hide-and-seek for at least three or four hours. Well, maybe Weezy would get home early. And if he wasn't in by midnight, she'd call Roy's folks and find out Roy wasn't home either. By one o'clock at the very latest, they would call the cops. The police would start looking for them at once and— Yeah, but *where* would they begin the search? Not out here in the junkyard. In town. And down at the beach. Then in the nearby hills. It would be late afternoon tomorrow, maybe even Thursday or Friday, before they came all the way out to Hermit Hobson's. As much as he wanted to stay near the myriad boltholes of the rubble-covered hilltop, he knew he could not keep out of Roy's grasp for forty-eight or thirty-six or even twenty-four hours. He'd be damned lucky to make it through to daylight.

He would have to walk home. Of course, he couldn't go back the way they had come, for if Roy suspected he'd left the junkyard and came looking for him, there was too great a danger that they would meet on a lonely stretch of road. A bicycle made little or no noise on a paved surface, and Colin was afraid he would not hear Roy coming in time to hide. He would have to trek overland, down the hill to the railroad tracks, along the tracks to the dry creekbed near Ranch Road, then into Santa Leona. That route would be more arduous than the other, especially in the dark, but it might also cut the distance from eight miles to seven or even six.

Colin was painfully aware that his planning was guided by one overriding consideration: cowardice. Hide. Run. Hide. Run. He seemed incapable of entertaining any alternative to those weak courses of action, and he felt miserably inadequate.

— So stay here. Turn the tables on Roy.

Fat chance.

— Don't run. Attack.

That's a pleasant fantasy, but it's impossible.

— It isn't. Become the aggressor. Surprise him.

He's faster and stronger than me.

— Then be devious. Set a trap.

He's too clever to fall for any trap I could set.

— How can you know if you don't try?

I know.

— How?

Because I'm me. And he's Roy.

Colin put a quick end to the interior dialogue because it was a waste of time. He understood himself all too well. He simply did not have within him the power or the will to transform himself. Before he tried to become the cat, he would have to be convinced that there was absolutely no percentage whatsoever in continuing to be the mouse.

This was one of those bleak and too-frequent moments in which he despised himself.

Pausing every few yards to reconnoiter the way ahead before pressing on, Colin crept from one car to another. He moved steadily toward the hill where Roy had attempted to push the Ford pickup into the train, for it was there that he most easily could get down to the railroad tracks. The night was much too still. Every rustle of his shoes in the brittle grass sounded like thunder and seemed certain to bring Roy down on him. Eventually, however, he came undiscovered to the far end of the junkyard.

In front of him, the open space between the last of the cars and the brow of the hill was approximately forty feet wide. At the moment it looked like a mile. The moon was shining unhindered, and that stretch of grass was bathed in far too much milky light to make a crossing feasible. If this area were being watched, he would be spotted before he had covered a quarter of the distance. Fortunately, scattered but solid masses of clouds had rolled in from the ocean during the past hour. Each time that a cluster of them shrouded the moon, the resultant darkness offered excellent cover. He waited for one of these brief eclipses. When the broad belt of grass fell under a shadow, he ran as silently as he could manage, up on his toes, holding his breath, to the brink, and then over.

The hillside was steep, but not so precipitous as to be unnegotiable. He went down fast because there was no other way to go; the pull of gravity was irresistible. He bounded wildly from one foot to the other, out of control, taking big, ungainly steps, and halfway to the bottom he found that he suddenly was dancing on a landslide. The dry, sandy soil collapsed under him. For an instant he rode it as if he were a surfer on a wave, but then he lost his footing, fell, and rolled the last twenty feet. He came to a stop in a cloud of dust, flat on his back, on the railroad right-of-way, one arm across the tracks.

Stupid. Stupid and clumsy. Stupid, clumsy idiot.

Jeez.

He lay still for several seconds, a bit winded, but surprised that nothing hurt. His pride was injured, of course, but not anything else.

The dust began to settle.

As he started to sit up, Roy called to him: 'Blood brother?'

Colin shook his head in disbelief and looked left, right, then up.

'Blood brother, is that you?'

The moon sailed out from behind the clouds.

In the wash of pale light, Colin saw Roy standing at the top of the eighty-foot slope, silhouetted against the sky, staring down.

He can't see me, Colin told himself. At least he can't see me as clearly as I see him. He's there with the sky behind him; I'm here in the shadows.

'It *is* you,' Roy said.

He charged down the hillside.

Colin got up, stumbled over the railroad tracks, and hurried into the wasteland beyond.

26

Colin felt terribly vulnerable as he raced across the field. As far as the moonlight revealed, there was no cover, no place for him to hide. He had the crazy thought that a giant shoe was going to come down on him at any second, squashing him as if he were a bug scurrying across a vast kitchen floor.

In the stormy season, rain saturated the hillsides, then gushed off the slopes into natural drainage channels that cut through the flat land west of the railroad tracks. At least once every winter, the gullies overflowed, and the plain became a lake, part of the water-retention system created by the county flood-control project. Because the earth was underwater an average of two months every winter, it boasted very little vegetation even in the summer. There were patches of grass that had a tenuous hold on the silt, beds of the wildflowers that thrived nearly everywhere in California, and prickly tumbleweed; but there were no trees, no dense undergrowth, and no bushes in which Colin could conceal himself.

He got off the bare land as quickly as he could by jumping down into a small arroyo. The gulch was fifteen to twenty feet in width and more than seven feet deep, with almost vertical walls. During a winter storm, it was a surging river, wild and muddy and dangerous, but now it held not one drop of water. He sprinted along a straightaway, pain stabbing through his calves and side, lungs burning. As he came to a broad curve in the arroyo, he glanced back for the first time since he'd crossed the railroad tracks. So far as he could see, Roy had not yet come down into the big ditch in pursuit of him. He was surprised that he had such an encouraging lead, and he wondered if it were possible that Roy had not seen where he'd gone.

Beyond the bend, seeking shelter, he turned into a secondary watercourse that branched off the main channel. This was about ten feet wide at its mouth, but the walls rapidly drew nearer to each other as he progressed to the source. The floor rose steadily until the depth of the gully decreased from seven to five feet. When he had gone no more than a hundred yards, the passageway had narrowed to six feet. If he stood erect, his head would be above ground level. At that point the channel split into a pair of short, dead-end corridors that cut no more than four feet below the surface of the field. He moved into one of these cul-de-sacs, wedged himself into it, each shoulder pressed firmly against a sandy embankment. He sat down, drew his knees up to his chin, clamped his arms around his legs, and tried to be invisible.

— Rattlesnakes.

Oh Jeez.

— Better think about it.

No.

— This is rattlesnake country.

Just shut up.

206

— Well, it is.

They don't come out at night.

— The worst things always come out at night.

Not rattlesnakes.

— How do you know?

I read it in a book.

— What book?

Can't remember the title.

— There wasn't any book.

Just shut up.

— Rattlesnakes all over the place.

Jeez!

He hunched down in the dirt, listening for rattlesnakes, waiting for Roy; and a long time passed during which he was not bothered by either nemesis. Every few minutes he checked his digital watch, and when he had been in the ditch for half an hour, he decided it was time to leave. If Roy had been searching the network of drainage canals all this time, he would have come close enough for Colin to be aware of him, or at least he would have made a noise in the distance; but he had not. Evidently he had abandoned the pursuit, perhaps because he'd lost track of Colin in the dark, hadn't seen in which direction he had gone, and had no clear idea where to look for him. If true, it was a tremendous piece of luck. But Colin felt that he would be pushing Fate too hard if he stayed where he was, in this den of vipers, expecting to be safe forever from rattlesnakes.

He crawled out of the trench, stood, and studied the scarred, moonlit landscape. Within his limited circle of vision, there was no sign of Roy.

With extreme caution, stopping again and again to listen to the night, Colin headed southeast.

Repeatedly, at the corners of his vision, there was movement; but it always proved to be a clump of tumbleweed rolling in front of the wind. Eventually he recrossed the flat land and reached the railroad tracks once more. He was at least a quarter of a mile south of the junkyard, and he quickly began to put even more distance between himself and Hermit Hobson's place.

An hour later, when he reached the intersection of the tracks and Santa Leona Road, he was weary to his bones. His mouth was dry. His back ached. Every muscle in his legs was knotted and throbbing.

He considered following the highway into town. It was tempting: fairly straight and direct, with no holes or ditches or obstacles hidden in its shadows. He already had shortened the trek as much as he possibly could by going overland. From this point on, continued avoidance of the roads would only prolong the journey.

He took a few steps on the blacktop but realised again that he did not dare pursue the easy route. He almost surely would be attacked before he reached the edge of town, where people and lights would make murder more difficult than it would be in the lonely countryside.

— Hitchhike.

There's no traffic at this hour.

— Someone will come along.

Yeah. Maybe Roy.

He left Santa Leona Road. He veered southwest from the railway line, striking out through more scrubland where only he and the tumbleweeds moved.

Within half a mile, he came to the dry creek-bed that paralleled Ranch Road. It had been widened and deepened for flood-control purposes, and the walls of it were not earth but concrete. He descended on one of the regularly spaced service ladders, and when he stood on the floor of the creek, the rim was twenty feet above him.

Two miles farther, in the heart of town, he climbed up another ladder and through a safety railing. He was on the sidewalk along Broadway.

Although 1A.M. was fast approaching, there were still people on the streets: several in passing cars; a few in an all-night diner; an attendant at a filling station. An elderly man walked arm-in-arm with a pixie-faced, white-haired woman, and a young couple strolled past the closed stores, window-shopping in spite of the hour.

Colin had an urge to rush up to the nearest of them and blurt out the secret, the story of Roy's madness. But he knew they would think he was a lunatic. They didn't know him, and they didn't know Roy. None of it would make sense to strangers. He wasn't even sure it made sense to him. And even if they did comprehend and believe, they couldn't help him.

His first ally would have to be his mother. When she heard the facts, she would call the police, and they would respond to her much more quickly and seriously than they would to a fourteen-year-old boy. He had to get home and tell Weezy all about it.

He hurried along Broadway toward Adams Avenue, but after only a few steps he stopped because he suddenly realised that he would have to undertake the last part of his journey with the same caution that had marked it thus far. Roy might intend to ambush him within a few feet of his front door. In fact, now that he thought about it, he was positive that's what would happen. Roy would most likely lie in wait directly across the way from the Jacobs' house; half that block was a pocket park with many hiding places from which he could observe the entire street. The instant he saw Colin approaching the house, he would move; he would move real fast. For just a moment, as if briefly cursed with a clairvoyant's vision, Colin could see himself being clubbed to the ground, being stabbed, being left there in blood and pain to die within inches of safety, on the threshold of sanctuary.

He stood in the middle of the sidewalk, trembling. He stood there for quite a while.

— Got to move, kid.

Where?

— Call Weezy. Ask her to come get you.

She'll tell me to walk. It's only a few blocks.

— So tell her why you can't walk.

Not on the phone.

— Tell her Roy's out there, waiting to kill you.

I can't make it sound right on the phone.

— Sure you can.

No. I've got to be there when I tell her. Otherwise, it won't sound right, and she'll think it's a joke. She'll be mad.

— You've got to try to do it on the phone so she'll come get you. Then you'll get home safely.

I can't do it on the phone.

— What's the alternative?

Finally he walked back to the service station near the dry creekbed. A telephone booth stood on one corner of the property. He dialed the number and listened to it ring a dozen times.

She wasn't home yet.

210

Colin slammed down the receiver and left the booth without recovering his dime.

He stood on the sidewalk, hands fisted at his sides, shoulders hunched. He wanted to punch something.

— The bitch.

She's your mother.

— Where the hell is she?

It's business.

— What's she doing?

It's business.

— Who's she with?

It's just business.

— I'll bet.

The service-station attendant started closing for the night. The banks of fluorescent lights above the pumps blinked out.

Colin walked west on Broadway, through the shopping district, just passing time. He looked in store windows, but he didn't see anything.

At ten minutes past one, he went back to the telephone booth. He dialed his home number, let it ring fifteen times, then hung up.

— Business my ass.

She works hard.

— At what?

He stood there for several minutes, one hand on the receiver, as if he were expecting a call.

— She's out screwing around.

It's business. A business dinner.

— This late?

A long, late business dinner.

He tried the number again.

No answer.

He sat down on the floor of the booth, in the darkness, and hugged himself.

211

— She's out screwing around when I need her.

You don't know for sure.

— I know.

You can't.

— Face it. She screws like everyone else.

Now you sound like Roy.

— Sometimes Roy makes sense.

He's crazy.

— Maybe not about everything.

At one-thirty he stood up, popped a dime into the phone, and called home again. It rang twenty-two times before he hung up.

It might be safe to walk home now. Wasn't it too late for Roy to keep a vigil? He was a killer, but he was also a fourteen-year-old boy; he couldn't stay out all night. His folks would wonder where he was. They might even call the cops. Roy would be in terrible trouble if he stayed out all night, wouldn't he?

Maybe. And maybe not.

Colin wasn't sure that the Bordens really cared what Roy did or what happened to him. So far as Colin knew, they had never set down rules for their son, other than the one about staying away from his father's trains. Roy did pretty much what he wanted, when he wanted.

Something was wrong with the Borden family. The relationships were curious, indefinable. Theirs was not a traditional parent-child arrangement. Colin had met Mr and Mrs Borden only twice; but both times he had sensed the strangeness in them, in their attitudes toward each other, and in their treatment of Roy. Mother, father, and son seemed like strangers. There was a peculiar stiffness in the way they talked among themselves, as if they were reciting lines from a script they hadn't learned very well. They were so *formal.* They almost seemed . . . afraid of one another. Colin had been aware of a coldness in the center of the family, but he had never spent much time wondering about it. Now that he gave it some thought, however, he realised that the Bordens were like people living in a rooming house; they smiled and nodded when they passed in the hall; they said hello when they met in the kitchen; but otherwise they led separate, distant lives. He didn't know why that was true. Something had happened to turn them away from one another. He couldn't imagine what it might have been. But he was certain that Mr and Mrs Borden wouldn't care very much if Roy stayed out until daybreak or even disappeared forever.

Therefore it wasn't safe for him to walk home. Roy would be waiting.

Colin dialed the number again, and he was surprised when his mother answered on the second ring.

'Mom, you've got to come get me.'

'Skipper?'

'I'll wait for you at—'

'I thought you were upstairs, asleep.'

'No. I'm over at—'

'I just got in. I thought you were home. What are you doing out at this hour?'

'It's not my fault. I was—'

'Oh, my God, have you been hurt?'

'No, no. I just—'

'You're hurt.'

'No, just a few scrapes and bruises. I need—'

'What happened? What's happened to you?'

213

'If you'd shut up and listen, you'll find out,'
Colin said impatiently.

She was stunned. 'Don't you snap at me. Don't
you dare.'

'I need help!'

'What?'

'You've got to help me.'

'Are you in trouble?'

'Real bad trouble.'

'What the hell have you done?'

'It's not what *I've* done. It's—'

'Where are you?'

'I'm over here at—'

'Have you been arrested?'

'What?'

'Is it *that* kind of trouble?'

'No, no. I'm—'

'Are you at the police station?'

'Nothing like that. I'm—'

'Where are you?'

'Near the Broadway Diner.'

'What trouble have you caused at the diner?'

'That's not it. I—'

'Let me talk to someone there.'

'Who? What do you mean?'

'Let me talk to a waitress or someone.'

'I'm not *in* the diner.'

'Where the hell are you?'

'In a phone booth.'

'Colin, what's the matter with you?'

'I'm waiting for you to come get me.'

'You're only a few blocks from home.'

'I can't walk. He's waiting for me along the
way.'

'Who?'

'He wants to kill me.'

A pause.

'Colin, you come straight home.'

'I can't.'

'This minute. I mean it.'

'I can't.'

'I'm getting angry, young man.'

'Roy tried to kill me tonight. He's still out there, waiting for me.'

'This isn't funny.'

'I'm not joking!'

Another pause.

'Colin, did you take something?'

'Huh?'

'Did you take a pill or something?'

'Drugs?'

'Did you?'

'Jeez.'

'Did you?'

'Where would I get drugs?'

'I know you kids can get them. It's as easy as buying aspirins.'

'Jeez.'

'It's a big problem these days. Is that it? Are you high and having trouble getting down?'

'Me? You really think that's a problem with *me*?'

'If you've been popping pills—'

'If that's what you really think—'

'— or if you've been drinking—'

'— then you don't know me at all.'

'— mixing booze and pills—'

'If you want to hear about it,' Colin said sharply, 'you'll have to bring the car and pick me up.'

'Don't use that tone with me.'

'If you don't come,' he said. 'then I guess I'll just rot here.'

He banged the receiver into the cradle and left the telephone booth.

'Shit!'

He kicked an empty soda can that was lying beside the walkway. It spun and rattled across the street.

He went to the Broadway Diner and stood at the curb, looking east, where Weezy would turn the corner if she bothered to come for him.

He was shaking uncontrollably with anger and fear.

He felt something else, too, something dark and devastating, something far more disturbing than anger, far more debilitating than fear, something uglier, like a terrible loneliness, but much worse than loneliness. It was a suspicion – no, a conviction – that he had been abandoned, forgotten, and that no one in the whole world cared or would ever care enough about him to really find out what he was like and what his dreams were. He was an outcast, a creature somehow vastly different from all other people, an object of scorn and derision, an outsider, secretly loathed and ridiculed by everyone who met him, even by those few who professed to love him.

He felt as if he would vomit.

Five minutes later she drew alongside him in the blue Cadillac. She leaned across the front seat and opened the door on the passenger's side.

When he saw her, he lost the grip that he'd had on himself ever since the nightmare at Hermit

216

Hobson's place. Tears streamed down his face. By the time he got into the car and closed the door, he was sobbing like a baby.

27

She didn't believe him. She refused to call the cops, and she wouldn't disturb the Bordens with a call at that hour.

At nine-thirty the following morning, she talked to Roy on the phone. Then she talked to his mother. She insisted on privacy, so Colin didn't even hear her side of the conversation.

After she had spoken with the Bordens, she tried to make Colin recant his story. When he wouldn't she became furious.

At eleven o'clock, after an extended argument, she and Colin went to the junkyard. Neither of them spoke during the drive.

She parked at the end of the dirt lane, near the shack. They got out of the car.

Colin was uneasy. Echoes of last night's terror still reverberated in his mind.

His bicycle was lying near the front porch steps. Roy's bike was gone, of course.

'You see,' he said. 'I was here.'

She didn't respond. She wheeled the bike around to the back of the car.

Colin followed her. 'It happened exactly the way I said it did.'

She unlocked the trunk. 'Help me.'

They lifted the bicycle into the back of the car, but it wouldn't fit well enough to allow the compartment to be closed and locked. She found a spool of wire in the tool kit and used a length of that to tie down the trunk lid.

'Doesn't the bicycle prove anything?' Colin demanded.

She turned on him. 'It proves you were here.'

'Like I said.'

'But not with Roy.'

'He tried to kill me!'

'He tells me he was home last night from nine-thirty on.'

'Well, of course that's what he'd tell you! But—'

'That's also what his mother tells me.'

'It's not true.

'Are you calling Mrs Borden a liar?'

'Well, she probably doesn't know she's lying.'

'What's that supposed to mean?'

'Roy probably told her he was home, in his room, and she believed him.'

'She knows he was home, not just because he told her so, but because she was home last night, too.'

'But did she actually talk to him?'

'What?'

'Last night? Did she talk to him? Or did she just assume he was up in his room?'

'I didn't grill her in detail about—'

'Did she actually see him last night?'

'Colin—'

'If she didn't actually see him,' Colin said excitedly, 'she can't know for sure that he was up there in his room.'

'That's ridiculous.'

'No. It isn't. They don't talk to each other much in that house. They don't pay attention to each other. They don't go looking for each other to strike up a conversation.'

'She'd know he was there when she looked in to say good night.'

'But that's just what I'm trying to tell you. She'd never do that. She'd never go out of her way to say good night to him. I know it. I'd bet on it. They don't act like other people. There's something really strange about them. There's something wrong in that house.'

'What do you think it is?' she asked angrily. 'Are they invaders from another planet?'

'Of course not.'

'Like in one of those crazy goddamned books you're always reading?'

'No.'

'Should we call Buck Rogers to save us?'

'I just . . . I was only trying to say that they don't seem to love Roy.'

'That's an awful thing to say.'

'I'm pretty sure it's true.'

She shook her head, amazed. 'Did it ever occur to you that you might be too young to fully understand an emotion as complex as love, let alone all the forms it can take? My God, you're an inexperienced fourteen-year-old boy! Who are you to judge the Bordens on something like that?'

'But if you could see the way they act. If you could hear the way they talk to each other. And they never do anything together. Even we do more things together than the Bordens do.'

'Even we? What do you mean by that?'

'Well, we don't do many things together, do we? I mean as a family.'

There were things in her eyes that he didn't want to see. He looked away.

221

'In case you've forgotten,' she said, 'I'm divorced from your father. And also in case it somehow slipped your mind, it was a bitter divorce. The pits. So what the hell do you expect? Do you think the three of us should go on picnics now and then?'

Colin shuffled his feet in the grass. 'I mean even just you and me. The two of us. We don't see much of each other, and the Bordens see even less of Roy.'

'When do I have time, for God's sake?'

He shrugged.

'I work hard,' she said.

'I know.'

'Do you think I like working hard as I do?'

'You seem to.'

'Well, I don't.'

'Then why—'

'I'm trying to build a future for us. Can you understand? I want to be sure we never have to worry about money. I want security. Big security. But you don't appreciate it.'

'I do. I know you work hard.'

'If you appreciated what I'm doing for us, for you, then you wouldn't have tried to upset me with this bullshit story about Roy trying to kill you and—'

'It's not bullshit.'

'Don't use that word.'

'What word?'

'You know what I mean.'

'Bullshit?'

She slapped his face.

Shocked, he put a hand to his cheek.

'Don't smirk at me,' she said.

'I wasn't.'

222

She turned away from him. She walked a few steps into the grass and stared at the junkyard for a while.

He almost cried. But he didn't want her to see him crying, so he bit his lip and held the tears back. After a while, the hurt and humiliation were replaced by anger, and then he didn't have to bite his lip any more.

When she gathered her composure, she came back to him. 'I'm sorry.'

'It's OK.'

'I lost my temper, and that's a bad example to set.'

'It didn't hurt.'

'You upset me so much.'

'I didn't want to.'

'You upset me because I know what's going on.'

He waited.

'You came out here last night on your bike,' she said. 'But not with Roy. I know who you came with.'

He said nothing.

'Oh,' she said, 'I don't know their names, but I know what kind of kids they are.'

He blinked. 'Who're you talking about?'

'You know who I'm talking about. I'm talking about these other friends of yours, these smart-ass kids you see standing on street corners these days, the punks on those skateboards who try to run you off in the gutter when you walk by them.'

'You think kids like that would want anything to do with me? I'm one of the people they'd run into the gutter.'

'You're being evasive.'

'I'm telling the truth. Roy was the only friend I had.'

'Nonsense.'

'I don't make friends easily.'

'Don't lie to me.'

He was silent.

'Since we moved to Santa Leona,' she said, 'you've gotten mixed up with the wrong kids.'

'No.'

'And last night you came out here with some of them because this is probably a popular place – in fact, it's just an ideal place – to sneak away and smoke some dope and do ... all sorts of other things.'

'No.'

'Last night you came here with them, popped a few pills – God knows what they were – and then you tripped out.'

'No.'

'Admit it.'

'It's not true.'

'Colin, I know you're basically a good boy. You've never been in any trouble before. Now you've made a mistake. You've let some other kids lead you astray.'

'No.'

'If you'll just admit it, if you'll face up to it, I won't be mad at you. I'll respect you for accepting your medicine. I'll help you, Colin, if you'll just give me a chance.'

'Give *me* a chance.'

'You popped a couple of pills—'

'No.'

'— and for a few hours you were really gone, really out of it.'

'No.'

'When you finally came around, you realised you'd wandered away, back toward town, without your bike.'

'Jeez.'

'You weren't sure how to get back here and find your bike. Your clothes were torn, filthy, and it was one o'clock in the morning. You panicked. You didn't know how you were going to explain all that, so you made up this foolish story about Roy Borden.'

'Will you listen?' He was barely able to keep from screaming at her.

'I'm listening.'

'Roy Borden *is* a killer. He—'

'You disappoint me.'

'Look at what I am, for Christ's sake!'

'Don't talk like that.'

'Can't you see me?'

'Don't shout at me.'

'Can't you see what I am?'

'You're a boy in trouble and getting deeper.'

Colin was furious with her because she was forcing him to reveal himself in a way he never had done before. 'Do I look like one of those kids? Do I look like the kind of guy they'd even bother to say hello to? They wouldn't even take time to spit on me. To them, I'm just a skinny, bashful, near-sighted creep.' Tears shimmered in the corners of his eyes. He hated himself for being unable to hold them back. 'Roy was the best friend I had. He was the *only* friend. Why would I make up a crazy story just to get him in trouble?'

'You were confused and desperate.' She stared at him as if her gaze would crack him and reveal the truth as she imagined it to be. 'And according to Roy, you were mad at him because he wouldn't come out here with you and the others.'

Colin gaped at her. 'You mean you got this whole theory from Roy? This whole dumb thing about me taking drugs – it comes from *Roy*?'

'I suspected it last night. When I mentioned it to Roy, he said I was right. He told you were very upset with him because he wouldn't come to the party—'

'He tried to kill me!'

'— and because he wouldn't contribute any money to buy the pills.'

'There weren't any pills.'

'Roy says there were, and it explains a lot.'

'Did he name even one of these wild dopers I'm supposed to be hanging out with?'

'They're none of my concern. It's you I'm worried about.'

'Jeez.'

'I *am* worried about you.'

'But for the wrong reason.'

'Playing with drugs is stupid and dangerous.'

'I didn't do anything.'

'If you want to be treated like an adult, you've got to start acting like one,' she said in a lecturing tone that galled him. 'An adult admits his mistakes. An adult always accepts the consequences of his acts.'

'Not most of the adults I see.'

'If you persist in this bullheaded attempt to—'

'How can you believe him instead of me?'

'He's a very nice boy. He—'

'You've only talked to him a couple of times!'

'Often enough to know he's a well-rounded boy and very mature for his age.'

'He's not! He's not like that at all. He's lying!'

226

'His story certainly rings truer than yours,' Weezy said. 'And he strikes me as a sensible boy.'

'You think I'm not sensible?'

'Colin, how many nights have you gotten me out of bed because you were convinced something was crawling around in the attic?'

'Not that often,' he mumbled.

'Yes. That often. Quite often. And was there ever anything there when we looked?'

He sighed.

'Was there?' she insisted.

'No.'

'How many nights have you been absolutely certain that something was lurking outside the house, trying to get in through your window?'

He didn't answer.

She pressed her advantage. 'And do level-headed boys spend all of their time building plastic models of movie monsters?'

'Is that why you don't believe me? Because I watch a lot of horror movies? Because I read science fiction?'

'Stop that. Don't try to make me sound simple-minded,' she said.

'Shit.'

'You're also picking up bad language from this crowd you're running around with, and I won't allow it.'

He walked away from her, into the junkyard.

'Where are you going?'

As he walked away, he said, 'I can show you proof.'

'We're leaving,' she said.

'Go ahead.'

'I should have been at the gallery an hour ago.'

'I can show you proof, if you'll bother to look at it.'

He walked through the junkyard, toward the point at which the hill dropped down to the railroad tracks. He didn't know for sure if she was following him, but he tried to act as if he had no doubt about it. He believed that looking back would be a sign of weakness, and he felt that he had been a weakling for too damned long.

Last night Hermit Hobson's collection of wrecks had been a sinister labyrinth. Now, in the bright daylight, it was only sad, a very sad and lonely place. By squinting slightly, you could look through the dead and pitted surface, through the sorry present, and see the past glowing in all of it. Once, the cars had been shiny and beautiful. People had invested work and money and dreams in these machines, and all that had come to this: rust.

When he reached the western end of the junkyard, he had trouble believing what he could plainly see. The proof he had intended to show Weezy was gone.

The dilapidated pickup still stood ten feet from the brink, where Roy had been forced to abandon it, but the corrugated metal runners were not there any more. Although the truck had stopped with its angled front wheels in the dirt, the rear wheels had remained squarely on the tracks. Colin clearly remembered that. But now all four wheels rested upon bare earth.

Colin realised what had happened and knew that he should have expected it. Last night, when he had hidden successfully from Roy in the arroyo west of the railway line, Roy had not rushed immediately into town to wait for him at the house, but had finally given up the chase and had come back here to erase all traces of his plan to wreck the train. He had carted away every loose section of the makeshift track that he'd constructed for the truck. Then he had even jacked up the rear wheels of the Ford to retrieve the last two incriminating sheets of metal that were pinned under them.

The grass behind the truck, which surely must have been smashed flat when the Ford passed over it, now stood nearly as tall and undisturbed as the grass on all other sides of the junker; it swayed gently in the breeze. Roy had taken time to rake it, thereby removing the twin impressions of the pickup's wake. On closer inspection, Colin saw that the resilient blades of grass had sustained minor damage. A few were broken. A few more were bent. Some were pinched. But those subtle signs would not be proof enough to convince Weezy that his story was true.

Although it was twenty feet closer to the brow of the hill than any of the other wrecks, the Ford looked as if it had been in that same spot, undisturbed, for years and years.

Colin knelt beside the pickup and reached behind one of the rusty wheels. He brought out a cold gob of grease.

'What are you doing?' Weezy asked.

He turned to her and held up his greasy hand. 'This is all I can show you. He took away everything else, all the other proof.'

'What's that?'

'Grease.'

'So?'

It was hopeless.

229

Part Two

28

For seven days Colin remained in the house.

Restricted to quarters was one part of his punishment. His mother made certain that he endured the confinement; she called home six or eight times every day, checking on him. Sometimes two or three hours would pass between the calls, and sometimes she would ring him three times in thirty minutes. He did not dare sneak out.

Actually, he didn't want to go anywhere. He was well accustomed to loneliness, comfortable and satisfied with just his own company. For most of his life, his room had been the largest part of his world, and for a while at least it would serve admirably as his entire universe. He had his books, horror comics, monster models, and radio; he could entertain himself for a week or a month or even longer. And he was afraid that if he set foot outside the door, Roy Borden would get him.

Weezy had also made it clear that when he had served his one-week sentence he would be on probation for a long time. For the remainder of the summer he would have to be home before dark. He didn't tell her how he felt about that when she laid down the rule, but in fact he didn't think of it as punishment. He had no intention of going anywhere at night. As long as Roy was running around loose, Colin would view every sunset with dread, as if he were a character in Bram Stoker's *Dracula*.

In addition to imposing a curfew, Weezy took away his allowance for one month. He wasn't bothered by that either. He had a big metal bank in the shape of a flying saucer, and it was full of coins and dollar bills that he had saved over the past two years.

He was distressed only by the fact that the restrictions would interfere with his courtship of Heather Lipshitz. He'd never had a girlfriend. No girl had ever been interested in him before. Not even a little bit. Now that he finally had a chance with a girl, he didn't want to spoil it.

He called Heather and explained that he had been grounded and could not keep their movie date. He didn't tell her the truth about why he had been restricted to the house; he didn't mention that Roy had attempted to kill him. She didn't know him well enough yet to accept such a wild story. And of all the people in Colin's life, Heather was the one whose opinion mattered the most right now; he didn't want her to think he was a nut case. When he explained his situation, she was very understanding, and they rescheduled their date for the following Wednesday, when he would be allowed out of the house again. She didn't even mind that they would have to go to the early show and that he would have to be home by dark to satisfy the curfew his mother had imposed. For twenty minutes they chatted about movies and books, and she was easier to talk to than any girl he had ever known.

When he hung up he felt better than he had before he'd telephoned her. For a third of an hour, at least, he had been able to push thoughts of Roy Borden to the back of his mind.

He called Heather every day during the week that he was grounded, and they were never at a loss for words. He learned a great many things about her, and the more he learned the more he liked her. He hoped he was making an equally good impression on her, and he was impatient to see her again.

He expected Roy to show up at the door some afternoon, or at least to call and make a lot of threats; but the days passed uneventfully. He considered taking the initiative, just to see what would happen. Once or twice each day, he picked up the telephone, but he never got farther than dialing the first three digits of the Borden number. Then the shakes always took him, and he hung up.

He read half a dozen new paperbacks: a science fiction, sword and sorcery, occult stories, stuff that was filled with monstrous villains, the sort of thing he liked the most. But there must have been something wrong with the plots or with the writers' prose styles, because he didn't get that familiar cold thrill from them.

He reread a few pieces that he had found hair-raising when he'd first encountered them a couple of years ago. He discovered that he still could appreciate the color and suspense of Heinlein's *The Puppet Masters*, but the terror that it had communicated to him so forcefully when he had first read it was no longer there. John Campbell's *Who Goes There?* and Theodore Sturgeon's scariest stories – *It* and *The Professor's Teddy-Bear* among others – still pulsed with a rich vision of evil, but they no longer made him look over his shoulder while he turned the pages.

He had trouble sleeping. If he closed his eyes for more than a minute, he heard strange sounds: the furtive but insistent noises someone might make if he were trying to get into the bedroom through the locked door or window. Colin heard something in the attic, too, something heavy that kept dragging itself back and forth, as if it were looking for a weak spot in his bedroom ceiling. He thought about the things his mother had said with such scorn, and he told himself there was nothing in the attic, told himself that it was just his overactive imagination, but he continued to hear it nonetheless. After two bad nights, he surrendered to the fear and stayed up reading until dawn; then in the early light, he was able to sleep.

29

Wednesday morning, eight days after the events at Hermit Hobson's junkyard, Colin was no longer restricted to quarters. He was reluctant to leave the house. He studied the surrounding grounds through all the first-floor windows; and although he could detect nothing out of the ordinary, his own front lawn seemed to him far more dangerous than any battlefield in any war there'd ever been, in spite of the lack of bursting bombs and whistling bullets.

—Roy wouldn't try anything in broad daylight.

He's crazy. How can you know what he'll do?

—Go. Go on. Get out and do what you have to do.

If he's waiting . . .

—You can't hide here for the rest of your life.

He went to the library. As he cycled along the sunny streets, he looked repeatedly behind. He was fairly sure that Roy was not following him.

Though Colin slept only three hours the night before, he was waiting at the front doors of the library when Mrs Larkin, the librarian, opened for business. He'd gone to the library twice a week since they'd moved to town, and Mrs Larkin had quickly learned what he liked. When she saw him standing on the steps, she said, 'We received the new Arthur C. Clarke novel last Friday.'

'That's swell.'

'Well, I didn't put it out on the shelf right away because I thought you'd be in the same day or Saturday at the latest.'

He followed her into the big, cool, stucco building, into the main room where their footsteps were smothered by the mammoth stacks of books, and where the air smelled of glue and yellowing paper.

'When you hadn't showed up by Monday afternoon,' Mrs Larkin said, 'I felt I couldn't hold the book any longer. And now, wouldn't you just know it, someone checked it out a few minutes till five yesterday afternoon.'

'That's all right,' Colin said. 'Thanks a lot for thinking about me.'

Mrs Larkin was a sweet-tempered, red-haired woman with too little brow, too much chin, too little bosom, and too much behind. Her glasses were as thick as Colin's. She loved books and bookish people, and Colin liked her.

'I mainly came to use one of the microfilm readers,' he said.

'Oh, I'm sorry, but we don't have any science fiction on microfilm.'

'I'm not interested in science fiction today. What I'd like to see is back issues of the Santa Leona *News Register*.'

'Whatever for?' She made a face, as if she'd bitten into a lemon. 'Perhaps I'm being a traitor to my own hometown when I say this, but the *News Register* is just about the dullest reading you can find. Lots of stories about bake sales and church socials, and reports of City Council meetings where silly politicians argue for hours about whether or not they should fill the potholes on Broadway.'

238

'Well . . . I'm sort of looking ahead to starting school in September,' Colin said, wondering if that sounded as ridiculous to her as it did to him. 'English composition always gives me a little bit of trouble, so I like to think ahead.'

'I can't believe that anything in school gives you trouble,' Mrs Larkin said.

'Anyway . . . I have this idea for an essay about summer in Santa Leona, not my summer but summer in general, and summer historically. I want to do some research.'

She smiled approvingly. 'You're an ambitious young man, aren't you?'

He shrugged. 'Not really.'

She shook her head. 'In all the years I've worked here, you're the first boy who's come in during summer vacation to prepare for next fall's school assignments. I'd call that ambitious. I surely would. And it's refreshing, too. You keep that attitude, and you'll go a long way in this world.'

Colin was embarrassed because he did not deserve the praise and because he had lied to her. He felt his face turn red, and he suddenly realised that this was the first time he had blushed in a week, maybe longer than that, which was some kind of record for him.

He went to the microfilm alcove, and Mrs Larkin brought spools of film that contained every page of the *News Register* for June, July, and August of last year, and for the same three months of the year before that. She showed him how to use the machine, watched over his shoulder until she was certain that he had no questions, then left him to his work.

Rose.

239

Something Rose.

Jim Rose?

Arthur Rose?

Michael Rose?

He remembered the last name by associating it with the flower, but he couldn't quite recall what the boy's first name had been.

Phil Pacino.

He remembered that one because it was like Al Pacino, the movie actor.

He decided to start with Phil. He lined up the spools of last summer's newspapers.

He assumed both deaths would be front-page news, so he skimmed, looking for bold headlines.

He couldn't remember the date Roy had given. He started with June and worked all the way through to the first of August before he found the story.

LOCAL BOY DIES IN FIRE

He was reading the last paragraph of the article when he sensed a change in the air and knew that Roy was behind him. He whirled, bolting up from the swivel chair as he turned – but Roy wasn't there. No one was there. No one was at the worktables. No one was browsing through the stacks. Mrs Larkin wasn't at her desk. He had imagined it.

He sat down and read the article again. It was exactly as Roy said. The Pacino house had burned to the ground, a total loss. In the rubble, firemen had found the blackened body of Philip Pacino, age fourteen.

Colin felt beads of sweat pop out on his

forehead. He wiped his face with one hand and dried his hand on his jeans.

He went through the papers for the next week with special care, looking for follow-up stories. There were three.

FIRE MARSHAL'S REPORT

PLAYING WITH MATCHES

According to the final, official statement, Philip Pacino had caused the blaze. He had been playing with matches near a workbench on which he constructed model airplanes. Apparently there had been a number of highly flammable items on the bench, including several tubes and pots of glue, a can of lighter fuel, and an open bottle of paint remover.

The second follow-up was a page-two report of the boy's funeral. The story contained tributes from Philip's teachers, teary remembrances from his friends, and excerpts from the eulogy. A photograph of the grieving parents headed the three-column piece.

Colin read it twice with great interest because one of Philip Pacino's friends quoted in the story was Roy Borden.

Two days later there was a long editorial that was hard-hitting by the *News Register*'s standards.

PREVENTING TRAGEDY

WHO'S RESPONSIBLE

In none of the four pieces was there the slightest

indication that the police or the fire department suspected murder and arson. From the beginning they had assumed it was an accident, the result of carelessness or adolescent foolishness.

But I know the truth, Colin thought.

He was weary. He had been at the microfilm reader for almost two hours. He switched off the machine, stood up, and stretched.

He didn't have the library to himself any more. A woman in a red dress was looking through the magazine rack. At one of the tables in the center of the room, a chubby, balding priest was reading an enormous book and assiduously taking notes.

Colin walked to one of the two, big, mullioned windows at the east end of the room and sat sideways on the two-foot-deep sill. He stared through the dusty glass, thinking. Beyond the window lay a Roman Catholic cemetery, and at the far end of the graveyard, Our Lady of Sorrows Church watched over the remains of its ascended parishioners.

'Hi there.'

Colin looked up, surprised. It was Heather.

'Oh hi,' he said. He started to get up.

'Don't move on my account,' she said in a soft, library voice. 'I can't stay long. I have some errands to run for my mother. I just stopped in to pick up a book, and I saw you sitting here.'

She was wearing a maroon T-shirt and white shorts.

'You look terrific,' Colin said, keeping his voice as low as hers.

She smiled. 'Thank you.'

'I really mean it.'

'Thank you.'

'Absolutely terrific.'

242

'You're embarrassing me.'

'Why? 'Cause I said you look terrific?'

'Well . . . in a way, yeah.'

'You mean you'd feel better if I said you looked awful?'

She laughed self-consciously. 'No. Of course not. It's just that . . . no one ever told me I looked terrific before.'

'You've got to be kidding.'

'No.'

'No guy ever told you that? What are they – all blind or something?'

She was blushing. 'Well, I know I'm not really all that terrific.'

'Sure you are.'

'My mouth's too big,' she said.

'No, it's not.'

'Yes, it is. I've got a very wide mouth.'

'I like it.'

'And my teeth aren't the greatest.'

'They're very white.'

'And a couple of them are kind of crooked.'

'Not so that anyone would notice,' Colin said.

'I hate my hands,' she said.

'Huh? Why?'

'My fingers are so stubby. My mother has long, elegant fingers. But mine look like little sausages.'

'That's silly. You have nice fingers.'

'And my knees are knobby,' she said.

'Your knees are perfect,' he said.

'Just listen to me,' she said nervously. 'A boy finally says I look nice, and I try to make him change his mind.'

Colin was amazed to discover that even a very pretty girl like Heather could have doubts about herself. He always had thought that those kids he

243

admired – those golden, blue-eyed, strong-limbed California boys and girls – were a race above all others, superior creatures who glided through life with perfect self-confidence, with an unshakable sense of worth and purpose. He was both pleased and displeased to discover this crack in the myth. He suddenly realised that those special, radiant kids were not really very different from him, that they were not so superior as he had thought they were, and this discovery buoyed him. On the other hand, he felt as if he had lost something important – a pleasant illusion that, at times, had warmed him.

'Are you waiting for Roy?' Heather asked.

He shifted uneasily in his windowsill seat. 'Uh . . . no. I'm just doing some . . . research.'

'I thought you were looking out the window for Roy.'

'Just resting. Taking a break.'

'I think it's nice how he shows up every day,' she said.

'Who?'

'Roy.'

'Shows up where?'

'There,' she said, gesturing toward something beyond the window.

Colin looked through the glass, then back at the girl. 'You mean he goes to church every day?'

'No. The graveyard. Don't you know about it?'

'Tell me.'

'Well . . . I live in the house across the street. The white one with the blue trim. See it?'

'Yeah.'

'Most times when he comes, I see him.'

'What's he do there?'

'He visits his sister.'

244

'He has a sister?'

'Had. She's dead.'

'He never said a word.'

Heather nodded. 'I don't think he likes to talk about it.'

'Not a word.'

'One time I told him it was really nice, you know, how he stopped at her grave so faithfully. He got mad at me.'

'He did?'

'Mad as hell.'

'Why?'

'I don't know,' Heather said. 'At first I thought maybe he still felt the pain of her death. I thought maybe it still hurt him so much he didn't want to talk about it. But then later it seemed like he was mad because I'd caught him doing something wrong. But he wasn't doing anything wrong. It's kind of weird.'

Colin thought about this news for a moment. He stared at the sunny graveyard. 'How'd she die?'

'I don't know. It happened before my time. I mean, we didn't move to Santa Leona until three years ago. She was dead long before that.'

A sister.

A dead sister.

Somehow, that was the key.

'Well,' Heather said, unaware of the importance of the information she had given him, 'I've got to be going. My mother gave me a shopping list. She expects me back with everything in an hour or so. She doesn't like people who are late. She says tardiness is a sign of a sloppy, selfish person. I'll see you at six o'clock.'

'I'm sorry we have to go to the early show,' Colin said.

'That's all right,' she said. 'It's the same movie no matter what time it's shown.'

'And like I said, I've got to be home by nine o'clock or so, before it gets completely dark. That's a real drag.'

'No,' she said. 'That's OK, too. You're not going to be punished forever. The curfew's only for a month, right? Don't worry about it. We'll have fun. See you later.'

'Later,' he said.

He watched her walk across the quiet library. When she was gone, he turned his gaze to the graveyard once more.

A dead sister.

30

Colin had no trouble finding the tombstone; it was like a beacon. It was bigger and shinier and fancier than any other rock in the graveyard. Mr and Mrs Borden had spared no expense in the matter. It was a very elaborate stone, done in sections, constructed both of granite and marble, joined together almost seamlessly. Every aspect of it was artfully shaped and highly polished. Wide, beveled letters were cut deep into the richly veined, mirror surface of the marble.

BELINDA JANE BORDEN

According to the data on the marker, she had died more than six years ago, on the last day of April. The monument at the head of the grave was surely several times the size of the body that it memorialised, for Belinda Jane was only five years old when they put her in the ground.

Colin returned to the library and asked Mrs Larkin for the spool of microfilm that contained the six-year-old, April 30 edition of the *News Register*.

The story was on page one.

Roy had killed his baby sister.

Not murder.

Just an accident. A horrible accident.

247

Nothing anyone could have done to prevent it.

An eight-year-old boy finds his father's car keys on the kitchen counter. He gets it in his head to take a ride around the block. That'll prove he's bigger and better than anyone gives him credit for. It'll prove he's even big enough to play with Dad's trains, or at least big enough to sit at Dad's side and just watch the trains, which is something he's not permitted to do but which he wants to do very badly. The car is parked in the driveway. The boy puts a pillow on the seat so that he can see over the steering wheel. But then he discovers that he can't quite reach the brake or the accelerator. He searches for a tool, and beside the garage he finds a piece of lumber, a three-foot length of two-by-two white pine that is just about exactly what he needs. He figures he can use the lumber to push the pedals that his feet won't reach. One hand to hold the two-by-two, and one hand for steering. In the car he starts the engine and fumbles with the gearshift. His mother hears. Comes out of the house. She's in time to see her little girl walk behind the car. She shouts at both the boy and the girl, and each of them waves at her. The boy finally throws the car into reverse as the mother rushes toward him, and at the same instant he thumps the accelerator with the wooden prod. The automobile goes backward. Fast. Just shoots backward. Strikes the child. She goes down hard. Goes down with one short scream. A tire thumps across her fragile skull. Her head bursts like a blood-filled balloon. And when the men in the ambulance arrive, they find the mother sitting on the lawn, legs akimbo, face blank, saying the same thing over and over again. 'It just popped. Just popped open. Just like that.

Her little head. It just popped.'
   Popped.
   Popper.
   Colin switched off the machine.
   He wished he could switch off his mind.

31

He got home a few minutes before five o'clock.
  Weezy walked in one minute later.
  'Hello, Skipper.'
  'Hi.'
  'Have a good day?'
  'It was OK.'
  'What'd you do?'
  'Not much.'
  'I'd like to hear about it.'
He sat down on the sofa.
  'I went to the library,' he said.
  'What time was that?'
  'Nine this morning.'
  'You were gone when I got up.'
  'I went straight to the library.'
  'And after that?'
  'Nowhere.'
  'When did you come home?'
  'Just now.'
She frowned.
  'You were at the library all day?'
  'Yeah.'
  'Come on now.'
  'I was.'
She paced the middle of the living room.
He stretched out on his back, on the sofa.
  'You're making me angry, Colin.'

'It's true. I like the library.'

'I'll restrict you to the house again.'

'Because I went to the library?'

'Don't get smart with me.'

He closed his eyes.

'Where else did you go?'

He sighed.

'I guess you want a juicy story,' he said.

'I want to know everywhere you went today.'

'Well,' he said, 'I went down to the beach.'

'Did you stay away from those kids, like I told
you to?'

'I had to meet someone at the beach.'

'Who?'

'A dope pusher I know.'

'What?'

'He deals out of his van at the beach.'

'What are you saying?'

'I bought a mayonnaise jar full of pills.'

'Oh my God.'

'Then I brought the pills back here.'

'Here? Where? Where are they?'

'I split them up into cellophane ten-packs.'

'Where have you hidden them?'

'I took them into town and sold them retail.'

'Oh Jesus. Oh my God. What have you gotten
into? What's *wrong* with you?'

'I paid five thousand bucks for the dope and
sold it for fifteen thousand.'

'Huh?'

'That's ten thousand clear. Now, if I can make
that much profit every day for one month, I can
get enough money together to buy a clipper ship
and smuggle tons of opium from the Orient.'

He opened his eyes.

She was red-faced.

'What the *hell* has gotten into you?' she demanded.

'Call Mrs Larkin,' he said. 'She'll probably still be there.'

'Who is Mrs Larkin?'

'The librarian. She'll tell you where I was all day.'

Weezy stared at him for a moment, then went into the kitchen to use the telephone. He couldn't believe it. She actually called the library. He was humiliated.

When she came back to the living room, she said, 'You *were* at the library all day.'

'Yeah.'

'Why'd you do that?'

"Cause I like the library.'

'I mean, why'd you make up that story about buying pills down at the beach?'

'I thought that's what you wanted to hear.'

'I suppose you think it's funny.'

'Kind of funny.'

'Well, it's not.'

She sat down in an armchair.

'All the conversations I've had with you during the past week – haven't any of them sunk in?'

'Every word,' he said.

'I've told you that if you want to be trusted, you've got to earn that trust. If you want to be treated like an adult, you've got to behave like one. You seem to listen, and I let myself hope we're getting somewhere, and then you pull a silly stunt like this. Do you understand what that does to me?'

'I think I do.'

'This childish thing you did, making up this story about buying pills down at the beach . . . it

253

just makes me distrust you all the more.'

For a while neither of them spoke.

At last Colin broke the silence. 'Are you eating at home tonight?'

'I can't, Skipper. I've got—'

'—a business engagement.'

'That's right. But I'll make your supper before I go.'

'Don't bother.'

'I don't want you eating junk.'

'I'll make a cheese sandwich,' he said. 'That's as good as anything.'

'Have a glass of milk with it.'

'OK.'

'What are your plans for the evening?'

'Oh, I guess maybe I'll go to the movies,' he said, purposefully failing to mention Heather.

'Which theater?'

'The Baronet.'

'What's playing?'

'A horror flick.'

'I wish you'd outgrow that sort of trash.'

He said nothing.

She said, 'You'd better not forget your curfew.'

'I'm going to the early show,' Colin said. 'It lets out by eight o'clock, so I'll be home before dark.'

'I'll check on you.'

'I know.'

She sighed and stood up. 'I'd better shower and change.' She walked to the hallway, then turned and looked at him again. 'If you'd behaved differently a little while ago, maybe I wouldn't find it necessary to check on you.'

'Sorry,' he said. And when he was alone, he said, 'Bullshit.'

32

Colin's first date with Heather was wonderful. Although the horror movie was not as good as he had hoped it would be, the last half hour was very scary; Heather was more frightened than he was, and she leaned toward him, held his hand in the dark, seeking reassurance and security. Colin felt uncharacteristically strong and brave. Sitting in the cool theater, in the velveteen shadows, in the pale, flickering light cast back by the screen, holding his girl's hand, he thought he knew what heaven must be like.

After the movie, as the sun settled toward the Pacific, Colin walked her home. The air from the ocean was sweet. Overhead, the palms swayed and whispered.

Two blocks from the theater, Heather tripped on a hoved-up piece of sidewalk. She didn't fall or even come close to losing her balance, but she said, 'Damnit!' She blushed. 'I'm so damned clumsy.'

'They shouldn't let the sidewalk deteriorate like that,' Colin said. 'Someone could get hurt.'

'Even if they made it perfectly straight and smooth, I'd probably trip on it.'

'Why do you say that?'

'I'm such a klutz.'

'No, you aren't,' he said.

'Yes, I am.' They started to walk again, and she said, 'I'd give anything to be just half as graceful as my mother.'

'You are graceful.'

'I'm a klutz. You should see my mother. She doesn't walk – she *glides*. If you saw her in a long dress, something long enough to cover her feet, you'd think she wasn't really walking at all. You'd think she was just floating along on a cushion of air.'

For a minute they walked in silence.

Then Heather sighed and said, 'I'm a disappointment to her.'

'Who?'

'My mother.'

'Why?'

'I don't measure up.'

'Up to what?'

'To her,' Heather said. 'Did you know that my mother was Miss California?'

'You mean like in a beauty contest?'

'Yeah. She won. She won a lot of other contests, too.'

'When was this?'

'She was Miss California seventeen years ago, when she was nineteen.'

'Wow!' Colin said. 'That's really something.'

'When I was a little girl, she entered me in lot of beauty pageants for children.'

'Yeah? What titles did you win?'

'None,' Heather said.

'I find that hard to believe.'

'It's true.'

'What were the judges – blind? Come on, Heather. You must have won something.'

'No, really. I never placed better than second. And I was usually just third.'

'Usually? You mean most of the time you won either second or third place?'

'I placed second four times. I got third place ten times. And five times I didn't place at all.'

'But that's fantastic!' Colin said. 'You made it to the top three spots in fourteen out of nineteen tries!'

'In a beauty contest,' Heather said, 'the only thing that counts is being No. 1, winning the title. In children's contests, nearly everyone gets to be No. 2 or No. 3 every once in a while.'

'Your mother must have been proud of you,' Colin insisted.

'She always said she was, every time that I came in second or third. But I always got the impression she was really very disappointed. When I hadn't won a first place by the time I was ten, she stopped entering me in the contests. I guess she figured I was a hopeless case.'

'But you did great!'

'You forget that she was No. 1,' Heather said. 'She was Miss California. Not No. 3 or No. 2. No. 1.'

He marveled at this lovely girl who didn't seem to know how truly lovely she was. Her mouth was sensuous; she thought it was merely too wide. Her teeth were straighter and whiter than most kids' teeth; she thought they were a bit crooked. Her hair was thick and shiny; she thought it was lank and dull. Graceful as a cat, she called herself a klutz. She was a girl who ought to be brimming with self-assurance; instead, she was plagued by self-doubt. Beneath her sparkling surface she was just as uncertain and worried about life as Colin was; and suddenly he felt very protective toward her.

'If I'd been one of the judges,' he said, 'you'd have won all of those contests.'

She blushed again and smiled at him. 'You're sweet.'

A moment later they reached her house and stopped at the end of the front walkway.

'You know what I like about you?' she asked.

'I've been wracking my brain, trying to figure out what it could possibly be,' he said.

'Well, for one thing, you don't talk about the same stuff that all the other boys talk about. They all seem to think that guys aren't supposed to be interested in anything but football and baseball and cars. All of that stuff bores me. And besides, you don't just talk – you *listen*. Almost no one else listens.'

'Well,' he said, 'one of the things I like about you is that you don't care that I'm not much like other boys.'

They stared self-consciously at each other for a moment, and then she said, 'Call me tomorrow, OK?'

'I will.'

'You better be getting home. You don't want to make your mother angry.'

She planted a shy little kiss on the corner of his mouth, turned away, and hurried into the house.

For a few blocks Colin drifted like a sleep-walker, meandering toward home in a pleasant daze. But suddenly he became aware of the darkening sky, the spreading pools of shadow, and the creeping night chill. He was not afraid of

258

violating the curfew, not afraid of his mother. But he was afraid of encountering Roy after dark. He ran the rest of the way home.

33

Thursday morning, Colin returned to the library and continued his search through the microfilm files of the local newspaper. He studied only two parts of each edition: the front page and the list of hospital admissions and discharges. Nevertheless, he needed more than six hours to find what he was looking for.

One year to the day after his baby sister's death, Roy Borden was admitted to the Santa Leona General Hospital. The one-line notice in the May 1 edition of the *News Register* didn't mention the nature of his illness; however, Colin was certain that it had to do with the strange accident that Roy had refused to discuss, the injury that had left such a great deal of terrible scar tissue on his back.

The name immediately below Roy's on the admissions roster was Helen Borden. His mother. Colin stared at that line for a long time, wondering. Because of the scars he had seen, he had expected to find Roy's name sooner or later, but the mother's appearance surprised him. Had she and her son been hurt in the same mishap?

Colin rolled the film back and carefully scanned every page of the April 30 and May 1 editions of the newspaper. He was looking for a story about an automobile wreck, or an explosion, or

261

fire, some sort of accident in which the Bordens had been involved. He found nothing.

He wound the film forward again, finished that spool and a few more, but uncovered only two additional bits of useful information, the first of which was rather puzzling. Two days after being admitted to Santa Leona General, Mrs Borden was transferred to a larger hospital, St Joseph's, over at the county seat. Colin wondered why she had been moved, and he could think of only one reason. She must have been so badly injured that she required very special care, something exotic that the smaller Santa Leona General could not provide.

He didn't discover anything more about Mrs Borden, but he did learn that Roy had spent exactly three weeks in the local hospital. Whatever the source of the wounds on his back, they clearly had been quite serious.

At a quarter till five, Colin finished with the microfilm and went to Mrs Larkin's desk.

'That new Arthur C. Clarke novel was just returned,' she said before Colin could speak. 'I've already checked it out for you.'

He didn't really want the novel right now, but he didn't want to appear ungrateful. He took it, looked at the jacket, front and back. 'Thanks a lot, Mrs Larkin.'

'Let me know what you think of it.'

'I was wondering if you could help me find a couple of books on psychology.'

'What kind of psychology?'

He blinked. 'There's more than one kind?'

'Well,' she said, 'under the general topic, we've got books on animal psychology, educational psychology, popular psychology, industrial psychology, political psychology, the psychology of the aged, of the young, Freudian psychology, Jungian psychology, general psychology, abnormal psychology—'

'Abnormal psychology,' Colin said. 'Yeah. That's what I've got to learn all about. But I also want a couple of general books that tell me how the mind works. I mean, I want to know why people do the things they do. I want something that covers the basics. Something easy, for beginners.'

'I think we can find what you need,' she said.

'I'd really appreciate it.'

As he followed her toward the stacks at the far end of the room, she said, 'Is this another idea for school?'

'Yeah.'

'Isn't abnormal psychology a rather heavy subject for a tenth-grade project?'

'It sure is,' he said.

34

Colin ate supper alone, in his room.

He called Heather, and they made a date to go to the beach on Saturday. He wanted to tell her about Roy's madness, but he was afraid she wouldn't believe him. Besides, he still didn't feel confident enough about their relationship to tell her that he and Roy were now enemies. Initially, she had seemed attracted to him because he and Roy were friends. Would she lose interest when she discovered he was no longer Roy's buddy? He wasn't sure, and he didn't want to risk losing her.

Later, he read the psychology books that Mrs Larkin had chosen for him. He finished both volumes by two in the morning. For a while he sat in bed, staring and thinking. Then, mentally exhausted, he slept without nightmares – and without a single thought for the monsters in the attic.

Friday morning, before Weezy woke, he went to the library, returned the psychology books, and checked out three more.

'Is the science-fiction novel good?' Mrs Larkin asked.

'Haven't started it yet,' Colin said. 'Maybe tonight.'

From the library he went down to the harbor. He didn't want to go home while Weezy was still there; he wasn't ready to endure another interrogation. He ate breakfast at the counter in a waterfront coffee shop. Later, he strolled to the southern end of the boardwalk, leaned against the railing, and watched the dozens of crabs that were sunning on the rocks a few feet below.

At eleven o'clock he went home. He let himself into the house with the spare key that was kept in the redwood planter near the front door. Weezy was long gone; the coffee in the pot was cold.

He got a Pepsi from the refrigerator and went upstairs with the three psychology books. In his room, sitting on the bed, he took only one swallow of the soda and read only one paragraph of the first book before he sensed that he was not alone.

He heard a muffled, scraping sound.

Something was in the closet.

—Ridiculous.

I heard it.

—You imagined it.

He had read two books on psychology, and he knew that he was probably guilty of transference. That's what the psychologists called it: transference. He couldn't face up to the people and things he was *really* afraid of, couldn't admit those fears to himself, so he transferred the anxiety to other things, to simple things — even simple-minded things — like werewolves and vampires and imaginary monsters that hid in the closet.

That's what he had been doing all of his life.

Yeah, maybe that's true, he thought. But I'm *sure* I heard something move in the closet.

He leaned away from the headboard. He held his breath and listened intently.

Nothing. Silence.

The closet door was shut tight. He couldn't remember if he had left it that way.

There! Again. A soft, scraping sound.

He slid off the bed and took a few steps toward the hall door, away from the closet.

The closet doorknob began to turn. The door eased open an inch.

Colin stopped. He desperately wanted to keep moving, but he was frozen in place as if a spell had been cast upon him. He felt as if he had been transformed into a specimen fly trapped in air that, through sorcery, had been turned to solid amber. From within that magic prison, he was watching a nightmare come to life; he stared at the closet, transfixed.

The door suddenly opened wide. There was no monster hiding among the clothes, no werewolf, no vampire, no hideous beast-god out of H.P. Lovecraft. Just Roy.

Roy looked surprised. He had started toward the bed, thinking his prey was there. Now he saw that Colin had anticipated him and was only a few steps from the open door that led to the second-floor hall. Roy stopped, and for an instant they stared at each other.

Then Roy grinned and raised his hands so that Colin could see what he held.

'No,' Colin said softly.

In Roy's right hand: a cigarette lighter.

'No.'

In his left hand: a can of lighter fluid.

'No, no, no! Get out of here!'

Roy took a step toward him. Then another.

'No,' Colin said. But he couldn't move.

Roy pointed the squeeze can and pressed on it. A jet of clear liquid arced through the air.

Colin ducked to the left, and the lighter fluid missed him, and he ran.

'Bastard!' Roy said.

Colin dashed through the open door and slammed it.

Even as the door was being drawn shut, Roy crashed into the other side.

Colin sprinted for the stairs.

Roy jerked open the door and rushed out of the bedroom. 'Hey!'

Colin descended two steps at a time, but he had gone only halfway when he heard Roy thundering down after him. He plunged on. He jumped the last four steps, into the first-floor hall, and ran to the front door.

'Got ya!' Roy shouted triumphantly behind him. 'Got ya, damnit!'

Before Colin could throw off the two locks on the door, he felt something cold and wet pouring down his back. He gasped in surprise and turned to Roy.

Lighter fluid!

Roy squirted him again, drenched the front of his thin cotton shirt.

Colin shielded his eyes with his hands. He was just in time. Flammable liquid splashed over his forehead, over his fingers, nose, and chin.

Roy laughed.

Colin couldn't breathe. The fumes choked him.

'What a popper!'

Finally the can of lighter fluid was empty. Roy threw it aside, and it clattered along the hardwood floor of the hallway.

Coughing, wheezing, Colin took his hands from his face and tried to see what was happening. The fumes stung his eyes; he closed them again. Tears oozed from beneath his eyelids. Though darkness had always terrified him, it had never been so awful as it was now.

'You stinking bastard,' Roy said. 'Now you'll pay for turning on me. Now you'll pay. You're gonna burn.'

Gasping for breath, barely able to get any air at all, temporarily blinded, hysterical, Colin threw himself toward the sound of the other boy's voice. He collided with Roy, clutched him, and held on.

Roy staggered backward and tried to shake loose, as if he were a cornered fox wrestling free of a determined terrier. He put his hands against Colin's chin, tried to force his head up and back, then grabbed him by the throat and attempted to strangle him. But they were face to face, and much too close for Roy to get sufficient leverage to be effective.

'Do it now,' Colin wheezed through the acrid fumes that filled his nose and mouth and limbs. 'Do it . . . and we'll . . . burn together.'

Roy tried again to throw him off. In the process, he stumbled and fell.

Colin went down with him. He held tightly to Roy; his life depended on it.

Cursing, Roy punched him, pummeled his back, slapped him alongside the head, pulled his hair. He even twisted Colin's ears until it seemed that they would come out by the roots.

Colin howled in pain and tried to fight back. But the moment he let go of Roy in order to hit him, Roy rolled away. Colin grabbed for him and missed.

Roy scrambled to his feet. He backed up against the wall.

Even through the veil of stinging tears brought

269

on by the fumes, Colin could see that the lighter
was still in Roy's right hand.

Roy snapped the flint wheel with his thumb. It
didn't spark, it but it surely would the next time
or the time after that.

Frantic, Colin launched himself at the other
boy, slammed into him, and knocked the lighter
out of his hand. It flew through the open arch-
away, into the living room, where it banged
against a piece of furniture.

'You *creep!*' Roy shoved him out of the way and
ran after the lighter.

Having imbibed nothing more than the reeky
air around him, Colin staggered drunkenly to the
front door. He threw off the deadbolt lock with no
difficulty, but then he fumbled with the stubborn
security chain for what seemed like hours.
Seemed. But of course couldn't be. Probably only
a few seconds. Or maybe even just fractions of a
single second. He had no real sense of time. He
was spinning. Floating. High on the fumes. He
was getting just enough air to keep him from
passing out but not one whiff more. That's why he
was having so much trouble with the security
chain. He was dizzy. The security chain seemed
to be evaporating in his fingers, just as the lighter
fluid was evaporating from his clothes and hands
and face. His ears were ringing. The security
chain. Concentrate on the security chain. Second
by second, his coordination was deteriorating,
getting sloppy. The damned security chain. Sloppier and sloppier. Sick and burning. Going to
burn. Like a torch. *The goddamned, fucking
security chain!* At last, in a burst of concentrated
effort, he tore the chain out of its slot and opened
the door wide. Expecting flames to explode along

his back at any second, he ran from the house, down the walk, across the street, and stopped at the edge of the small park. A wonderfully sweet wind washed over him and began to scour the fumes away. He drew several deep breaths, trying to regain a measure of sobriety.

On the far side of the street, Roy Borden came out of the house. He spotted his prey at once and loped to the end of the walk, but he didn't cross the roadway. He stood over there, hands on his hips, staring at Colin.

Colin stared back at him. He was still dizzy. He still had difficulty drawing his breath. But he was ready to scream for help and run like hell the instant that Roy stepped off the curb.

Realising that the game was lost, Roy walked away. In the first block, he looked back half a dozen times. In the second block, he glanced over his shoulder only twice. In the third block, he didn't look back at all, and then he turned the corner and was gone.

On the way into the house, angry with himself, Colin stopped by the redwood planter and took the key from its place under the ivy. He was amazed that he had been so unthinking, so stupid. He had brought Roy to the house half a dozen times during the past month. Roy had known where the spare key was kept, and Colin had been careless enough to leave it there. From now on, he would carry it with him; and thereafter, he would maintain his defenses with considerably more diligence than he had shown to date.

He was at war.

Nothing less.

He went inside and locked the door.

In the powder room at the end of the hall, he

stripped out of his saturated shirt and threw it on the floor, he scrubbed his hands vigorously, using lots of perfumed soap and hot water. Then he washed his face several times. Although he could still detect the fumes, the worst of the stench was gone. His eyes stopped tearing, and he was able to breathe normally once again.

In the kitchen he went directly to the telephone, but he hesitated with his hand on the receiver. He couldn't call Weezy. The only proof he had that Roy attacked him was the soaked shirt, and that was really no proof at all. Besides, by the time she got home, most of the lighter fluid would have evaporated, leaving no stains. The empty can was on the floor in the hallway, and Roy's fingerprints probably were all over it. But, of course, only the police had the equipment and expertise to test for prints and to prove whose they were, and the police would never take his story seriously. Weezy would think he had popped pills and hallucinated the whole thing, and he would be in trouble again.

If he explained the situation to his father and asked for help, the old man would call Weezy and demand to know what was happening. Pressed for an explanation, she would tell him a lot of silly stories about pills and pot and all-night drug parties. In spite of the fact that everything she would have to say would be clearly absurd, she would convince Frank because that was the kind of thing he would want to hear. The old man would accuse her of neglecting her duties as a parent. He'd be very self-righteous. He'd use her failure as an excuse to bring in his pack of hungry attorneys. A telephone call to Frank Jacobs would lead inevitably to another custody battle, and that was the last thing Colin wanted.

The only other people to whom he could turn were his grandparents. All four of them were alive. His mother's folks lived in Sarasota, Florida, in a big white stucco place with lots of windows and shiny terrazzo floors. His father's people had a small farm in Vermont. Colin hadn't seen his grandparents in three years, and he'd never been close to any of them. If he called them, they would call Weezy. His relationships wih them were not such that they would keep a secret for him. And they certainly wouldn't come across country to take his side in this little war, not in a million years; that was a pipe dream.

Heather? Perhaps it was time to tell her, to ask for her help and suggestions. He could not hide his separation from Roy forever. But what could she do? She was a slender, rather timid girl, very pretty and nice and smart, but not much good in a fight like this.

He sighed.

'Jeez.'

He took his hand off the telephone.

There was no one on earth from whom he could hope to get help. No one.

He was as alone as if he had been standing at the North Pole. Utterly, perfectly, unrelievedly alone. But he was accustomed to that.

When had it ever been different?

He went upstairs.

In the past, whenever the world seemed too harsh and difficult to handle, he simply retreated from it. He had squirreled away with his monster models, his comic-book collection, and his shelves of science-fiction and horror novels. His room had been a sanctuary, the eye of the hurricane, where the storm could not touch him, where it could even be forgotten for a while. His room had always done for him what a hospital did for a sick man and what a monastery did for a monk: It healed him and it made him feel that in some mystical way he was part of something far, far more important and *better* than everyday life. His room had been filled with magic. It had been his refuge and his stage, where he could either hide from the world and from himself, too – or act out his fantasies for an audience of one. His room had been his place to weep and his playground, his church and his laboratory, the repository of his dreams.

Now it was just a room like any other. A ceiling. Four walls. A floor. A window. A door. Nothing more than that. Just one more place to be.

When Roy had come in here alone, uninvited, unwanted, he had broken the delicate spell that made this place unique. He had surely snooped through all the drawers and books and monster model kits, and in doing that he had also pawed through Colin's soul without ever realising it. With his crude touch he had drained the magic out of everything in the room, just as a lightning rod draws magnificent bolts of energy from the sky and disperses them so widely in the earth that they cease to exist at all. Nothing here was special any longer, and none of it would be special again. Colin felt violated, raped; he felt used and discarded. But Roy Borden had stolen a great deal more than privacy and pride; he had also made off with what remained of Colin's shaky sense of security. And even more than that, much worse than that he was a thief of illusions; he had taken all of those false but wonderfully comforting beliefs that Colin had long cherished.

Colin was depressed, yet he was also aware of a strange new power that was beginning to shine within him. Although he nearly had been killed just minutes ago, he was less afraid at this moment than at any time in memory. For the first time in his life, he did not feel weak or inferior. He was still the same second-rate physical specimen that he had always been – skinny, myopic, poorly co-ordinated – but inside he felt all new, fresh, and capable of anything.

He did not cry, and he was proud of that.

At the moment there was no room in him for tears; he was filled with a need for revenge.

Part Three

Part Three

35

Colin spent the rest of Friday in his room. He read parts of the three psychology books that he'd brought home from the library, and he reread some pages as often as half a dozen times. When he wasn't studying, he stared at the wall, sometimes for as long as an hour, just thinking. And planning.

When he left the house early the next morning, the sky was high and bright and cloudless. He intended to meet Heather at twelve o'clock, spend the afternoon at the beach, and be home by nightfall; nevertheless, he took a flashlight with him.

He rode his bicycle down to the beach, then to the harbor, even though he didn't have any immediate business in either of those places. He was taking a roundabout route to his real destination in order to make certain that he wasn't followed. He could see that Roy wasn't close behind him, but perhaps the boy was watching from a distance through the same pair of high-power binoculars they had used when they were spying on Sarah Callahan. From the harbor, Colin cycled to the tourist information center at the north end of town. Satisfied that he had no tail, he finally struck out directly for Hawk Drive and the Kingman place.

Even in bright daylight, the abandoned house loomed threateningly at the top of the hill. Colin approached it with uneasiness that changed to quiet fear by the time he entered the gate and started up the broken flagstone walk. If he had been the state official in charge of the property, or the mayor of Santa Leona, he would have called for the complete and immediate destruction of the place for the good of the community. He still thought the house exuded a tangible evil, a menace that could be felt and seen as clearly as the California sunshine that now dazzled his eyes and warmed his face. Three large, black birds circled over the roof and finally perched on a chimney. The house seemed to be aware, watchful, infused with malignant life force. The weathered gray walls looked scabrous, diseased, cancerous. Rusting nails resembled old wounds: stigmata. Sunlight seemed unable to penetrate the mysterious spaces beyond the missing windowpanes, and from outside, at least, the inside of the mansion appeared to be as dark now as it would be at midnight.

Colin put his bicycle down in the grass, climbed the sagging porch steps, and looked through the shattered window where he and Roy had stood one night not long ago. On closer inspection, Colin saw that some light did reach into the house. The drawing room was visible in every detail. At one time it must have served as a clubhouse for a group of boys – for candy wrappers, empty soda cans, and cigarette butts were strewn across the bare, scarred floor. A faded and tattered *Playboy* centerfold was fixed above the fireplace, over the same mantel on which Mr Kingman had lined up the blood-splashed heads of his slaughtered family. The kids who had been using the house as a hangout had not been around for many months – a thick, undisturbed layer of dust covered everything.

The front entrance was unlocked, but the corroded hinges squeaked as Colin pushed on the warped door. The wind rushed in around him and stirred up a small cloud of dust in the foyer. Inside, the air was heavily tainted with the odors of mildew and dry rot.

As Colin prowled from room to room, he saw that vandals had been at work in every corner of the huge house. Boys' names, obscene words, dirty limericks, and crude drawings of male and female genitalia were scrawled wherever there was bare plaster or fairly plain wallpaper. Ragged holes – some only as large as a hand, others nearly as big as a door – had been knocked in the walls. Piles of plaster and splintered laths littered the place.

When Colin stood perfectly still, the old house was ethereally quiet. But when he moved, the arthritic structure responded to each step he took; its joints groaned on all sides of him.

Several times he thought he heard something creeping up behind him, but when he looked he was always alone. For the most part, he moved through the ruins without a thought for ghosts and monsters. He was surprised and pleased by his newly acquired bravery – and just a bit uncomfortable with it. Only a few weeks ago, he would have refused to cross the Kingman threshold by himself, even if there had been a million-dollar prize at stake.

He was in the mansion more than two hours. He did not overlook a room or even a closet. In

281

those chambers where all the windows were
boarded shut, he used the flashlight that he had
brought along. He spent most of the time on the
second floor, exploring every nook – and
planning a surprise or two for Roy Borden.

36

There was, after all, something that Heather could do to help him. In fact, she was perhaps the most essential part of the revenge plot that he concocted. Without her co-operation, he would have to find another way to get Roy. Colin didn't intend that she fight at his side. He wasn't relying on her strength or agility. He wanted to use her as bait.

If she agreed to help him, she would be in some danger. But he was certain that he could protect her. He was not the same weak and ineffectual Colin Jacobs who had moved to Santa Leona at the beginning of the summer, and his new aggressiveness would come as a surprise to Roy. A nasty surprise. And surprise was very definitely to his advantage.

Heather was waiting at the beach, in the shadow of the pier. She was wearing a one-piece blue swimsuit. She didn't wear two-piece suits or bikinis or anything like that because she didn't think she looked good enough in them. Colin thought she would have looked as appealing as any other teen-age girl on the beach, better than many of them, and he told her that. He could see that the compliment pleased her, but it was equally obvious that she did not really believe it.

They chose a spot on the hot sand to spread their beach towels. For a while they lay on their backs, in companionable silence, basking in the sun.

At last Colin turned on his side and rose up slightly, supporting himself on one bent elbow, and said, 'How much does it matter to you that I'm Roy Borden's friend?'

She frowned, but she didn't open her eyes or turn away from the sun. 'What do you mean?'

'How much does it matter?' he persisted, his heart beginning to pound.

'Why should it matter to me?' she asked. 'I don't understand.'

Colin took a deep breath and plunged ahead. 'Would you still like me if I wasn't Roy's friend?'

Now she turned her head toward him and opened her eyes. 'Are you serious?'

'Yeah.'

She rolled onto her side and rose on one elbow to face him. The wind stirred her hair. 'You mean you think maybe I'm interested in you only because you're the best friend of the school big shot?'

Colin blushed. 'Well . . .'

'That's a terrible thing to think,' she said, but she didn't sound angry.

He shrugged, embarrassed but still anxious to hear her answer.

'And it's insulting,' she said.

'I'm sorry,' he said quickly, placatingly. 'I didn't mean it that way. It's just . . . I had to ask. It's important to know if you—'

'I like you because you're you,' Heather said. 'I'm here right now because you're fun to be with. Roy Borden doesn't have anything to do with it. Actually, I'm here in spite of the fact that you're his buddy.'

284

'Huh?'

'I'm one of the few people at school who doesn't really care what Roy does or says or thinks. Most everyone wants to be his friend, but I don't particularly care if he even knows I exist.'

Colin blinked, surprised. 'You don't like Roy?'

She hesitated, then said, 'He's your friend. I don't want to talk against him.'

'But that's just it,' Colin said excitedly. 'He isn't my friend any more. He hates me.'

'What? What happened?'

'I'll tell you in a minute. Don't worry about that. I've been just about bursting to tell someone.' Colin sat up on his beach towel. 'But first I've got to know what you think of him. I thought you liked him. One of the first things you said to me was that you'd seen me with Roy. So I figured—'

'I was just curious about you and him,' she said. 'You didn't seem like the kind of guy who usually hangs around with him. And the better I've gotten to know you, the stranger it seems.'

'Tell me why you don't like him.'

She sat up, too.

The ocean wind was warm and salt-scented.

'Well,' she said, 'I don't exactly dislike him. Not a lot. I mean, not actively or passionately or anything. I don't really know him well enough for that. But I do know him well enough to know I could never be a fan of his. There's something sleazy about him.'

'Sleazy?'

'It's hard to put into words,' Heather said. 'But I always get the feeling that Roy's never . . . sincere. Not ever. Not about anything. Most of the time he seems to be putting on an act. Apparently, no one else ever notices it. But I get the feeling he's always manipulating people, using them one way or another, and then laughing about it inside.'

'Yeah!' Colin said. 'Oh yeah! Exactly. That's exactly what he's doing. And he's good at it. Not just with other kids. He can manipulate adults, too.'

'My mother met him once,' Heather said. 'I didn't think she was ever going to stop talking about him. She thought he was so charming, so polite.'

'My mother, too,' Colin said. 'She'd rather have him for a son than me.'

'So what happened?' Heather asked. 'Why aren't you and Roy friends any more?'

He told her everything, beginning with the day he had first met Roy. He told her about the cat in the birdcage. The games with the electric trains. Roy's story about killing two other boys just for kicks. Roy's desire to rape and kill Sarah Callahan, his neighbor. The nightmare at Hermit Hobson's automobile graveyard. The lighter-fluid attack. He told her everything that he'd learned in the library, the entire story of Belinda Jane Borden's hideous accidental death – and the eventual hospitalisation of both Roy and Mrs Borden.

Heather listened in stunned silence. Initially, her face registered doubt, but the skepticism gradually faded and was replaced by a look of growing if reluctant belief. She was horrified, and when Colin finally finished, she said, 'You've got to tell the police.'

He looked out at the rolling sea and the sky with its swooping gulls. 'No,' he said. 'They won't believe me.'

'Sure they will. You convinced *me*.'

'That's different. You're a kid, like me. They're adults. Besides, when they call my mother to ask her if she knows anything about it, she'll tell them I'm lying and that I've got a drug problem. God knows what they'll do to me then.'

'We'll tell my folks,' Heather said. 'They're not really all that bad. Better than yours, I guess. They actually listen now and then. We can convince them. I know we can.'

He shook his head. 'No. Roy charmed your mother before. Remember? He'll charm her all over again if he has to. She'll believe him, not us. And if your folks call Weezy to discuss it with her, she'll convince them I'm a crazed doper. They'll split us up. You won't be allowed to come near me. Then if Roy knows you believe me, he'll try to kill *both* of us.'

She was silent for a while. Then she shuddered and said, 'You're right.'

'Yeah,' he said miserably.

'What are we going to do?'

He looked at her. 'Did you say "we"?'

'Well, of course I said "we." What do you think – that I'd turn my back on you at a time like this? You can't handle it alone. No one could.'

Relieved, he said, 'I was hoping you'd say that.'

She reached out, took hold of his hand.

'I've got a plan,' he said.

'A plan for what?'

'For trapping Roy. There's a part in it for you.'

'What do I have to do?'

'You're the bait,' Colin said. He told her about his scheme.

When he was finished, she said, 'It's clever.'

'It'll work.'

'I'm not sure.'

287

'Why not?'

'Because I don't make very good bait,' she said. 'You need to use a girl that Roy would find . . . desirable . . . sexy. A girl he'd want real bad.' Her face colored. 'I'm just not . . . enough.'

'You're wrong about that,' Colin said. 'You're enough. You're more than enough. You're plenty.'

She looked away from him, looked down at her knees.

'Pretty knees,' Colin said.

'Knobby.'

'No.'

'Knobby and red.'

'No.'

Sensing that it was what she wanted him to do, he put a hand on her knee, moved it up her thigh a few inches, then down again, stroking softly.

She closed her eyes, trembled slightly.

He felt his own body responding.

'It would be dangerous,' she said.

He couldn't lie to her. He couldn't minimise the risk just to secure her co-operation. 'Yes,' he said. 'It would be very, very dangerous.'

She picked up a handful of sand and let it trickle slowly through her fingers.

He gently stroked her knee, her thigh. He couldn't believe he was touching her like that. He stared at his bold hand with excitement and amazement, as if it had acquired a will of its own.

'On the other hand,' she said, 'we'd have the advantage of planning.'

'And surprise.'

'And the gun,' she said.

'Yes. And the gun.'

'You're sure you can get the gun?'

'Positive.'

'OK,' she said. 'I'll do it. We'll trap him. Together.'

Colin's stomach rolled unpleasantly, powered by a strange mixture of energies: desire and fear in equal measure.

'Colin?'

'What?'

'Do you really think I'm . . . enough?'

'Yes.'

'Pretty?'

'Yes.'

She looked deep into his eyes, and then she smiled and turned away, stared out to sea.

He thought he saw tears in her eyes.

'You'd better go now,' she said.

'Why?'

'It'll work better if Roy doesn't realise you and I know each other. If he happens to see us here, together, he might not fall for the trick later.'

She was right. Besides, he had things to do, preparations to make. He got up and folded his beach towel.

'Call me tonight,' she said.

'I will.'

'And be careful.'

'You, too.'

'And Colin?'

'Yeah?'

'I think you're enough, too. You're plenty.'

He grinned and tried to think of something to say and couldn't think of anything and turned and raced off, toward the bicycle lockup in the parking lot.

37

The plan required one piece of expensive equipment, and Colin had to raise a considerable sum of money.

He went home from the beach, went up to his room, and opened the big metal bank that was shaped like a flying saucer. He shook it; a few tightly folded bills and a great many coins spilled onto the bedspread. He tallied the lot and found that he had exactly seventy-one dollars – which was approximately one third of what he needed.

He sat on the bed for a few minutes, staring at the money. He considered his options.

Finally he went to the closet and hauled out several large boxes that were filled with comic books, each in a sealed zip-lock plastic bag, preserved in mint condition. He sorted through them and pulled out some of the most valuable editions.

At one-thirty, he took sixty comic books down to Nostalgia House on Broadway. The store catered to collectors of science fiction, first-editon mysteries, comic books, and tapes of old radio shows.

Mr Plevich, the proprietor, was a tall, white-haired man with a bushy mustache. He stood with his big belly pressed against the counter while he looked through Colin's offering.

'S-s-some really n-nice items,' Mr Plevich said.

'What can you give me for them?'

'I c-can-t give you w-what they're worth,' Mr Plevich said. 'I've g-got to leave room for my p-p-profit.'

'I understand,' Colin said.

'Actually, I'd advise you against s-s-selling these now. They're all mint-c-condition f-f-first issues.'

'I know.'

'They're already w-worth a good d-d-deal more than you p-paid for them at the newsstand. If you hold on to them for t-t-t-two years or so, they'll probably t-triple in value.'

'Yeah. But I need the money now. I need it right away.'

Mr Plevich winked at him. 'You have a g-g-girlfriend?'

'Yeah. And her birthday's coming up,' Colin lied.

'You'll b-b-be sorry. A g-g-girlfriend will w-walk away sooner or later, but a g-good comic b-b-book c-can be enjoyed over and over again.'

'How much?'

'I was thinking one hundred d-d-dollars.'

'Two hundred.'

'Much t-too much. She d-doesn't n-n-need such an expensive g-g-g-gift. How about one hundred and t-twenty?'

'No.'

Mr Plevich looked through the batch of comics two more times, and they finally settled on one hundred and forty dollars, cash.

California Federal Trust stood on the corner, half a block from Nostalgia House. Colin gave one of the tellers the coins that had been in his flying-saucer bank, and she gave him some folding money.

With $211 stuffed in his pockets, he went to Radio Shack on Broadway and bought the best compact tape recorder he could afford. He already owned a cassette recorder, but it was bulky; and besides, the microphone didn't pick up anything further away than three or four feet. The one he bought for $189.95, on sale, $30 off the regular price, picked up and clearly recorded voices as far away as thirty feet; at least that's what the salesman said. Furthermore, it was only nine inches long, five inches wide, and just three inches thick; it could be hidden easily.

A few minutes after he got home and stashed the recorder in his room, his mother stopped by long enough to change clothes for a dinner date. She gave him money to eat at Charlie's Cafe. When she was gone, he made a cheese sandwich and washed it down with chocolate milk.

After supper he went up to his room and experimented with the new tape recorder for a while. It was a fine machine. In spite of its compact size, it provided a clear and remarkably lifelike reproduction of his voice. It was capable of picking up voices from as much as thirty feet away, as promised, but at its maximum range the fidelity was not adequate for Colin's purposes. He tested the machine again and again and determined that it could record a conversational tone of voice only up to twenty-five feet. That was good enough.

He went into his mother's bedroom and looked in the nightstands, then the dresser. The gun was in a dresser drawer. It was a pistol. There were two safety catches, and when you switched them off, a pair of red warning dots shone on the blue-black gun metal. When he had told Roy about the pistol, he had said it probably wasn't even loaded. But it was. He put the safeties on again and replaced the weapon; it rested on a pile of his mother's silky panties.

He called Heather, and they discussed the plan again, searching for potential problems that they had overlooked before. The scheme still appeared to be workable.

'Tomorrow, I'll talk to Mrs Borden,' Colin said.

'Do you think it's really necessary?'

'Yes,' he said. 'If I can get her to open up even a little bit and get it on tape, it'll help support our story.'

'But if Roy knows you've been talking to her, he might get suspicious. He might realise something's up, and we'll lose the advantage of surprise.'

'They don't communicate well in that family,' Colin said. 'Maybe she won't even tell Roy she talked to me.'

'And maybe she will.'

'We have to risk it. If she tells us something that helps explain Roy, something that explains his motivation, then we'll have an easier time getting the police to believe us.'

'Well . . . OK,' Heather said. 'But call me after you've talked to her. I want to hear all about it.'

'I will. And then tomorrow night we'll set the trap for Roy.'

She was silent a moment. Then she said, 'So soon?'

'There's no reason to wait any longer.'

'It wouldn't hurt to take an extra day or two to think about it. The plan, I mean. Maybe there's a hole in it. Maybe we're overlooking something.'

'We aren't,' he said. 'We've talked about it and thought about it enough. It'll work.'

'Well . . . all right.'

'You can always back out,' he said.

'No.'

'I won't hold it against you.'

'No,' she said. 'I'm going to help. You need me. We'll do it tomorrow night.'

Several hours later, Colin woke from a nightmare, sweating and shaking. He couldn't remember exactly what the dream had been about. The only thing he could recall was that Heather had been in it; her screams had awakened him.

38

At eleven-thirty Sunday morning, Colin went
down to the harbor and sat on a bench on the
boardwalk, where he could see every approach to
a store called Treasured Things. It was a gift shop
that survived off the tourists. In Treasured Things
you could buy postcards, lamps made out of
seashells, belts made out of seashells, paper-
weights made out of seashells, seashells made out
of chocolate, T-shirts bearing supposedly funny
slogans, books about Santa Leona, candles
shaped like the famous bell tower of Santa Leona
Mission, china plates painted with scenes of
Santa Leona, and a wide variety of other useless
junk. Roy Borden's mother worked in the shop
five afternoons a week, including Sundays.

Colin was carrying a folded nylon windbreaker. The new tape recorder was concealed in
it. Even with the stiff breeze coming in off the
ocean, the day was much too warm for a jacket,
but Colin didn't think Mrs Borden would notice
it. After all, there was no reason for her to be
suspicious of him.

A lot of people were strolling along the boardwalk, talking and laughing and window-
shopping and eating chocolate-covered bananas;
and a number of them were good-looking, leggy
young girls in shorts and bikinis. Colin forced

himself not to stare at them. He didn't want to be distracted, to miss Helen Borden, and then have to approach her in the busy gift shop.

He spotted her at ten minutes of twelve. She was a thin, birdlike woman. She walked briskly, head up, shoulders back, very businesslike.

He reached into the folded windbreaker and switched on the recorder, then got up and hurried across the wide boardwalk. He intercepted her before she reached Treasured Things.

'Mrs Borden?'

She stopped abruptly at the sound of her name and turned to him. She was clearly perplexed. She didn't recognise him.

'We've met twice,' he said, 'but only for a minute or two each time. I'm Colin Jacobs. Roy's friend.'

'Oh. Oh yes.'

'I have to talk to you.'

'I'm on my way to work.'

'It's important.'

She looked at her watch.

'Very, very important,' he said.

She hesitated, glanced at the gift shop.

'It's about your daughter,' he said.

Her head snapped around.

'It's about Belinda Jane,' he said.

Helen Borden's face was well tanned. At the mention of her dead daughter's name, the tan remained but the blood drained out of the skin beneath it. She looked suddenly old and sick.

'I know how she died,' Colin said.

Mrs Borden said nothing.

'Roy told me about it,' he lied.

The woman appeared to be frozen. Her eyes were cold.

298

'We talked for hours about Belinda,' Colin said.

When she spoke her thin lips barely moved. 'This is none of your business.'

'Roy made it my business,' Colin said. 'I didn't want to hear about it. But he told me secrets.'

She glared at him.

'Awful secrets,' he said. 'About how Belinda died.'

'That's no secret. I know how she died. I *saw*. It was . . . an accident. A horrible accident.'

'Was it? Are you absolutely sure?'

'What are you saying?'

'He told me these secrets, made me swear never to tell anyone. But I can't keep it in. It's too awful.'

'What did he tell you?'

'Why he killed her.'

'It was an accident.'

'He'd been planning it for months,' Colin lied.

She suddenly took him by the arm and led him across the boardwalk to an isolated bench by the railing. He was holding the windbreaker in that same arm, and he was afraid that she would discover the tape recorder. She didn't. They sat side by side with the sea at their backs.

'He told you he murdered her?'

'Yeah.'

She shook her head. 'No. It had to be an accident. It had to be. He was only eight years old.'

'I think maybe some kids are born bad,' Colin said. 'I mean, you know, not many. Just a few. But every once in a while, you know, you read about it in the papers, about how some young kid committed cold-blooded murder. I think maybe, you know, like one in a hundred thousand is born twisted. You know? *Born* evil. And whatever

299

a kid like that does, no matter how bad the things are that he does, you can't blame it on the way he was raised or the things he was taught because, you know, he was born to be the way he is.'

She stared intently at him as he rambled on, but he wasn't sure that she heard a word he said. When he finally stopped, she was silent for a while, and then she said, 'What does he want from me?'

Colin blinked. 'Who?'

'Roy. Why did he put you up to this?'

'He didn't,' Colin protested. 'Please, don't tell him I talked to you. Please, Mrs Borden. If he knew I was here, telling you this, he'd kill me.'

'Belinda's death was an accident,' she said. But she didn't sound convinced of that.

'You didn't always think it was accidental,' he said.

'How do you know?'

'That's why you beat Roy.'

'I didn't.'

'He told me.'

'He lied.'

'That's where he got the scars.'

She was nervous, fidgety.

'It was one year after Belinda died.'

'What did he tell you?' she asked.

'That you beat him because you knew he killed her on purpose.'

'He said that?'

'Yeah.'

She turned slightly on the bench so that she could look out to sea. 'I'd just finished cleaning and waxing the kitchen floor. It was clean as a whistle. Perfect. Absolutely spotless. You could have eaten off that floor. Then he came in with muddy shoes. He was mocking me. He didn't say a word, but when I saw him walking across that floor in his muddy shoes, I knew he was mocking me. He had killed Belinda, and now he was mocking me, and in some way one thing seemed as bad as the other. I wanted to kill him.'

Colin almost sighed with relief. He hadn't been sure that Mrs Borden had put the scars on her son's back. He had been operating on a hunch, and now that it had proved true, he felt more secure about the rest of his theory.

'I knew he'd killed her on purpose. But they wouldn't believe me,' she said.

'I know.'

'I always knew it. There was never a time I didn't know it. He killed his baby sister.' She was talking to herself now, looking out to sea and into the past as well. 'When I hit him, I was just trying to make him admit the truth. She deserved that much, didn't she? She was dead, and she deserved to have her killer punished. But they didn't believe me.'

Her voice trailed away, and she was silent for so long that Colin finally tried to get her talking again. 'Roy laughed about that. He thought it was funny that no one took you seriously.'

She didn't need much coaxing. 'They said I had a nervous breakdown. Sent me away to the county hospital. I had therapy. They called it that. Therapy. As if I was the crazy one. An expensive psychiatrist. He treated me as if I were a child. A foolish man. I was there a long time – until I realised that all I had to do was pretend that I'd been wrong about Roy.'

'You never were wrong.'

She looked at him. 'He told you why he killed Belinda?'

'Yeah.'

'What reason did he give?'

Colin shifted uneasily on the bench because he didn't have an answer to her question, and he didn't want her to realise that he had engaged her attention with a string of lies. He had been leading her on, trying to get her to say certain things that he wanted to have on the tape. She said some of them, but not all of them. He hoped to keep her confidence until he had everything he needed.

Fortunately, when he hesitated, Mrs Borden answered the question for him. 'It was jealousy, wasn't it? He was jealous of my little girl because after she was born he knew he'd never really be one of us.'

'Yeah. That's what he told me,' Colin said, though he wasn't sure what she meant.

'It was a mistake,' she said. 'We never should have adopted him.'

'Adopted?'

'He didn't tell you that?'

'Well . . . no.'

He'd blown it. She would wonder why Roy had revealed everything else, every ugly secret, but not this. Then she'd realise that Roy hadn't told him anything about Belinda Jane, that he was lying, that he was playing a bizarre game with her.

But she surprised him. She was so deeply involved in her memories, and so focused on the fact that her son had admitted to premeditated sororicide, that she didn't have the presence of mind to consider the curious gaps in Colin's knowledge.

'We wanted a child more than anything in the world,' she said, looking out to sea once more. 'A child of our own. But the doctors said we never could. My fault. There were ... things wrong with me. Alex, my husband, was terribly upset. Terribly. He had counted so much on a child of his own. But the doctors said it just wasn't possible. We went to half a dozen doctors, and they all said the same thing. Not remotely possible. Because of me. So I talked him into adoption. My fault again. Entirely my fault. It was the wrong thing to do. We don't even know who Roy's real parents were – or *what* they were. That bothers Alex. What kind of people did Roy come from? What was wrong with them? What flaws and sicknesses did they pass on to him? It was an awful mistake to take him in. By the time we'd had him a few months, I knew he was wrong for us. He was a good baby, but Alex didn't take to him. I'd wanted so much for Alex to have his child, but what *he* wanted was a child with his own blood in its veins. That was quite important to Alex. You can't imagine *how* important. An adopted child is different from your flesh, Alex says. He says you can't ever feel as close to it as you can to your own blood. He says it's like training a dangerous wild animal from the time it's a cub and keeping it as a pet; you just never know when it might turn on you because deep down it isn't at all like what you've tried to make it. And so that was another thing I'd done wrong: bringing someone else's child into our home. A stranger. And he turned on us. I'm always doing something wrong. I've failed Alex. All he ever wanted was a child of his own.'

When Colin had been sitting on the bench,

waiting for her to show up, he had expected to have trouble getting her to talk. But he had pushed the right button. She wouldn't shut up. She droned on and on, as if she were an Ancient Mariner robot, a machine with a tale to tell. And it looked to him as if she were also a machine with very little time left; beneath the cool veneer of businesslike efficiency, serious instabilities were generating a lot of inner heat. As he listened to what she said, he also listened for the sound of gears stripping and mainsprings breaking and vacuum tubes popping.

'We'd had Roy two and a half years,' she said, 'when I discovered that I was going to have a baby. The doctors were wrong about me. I almost died in labor, and there was no doubt afterward that she would be my first and last, but I *did* have her. They were wrong. In spite of all their complicated tests and consultations and sky-high fees, every one of them was wrong. She was a miracle child. God meant all along for us to have the impossible, the miracle child, that special blessing, and I was too impatient to wait. I didn't have faith enough. Not nearly enough. I hate myself for that. I talked Alex into the adoption. Then along came Belinda, the one we were *meant* to have. I had no faith. So after just five years, she was taken away from us. Roy took her away from us. The child we were never meant to have took away the one that God sent us. You see?'

Colin's fascination was changing to embarrassment. He didn't need or want to hear every sordid detail. He looked around self-consciously to see if anyone could overhear, but there was no one near the bench.

She turned away from the sea and stared into

his eyes. 'Why did you come here, young man? Why did you tell me Roy's secret?'

He shrugged. 'I thought you ought to know.'

'Did you expect me to do something to him?'

'Aren't you going to?'

'I wish I could,' she said with genuine malice. 'But I can't. If I start telling them that he killed my little girl, it'll be like before. They'll send me away to the county hospital again.'

'Oh.' That was what he had figured even before he spoke to her.

'Nobody will ever believe me when it comes to Roy,' she said. 'And who's going to believe you? I understand from your mother that there's some problems with drugs.'

'No. That's not true.'

'Who's going to believe either of us?'

'No one,' he said.

'What we need is proof.'

'Yeah.'

'Irrefutable proof.'

'Right.'

'Something tangible,' she said. 'Maybe . . . if you could get him to tell you all about it again . . . about how he killed her on purpose . . . and maybe have a tape recorder hidden some-place . . .'

Colin winced at the mention of a recorder. 'That's a thought.'

'There must be a way,' she said.

'Yeah.'

'We'll both think about it.'

'All right.'

'Think about a way to trap him.'

'OK.'

'And we'll meet again.'

'We will?'

'Here,' she said. 'Tomorrow.'

'But—'

'It's always been just me against him,' she said, leaning close to Colin. He could feel her breath against his face. And he could smell it, too: spearmint. 'But now there's you,' she said. 'Two people know about him now. Together we ought to be able to think of a way to get him. I want to get him. I want everyone to know how he *planned* to kill my little girl. When they know the truth, how can they expect me to keep him in my house? We'll send him back where he came from. The neighbors won't talk. How can they, after they know what he did? I'll be free of him. I want that more than anything.' Her voice fell to a conspiratorial whisper. 'You'll be my ally, won't you?'

He had the insane thought that she was going to go through the blood-brother ritual with him.

'Won't you?' she asked.

'OK.' But he didn't intend to meet with her again; she was almost as scary as Roy.

She put her hand on his cheek, and he started to pull away before he realised that she was only being affectionate. Her fingers were cold.

'You're a good boy,' she said. 'You did a good thing – coming to me like this.'

He wished she would take her hand away.

'I've always known the truth,' she said, 'but what a relief it is to have someone else who knows. You be here tomorrow. Same time.'

Just to be rid of her, he said, 'Sure.'

She got up abruptly and walked away, toward Treasured Things.

As Colin watched her go, he thought that she

306

was far more terrifying than any of the monsters he'd feared throughout his childhood and adolescence. Christopher Lee, Peter Cushing, Boris Karloff, Bela Lugosi – none of them had ever portrayed a character quite as chilling as Helen Borden. She was worse than a ghoul or a vampire, doubly dangerous because she was so well disguised. She looked rather ordinary, even drab, unremarkable in every aspect, but inside she was an awful creature. He could still feel where her icy fingers had pressed against his face.

He took the recorder out of the windbreaker and switched it off.

Incredibly, he was ashamed of himself for some of the things he had said about Roy, and for the way he had so eagerly played to her hatred of her son. It was true that Roy was sick; it was also true that he was a killer; but it was not true that he had always been that way. He wasn't, as Colin had said, 'born evil.' Fundamentally, he was not less of a human being than anyone else. He had not murdered his sister in cold blood. Judging from all the evidence that Colin had seen, Belinda Jane's death had been an accident. Roy's sickness had developed in the aftermath of that tragedy.

Depressed, Colin got off the bench and went out to the parking lot. He unchained his bike from the security rack.

He no longer wanted revenge against Roy. He just wanted to put a stop to the violence. He wanted to get the evidence so the proper authorities would believe and act. He was weary.

Although it was pointless to tell them, although they would never understand, Mr and Mrs Borden were killers, too. They had turned Roy into one of the living dead.

39

Colin called Heather.

'Did you talk to Roy's mother?' she asked.

'Yeah. And I got more than I bargained for.'

'Tell me.'

'It's too complicated over the phone. You've got to hear the tape.'

'Why don't you bring it here? My parents are gone for the day.'

'I'll be there in fifteen minutes.'

'Don't come by the front way,' she said. 'Roy just might happen to be at the cemetery across the street; you never can tell. Take the alley and come through the backyard.'

He made certain he wasn't followed, and she was waiting for him on the patio behind the house. They went into the cheery yellow-and-white kitchen, sat at the table, and listened to the taped conversation between him and Mrs Borden.

When Colin finally switched off the machine, Heather said, 'It's awful.'

'I know.'

'Poor Roy.'

'I know what you mean,' Colin said morosely.

'I'm kind of sorry I said those things about him. He can't help what he is, can he?'

'It affected me the same way. But we can't let

309

ourselves feel too sorry for him. Not yet. We don't dare. We've got to remember that he's dangerous. We've got to keep in mind that he'd happily kill me – and rape and kill you – if he thought he could get away with it.'

The kitchen clock ticked hollowly.

Heather said, 'If we played this tape for the police, it might convince them.'

'Of what? That Roy was an abused child? That he was maybe abused enough to grow up twisted? Yeah. Maybe it would convince them of that, all right. But it wouldn't prove a thing. It wouldn't prove that Roy killed those two boys or that he tried to wreck a train the other night or that he's trying to kill me. We need more than this. We have to go through with the rest of the plan.'

'Tonight,' she said.

'Yeah.'

40

Weezy came home at five-thirty, and they had an early supper together. She brought stuff from the deli: sliced ham, sliced turkey breast, sliced cheese, macaroni salad, potato salad, big dill pickles, and wedges of cheesecake. There was a lot of food, but neither of them ate much; she was always watching her figure, conscious of every extra ounce, and Colin was simply too worried about the coming night to have much of an appetite.

'You going back to the gallery?' he asked.

'In about an hour.'

'Be home at nine?'

''Fraid not. We close at nine, sweep the floor, dust the furniture, and open again at ten.'

'What for?'

'We're having a private, invitation-only show-ing of a new artist.'

'At ten o'clock at night?'

'It's supposed to be an elegant after-dinner affair. Guests will have their choice of brandy or champagne. Sound swell to you?'

'I guess.'

She put a daub of mustard on her plate, rolled up a slice of ham, dipped the ham in the mustard, and nibbled daintily. 'All of our best local customers are coming.'

'How late will it last?'

'Midnight or thereabouts.'

'Will you come home after that?'

'I expect so.'

He tasted the cheesecake.

'Don't forget your curfew,' she said.

'I won't.'

'You be home before dark.'

'You can trust me.'

'I hope so. For your sake, I hope so.'

'Call and check if you want.'

'I probably will.'

'I'll be here,' he lied.

After she had showered and changed and left for the evening, he went into her room and took the pistol from the dresser drawer. He put it in a small cardboard box. He also put the tape recorder, two flashlights, and a squeeze bottle of ketchup in the box. He took a dish towel out of the linen closet and cut it in half, the long way. He put the two strips of cloth with the other things. He went out to the garage and fetched a coil of rope from the wall, where it had been hanging ever since they moved into the house, and he added that to the bundle.

He had some time to kill before he could set out for the Kingman house. He went to his room and tried to work on one of his monster models. He couldn't do it. His hands wouldn't stop shaking.

An hour before nightfall, he picked up the box that contained the pistol, the tape recorder, and the other items. He left the house and strapped the package to the carrier on his bicycle. He followed an indirect route to the abandoned Kingman house at the top of Hawk Drive, and he was certain he was not followed.

312

Heather was waiting just inside the front door of the ruined mansion. She stepped out of the shadows when Colin arrived. She was wearing short blue shorts and a long-sleeved white blouse, and she was beautiful.

He put the bicycle on its side, out of sight in the tall dry grass, and he carried the cardboard box inside.

The house was always a strange place, but perhaps even stranger than usual at twilight. The slanting copper sunlight streamed through a few broken, shutterless windows and gave the place a somewhat bloody look. Motes of dust spun lazily in the fading beams. In one corner a huge spider web gleamed like crystal. The shadows crept as if they were living things.

'I look terrible,' Heather said as soon as he joined her in the house.

'You look great. Terrific.'

'My shampoo didn't work,' she said. 'My hair came out all stringy.'

'Your hair is nice. Very nice. You couldn't ask for prettier hair.'

'He's not going to be interested in me,' she said, quite sure of that. 'As soon as he sees that it's me you've got here, he'll just turn and walk out.'

'Don't be silly. You're perfect. Absolutely perfect.'

'Do you really think so?'

'I really do.' He gave her a warm, tender, lingering kiss. Her lips were soft, tremulous. 'Come on,' he said gently. 'We have to get the trap set.' He was involving her in an extremely dangerous situation, using her, manipulating her, not unlike Roy had manipulated him, and he hated himself for it. But he didn't call it off while there was still time.

313

She followed him, and as he started up the stairs toward the second floor, she said, 'Why not down here?'

He stopped, turned, looked down at her. 'The shutters have fallen or been torn off almost all the windows on the first floor. If we staged it down there, the lights would be visible outside the house. We might attract someone. Other kids. They might interrupt us before we've gotten what we want out of Roy. Some of the rooms on the second floor still have all their shutters.'

'If something goes wrong,' she said, 'it would be easier to get away from him if we were on the first floor.'

'Nothing's going to go wrong,' he said. 'Besides, we've got the gun. Remember?' He patted the box that he was carrying under his right arm.

He started up the steps again and was relieved to hear her following him.

The second-floor hall was gloomy, and the room he was interested in was dark except for threads of late-afternoon sun around the edges of the bolted shutters. He switched on one of the flashlights.

He had chosen a large bedroom just to the left of the head of the stairs. Ancient, yellowed wallpaper was peeling off the walls and hanging in long loops across the ceiling, like old bunting left over from a festive occasion a hundred years ago. The room was dusty and smelled vaguely of mildew, but it wasn't littered with rubble as many of the other chambers were; there were only scattered pieces of lath and a few chunks of plaster and a couple of ribbons of wallpaper on the floor along the far wall.

He handed Heather the flashlight and put down the box. He picked up the second light, turned it on, and propped it against the wall so that the beam shone up at the ceiling and was reflected back down.

'It's a spooky place,' Heather said.

'There's nothing to be scared of,' Colin said.

He took the tape recorder out of the box and placed it on the floor, near the wall that was opposite the door. He gathered up some of the rubble and carefully arranged it over the small machine, letting only the head of the microphone in the open, and concealing even that in a shady little pocket of tangled wallpaper.

'Does it look natural?' he asked.

'I guess so.'

'Look at it closely.'

She did. 'It's OK. It doesn't look arranged.'

'You can't see the recorder at all?'

'No.'

He retrieved the second flashlight and shone it on the pile of trash, looking closely for a glint of metal or plastic, a reflection that would betray the trick.

'OK,' he said at last, satisfied with his work. 'I think it'll fool him. He probably won't even give it a second look.'

'Now what?' she asked.

'We've got to make you look like you've been roughed up a bit,' Colin said. 'Roy won't believe a word of it unless you look like you put up a struggle.' He took the squeeze bottle of ketchup out of the box.

'What's that for?'

'Blood.'

'Are you serious?'

'I'll admit it's trite,' Colin said. 'But it ought to be effective.'

He squeezed some of the ketchup onto his fingers, then artfully smeared it along her left temple, matting her golden hair with it.

She winced. 'Yuch.'

Colin stepped back a couple of feet and studied her. 'Good,' he said. 'It's a little too bright right now. Too red. But when it dries a bit, it ought to look just about like the real thing.'

'If we'd really struggled, like you're going to tell him we did, then I'd be rumpled and dirty,' she said.

'Right.'

She pulled her blouse half out of her shorts. She stooped, wiped her hands over the dust-covered floor, and made long sooty marks on her shorts and blouse.

When she stood up, Colin regarded her critically, looking for the false note, trying to see her as Roy would see her. 'Yeah. That's better. But maybe one more thing might help.'

'What's that?'

'If the sleeve of your blouse was torn.'

She frowned. 'It's one of my better blouses.'

'I'll pay for it.'

She shook her head. 'No. I said I'd help. I'm in this all the way. Go ahead. Tear it.'

He jerked on the material on both sides of her left shoulder seam, jerked once, twice, three times. The stitching finally parted with a nasty sound, and the sleeve sagged on her arm, torn half away.

'Yeah,' he said. 'That sure does it. You're very, very convincing.'

'But now that I'm such a mess, will he want anything to do with me?'

'It's funny . . .' Colin stared at her thoughtfully. 'In a strange way, you're even more appealing than you were before.'

'Are you sure? I mean, I'm all dirty. And I wasn't all that fabulous when I was clean.'

'You look great,' he assured her. 'Just right.'

'But if this is going to work, he really has to want to . . . well . . . he has to want to rape me. I mean, he'll never get the chance. But he has to *want* to.'

Again, Colin was acutely aware of the danger into which he was putting her, and he didn't like himself very much.

'There's just one more thing I can do that might help,' she said.

Before he realised what she intended, she grasped the front of her blouse and tugged hard on it. Buttons popped; one of them struck Colin's chin. She tore the blouse open all the way, and for an instant he saw one small, beautiful, quivering breast and a dark nipple. But then the halves of the blouse fell part of the way together again, and he could see nothing more than the soft, sweet swell of flesh that marked the beginning rise of her breasts.

He looked up, met her eyes.

She was blushing fiercely.

For a long moment neither of them spoke.

He licked his lips. His throat was suddenly parched.

At last, trembling, she said, 'I don't know. Maybe it doesn't help much to have my blouse open a little. I mean, I don't have much to show.'

'Perfect,' he said weakly. 'It's the perfect touch.' He looked away from her, went to the cardboard box, and picked up the coil of rope.

'I wish I didn't have to be tied up,' she said.

'There's no other way,' he said. 'But you won't really be tied. Not tightly. The rope will just be wrapped around your wrists a few times; it won't be knotted there. You'll be able to get your hands free in a flash. And where there are knots, they'll be the kind that slip open easily. I'll show you how. You'll be able to get out of the ropes in a couple of seconds if you have to. But you *won't* have to. He won't get anywhere near you. He won't get his hands on you. Nothing will go wrong. I have the gun.'

She sat down on the floor, with her back against the wall. 'Let's get it over with.'

By the time he finished tying her, night had fallen outside, and there were not even threads of light at the unraveling edges of the aging, splintered shutters.

'It's time to make the phone call,' Colin said.

'I'm going to hate being alone in this place.'

'It'll only be a few minutes.'

'Can you leave both flashlights?' she asked.

He was moved by her fear; he knew what it was like. But he said, 'Can't. I'll need one to get in and out of the house without breaking my neck in the dark.'

'I wish you'd brought three.'

'You'll have enough light with one,' he said, knowing that it would be pathetically little comfort in this creepy place.

'Hurry back,' she said.

'I will.'

He stood up and walked away from her. At the doorway he turned and looked back. She was so vulnerable that he could hardly stand it. He knew he should return and take the ropes off her and send her home. But he had to trap Roy, get the truth on tape, and this was the easiest way to accomplish that.

He left the room and went down the stairs to the first floor, then out of the mansion by way of the front door.

The plan would work.

It *had* to work.

If something went wrong, his and Heather's bloody head might wind up on the mantel in the Kingman house.

41

Colin stepped into a telephone booth at a service station, four blocks from the Kingman mansion. He dialed the Borden number.

Roy answered. 'Hello?'

'Is that you, blood brother?'

Roy didn't respond.

'I was wrong,' Colin said.

Roy was silent.

'I called to say I was wrong.'

'Wrong about what?'

'Everything. About breaking our blood-brother oath.'

'What're you after?' Roy asked.

'I want to be friends again.'

'You're an asshole.'

'I mean it. I really want to be friends again, Roy.'

'It isn't possible.'

'You're smarter than all of them,' Colin said. 'You're smarter and tougher. You're right; they're all a bunch of jerks. The grown-ups, too. It's easy to manipulate them. I see that now. I'm not one of them. I never was. I'm like you. I want to be on your side.'

Roy was silent again.

'I'll prove I'm on your side,' Colin said. 'I'll do

what you wanted to do. I'll help you kill someone.'

'Kill someone? Colin, have you been popping
pills again? You aren't making sense.'

'You think I've got someone listening in on
this,' Colin said. 'Well, I don't. But if you're
worried about talking on the phone, then let's talk
face to face.'

'When?'

'Now.'

'Where?'

'The Kingman house,' Colin said.

'Why there?'

'It's the best place.'

'I can think of better.'

'Not for what we're going to do. It's private, and
that's what we need.'

'For what? What are you talking about?'

'We're going to screw her and then kill her,'
Colin said.

'Are you crazy? What kind of talk is that?'

'There's no one listening in, Roy.'

'You're a lunatic.'

'You'll like her,' Colin said.

'You must be full of dope.'

'She's foxy.'

'Who?'

'The girl I've got for us.'

'*You* lined up a girl?'

'She doesn't know what's going to happen.'

'Who is she?'

'She's my peace offering to you,' Colin said.

'What girl? What's her name?'

'Come and see.'

Roy didn't respond.

'Are you scared of me?' Colin asked.

'Hell, no.'

'Then give me a chance. Let's meet at the Kingman house.'

'You and your doper buddies are probably laying for me,' Roy said. 'You planning to gang up on me?'

Colin laughed sourly. 'You're good, Roy. You're real good. That's why I want to be on your side. Nobody's smarter than you are.'

'You've got to stop gobbing pills,' Roy said. 'Colin, dope kills. You're going to ruin yourself.'

'So come talk to me about it. Convince me to go straight.'

'I've got something to do for my father. I can't get out of it. I won't be able to get away from here for at least an hour.'

'OK,' Colin said. 'It's almost a quarter past nine. We'll meet at the Kingman place at ten-thirty.'

Colin hung up, opened the telephone-booth door, and ran like hell. He went back up the steep hill, fast as he could, arms tucked close to his sides.

He reached the Kingman house, went through the gate, up the walk. Inside, he climbed the creaking stairs and heard Heather hesitantly calling his name before he reached the second floor.

She was still in the first bedroom on the left, sitting as he had left her, roped, ravishing.

'I was afraid it was someone else,' she said.

'You OK?'

'One flashlight wasn't enough,' she said. 'It was too dark in here.'

'Sorry.'

'And I think this place has rats. I heard scratching noises in the walls.'

'We won't have to stay here much longer,' he said. He bent over the cardboard box and snatched out the two long strips of dish towel that he had brought from home. 'Things are moving fast now.'

'Did you talk to Roy?'

'Yeah.'

'He's coming?'

'He says he's got things to do for his father and can't get out of the house right away. He says he can't make it before ten-thirty.'

'Then it wasn't necessary to tie me up before you made the call,' she said.

'Yes, it was,' he said. 'Don't pull the ropes apart. He's on his way now.'

'I thought you said ten-thirty.'

'He was lying.'

'How do you know?'

'I just *know*. He's trying to get here ahead of me and set a trap. He thinks I'm as naïve as I used to be.'

'Colin . . . I'm scared.'

'It'll be all right.'

'Will it?'

'I have the gun.'

'What if you have to use it?'

'I won't have to.'

'He might force you to.'

'Then I will. I'll use it if he forces me.'

'But then you'd be guilty—'

'Of self-defense,' Colin said.

'*Can* you use it?'

'In self-defense. Sure. Of course.'

'You aren't a killer.'

'I'll just wound him if I have to,' he said. 'Now we've got to hurry. I've got to put the gag on you.

It has to be tight if it's going to look convincing, but tell me if I make it too tight for comfort.' He fashioned a gag from the two pieces of dish towel, then said, 'OK?'

She made an unintelligible sound.

'Shake your head – yes or no. Is it too tight?'

She shook her head: no.

He could see the doubts were growing by the second; she wished she'd never gotten into this. Genuine fear sparked in her eyes, but that was good; it made her look as if she really were the helpless victim that she was pretending to be. Roy, possessed of the instincts of a cunning, vicious animal, would instantly recognise her terror and would be convinced by it.

Colin went to the tape recorder, lifted a piece of trash that was covering it, switched it on, carefully replaced the camouflage, and looked at Heather again. 'I'm going out to the head of the stairs to wait for him. Don't worry.'

He left the room, taking the pistol, one flashlight, and the cardboard box that now contained only the squeeze bottle of ketchup. He put the ketchup and the box in another room, then went to the head of the stairs and switched off his light.

The house was very dark.

He tucked the pistol under his belt, against the small of his back, where Roy couldn't see it. He wanted to appear unarmed, defenseless, in order to sucker Roy upstairs.

Colin was breathing noisily, virtually gasping, not because he was physically exhausted, but because he was afraid. He concentrated on breathing quietly, but it wasn't easy.

Something crashed downstairs.

He held his breath, listened.

Another noise.

Roy had arrived.

Colin looked at his read-out watch. Exactly fifteen minutes had passed since he'd left the telephone booth.

It was exactly as Colin had told Heather: Roy had lied about not being able to make it until ten-thirty. He had just wanted to be sure he was the first person in the house. If a trap was going to be laid for him, he intended to be there in the shadows to watch it being set.

Colin had anticipated this development, and he felt good about that. Standing in the dark hall, he smiled.

Something moved in the wall beside him, and he jumped. A mouse. Nothing more than that. It wasn't Roy. He could still hear Roy downstairs. Just a mouse. Maybe a rat. At worst, a couple of rats. Nothing to worry about. But he knew he had better guard against overconfidence, because if he didn't, he would be nothing but food for those rats before the night was out.

Footsteps.

A flashlight, hooded by a hand.

The light moved to the foot of the stairs.

Roy was coming up.

Suddenly, Colin felt that the plan was childish, stupid, naïve. It would never work. Not in a million years. He and Heather were going to die.

He swallowed hard and switched on his own light, shone it down the steps. 'Hello, Roy.'

42

Roy stopped, pointed his flashlight at Colin.

For several seconds they stared at each other. Colin could see the hatred in Roy's eyes, and he wondered if his own fear was equally visible.

'You're here already,' Roy said.

'The girl's up here.'

'There isn't any girl.'

'Come see.'

'Who is she?'

'Come see,' Colin said.

'What's the trick?'

'There isn't one. I told you on the phone. I want to be on your side. I've tried being on *their* side. It didn't work. They don't believe me. They don't care about me. None of them. I hate them, all of them. My mother, too. You were right about her. She's a fucking bitch. You were right about all of them. They'll never help me. Never. They're no good to me at all. And I don't want to have to run from you forever. I don't want to have to be looking over my shoulder for the rest of my life. You can't be beat. You'll get me sooner or later. You're a winner. You win at everything eventually. I see that now. I'm tired of being a loser. That's why I want to be on your side. I want to win. I want to get even with them, all of them. I'll do anything you want to do, Roy. Anything.'

'So you got a girl for us.'

'Yeah.'

'How'd you get her up there?'

'I saw her yesterday,' Colin said, trying to sound excited, as if he hadn't carefully worked out every word of what he was about to say. 'I was riding my bike, just cruising, thinking, trying to think of some way to make up with you. I passed here, and I saw her sitting on the front walk. She had a drawing tablet. She's interested in art. She was sketching the mansion. I stopped and talked to her, and I found out she'd been working on sketches of the place for a few days. She said she was coming back this evening, so she could draw the place with late-afternoon shadows. I knew right away she was what I was looking for. I knew if I gave her to you that we'd be friends again. She's foxy as hell, Roy. She's really something. I set up a trap for her. Now she's up here, in one of the bedrooms, tied up and gagged.'

'Just like that?' Roy asked.

'Huh?'

'You just set a trap and single-handedly tied and gagged her. It was that easy?'

'Hell, no!' Colin said. 'It wasn't easy at all. I had to hit her. Knocked her out. Bloodied her up a little. But I got her. You'll see.'

Roy stared up at him, thinking about it, making up his mind to either stay or leave. His icy eyes gleamed in the thin, cold light.

'Are you coming?' Colin asked. 'Or are you afraid to really do it to her?'

Roy slowly climbed the steps.

Colin backed away from the head of the stairs to the open door of the room where Heather waited.

Roy stepped into the second-floor hallway.

The two boys were no more than fifteen feet apart.

'In here,' Colin said.

But Roy stayed against the far wall and moved toward the door of the room opposite the one where Colin wanted him to go.

'What are you doing?' Colin asked.

'I want to see who else is here,' Roy said.

'No one. I told you.'

'I want to see for myself.'

Keeping one eye on Colin, Roy shone his light into the room across the hall. Colin thought of the cardboard box he had left in there, and his heart began to pound furiously. He knew the trick would be exposed and the plan ruined if Roy saw the bottle of ketchup. But the box must not have looked out of place among the other trash that littered the floors of the rotting mansion, for Roy didn't go into the room to investigate it. He moved on down the hall to see whether the rest of the second floor was deserted.

Colin waited in the doorway until Roy had looked in all the other rooms.

'No one,' Roy said.

'I'm being straight with you.'

Roy started toward him.

Colin backed into the bedroom and went quickly to Heather. He stood beside her.

She looked as if she might scream in spite of the gag in her mouth. Colin wanted to smile and reassure her, but he didn't dare; Roy might step inside and see the exchange, and then he would realise they were in collusion.

Roy entered cautiously. Shadows danced out from his moving flashlight beam. When he saw the girl, he stopped, surprised. He was only fifteen feet away, and he was blocking the only exit; this was the moment of truth. 'Is that . . . Heather?'

'Yeah,' Colin said thickly. 'You know her? Isn't she something?'

Roy looked her over with growing interest. Colin saw the boy's eyes lingering on the curve of her smooth, sleek calves, then her knees, then her taut thighs. For a minute Roy didn't seem capable of lifting his gaze from those slender shapely legs. Then he finally looked up at her ruined blouse, at the swell of breasts that were partly visible through the torn material. He looked at the ropes, at the gag in her mouth, and at her wide, frightened eyes. He saw that she was genuinely afraid, and her fear pleased him. He smiled and turned to Colin. 'You did it.'

Colin knew the trick had worked. Roy couldn't conceive of Colin and Heather setting a trap all by themselves, without adults to back them up. As soon as Roy had seen that they were alone in the mansion, that there were no reinforcements waiting in another room, he had been convinced. The Colin he knew was too much of a coward to try anything like that. But the Colin he knew no longer existed. The new Colin was a stranger to him.

'You really, really did it,' Roy said.

'Didn't I tell you?'

'Is that blood on her head?'

'I had to hit her pretty hard. She was unconscious for a while,' Colin said.

'Jesus.'

'Now do you believe me?'

'You really want to fuck her?' Roy asked.

'Yeah.'

330

'Then kill her?'

'Yeah.'

Heather protested through her gag, but her voice was weak and unintelligible.

'How will we kill her?' Roy asked.

'You have your penknife with you?'

'Yeah.'

'Well,' Colin said. 'I've got mine, too.'

'You mean – stab her?'

'Just like you did the cat.'

'With penknives, it'll take a long time.'

'The longer the better – right?'

Roy grinned. 'Right.'

'So are we friends again?'

'I guess we are.'

'Blood brothers?'

'Well . . . all right. Sure. You've made up for what you did.'

'You'll stop trying to kill me?'

'I'd never hurt a blood brother.'

'You tried to hurt me before.'

'Because you stopped acting like a blood brother.'

'You won't throw me off a cliff like you did Steve Rose?'

'He wasn't my blood brother,' Roy said.

'You won't squirt lighter fluid on me and set me on fire like you did Phil Pacino?'

'He wasn't my blood brother either,' Roy said impatiently.

'You tried to set me on fire.'

'Only when I thought you betrayed our oath. You didn't want to be my blood brother any more, so you were fair game. But now you want to uphold the oath, so you're safe. I won't hurt you now. Not ever. In fact, it's just the opposite. Don't

you see? You're my blood brother. I'd die for you
if I had to.'

'OK,' Colin said.

'But don't ever turn against me again like you
did before,' Roy said. 'I guess a blood brother
ought to be given a second chance. But not a
third.'

'Don't worry,' Colin said. 'We're together from
here on out. Just the two of us.'

Roy looked down at Heather again and licked
his lips. He put one hand on his crotch and
rubbed himself through his jeans. 'We're going to
have fun,' Roy said, 'and this little bitch is just the
start of it. You'll see, Colin. You understand now.
You understand how it's us against them. We're
going to have a barrel of laughs. It'll be a real
popper.'

Conscious of the tape recorder, his heart
exploding as Roy took a step toward Heather,
Colin said. 'If you want, some night we'll go back
out to the junkyard and push that old truck down
on the tracks, in front of a train.'

'Nah,' Roy said. 'We can't do that any more. Not
now that you've told your old lady about it. We'll
figure something else.' He took another step
toward Heather. 'Come on. Let's get that gag out
of her mouth. I have something else I'm aching to
put between her pretty lips.'

Colin reached behind his back and pulled the
pistol from his belt. 'Don't touch her.'

Roy didn't even look at him. He moved toward
Heather.

Colin shouted: 'I'll blow your head off, you son-
of-a-bitch!'

Roy was stunned. At first he didn't comprehend, but then he saw Heather shrugging off the

332

ropes that bound her wrists, and he realised that he had been tricked after all. The blood left his face, and he was white with rage.

'All of this was recorded,' Colin said. 'I've got it on tape. Now I'll be able to make someone believe me.'

Roy started toward him.

'Don't move!' Colin said, jabbing the pistol at him.

Roy stopped.

Heather removed her gag.

'You all right?' Colin asked her.

'I'll be better when we're out of here,' she said.

To Colin, Roy said, 'You creepy little bastard. You don't have the guts to shoot anyone.'

Brandishing the pistol, Colin said. 'Take one more step, and you'll find out you're wrong.'

Heather had frozen in the act of disentangling her legs from the ropes.

Everyone was perfectly silent for a moment.

Then Roy took the step.

Colin pointed the gun at Roy's feet and squeezed off a warning shot.

Except the gun didn't fire.

He tried again.

Nothing.

'You told me your mother's gun wasn't loaded,' Roy said. 'Remember?' His face was split by a rictuslike grin of fury.

Frantically, desperately, Colin squeezed the trigger again. Again. *Again!*

Still nothing.

He *knew* it was loaded. He had checked. Damnit, he had seen the bullets!

Then he remembered the safeties. He'd forgotten to switch them off.

Roy pushed him, and Heather screamed.

Before he could slip the two small switches on the gun, Colin went down under the bigger boy, and they rolled over and over again on the thick carpet of dust, and Colin's head banged hard against the floor, and Roy backhanded him across the face, swung once, twice, three times with fists like blocks of marble, hitting Colin in the ribs and then in the stomach, knocking the wind out of him, and Colin tried to use the gun as a club, but Roy seized his wrist and wrenched the weapon out of his hand, used it as Colin had tried to use it, swung it, struck Colin alongside the head, twice, and blackness welled up, a welcoming warm, velvety, immensely appealing blackness.

Colin realised that one or two more blows would either render him unconscious or kill him, and then he would be no help whatsoever to Heather. There was only one thing he could do; he went limp and played dead. Roy stopped beating him and sat on him, gasping. Then, just for good measure, he slammed the gun into Colin's skull once more.

Pain exploded from Colin's left ear, through his cheek, into the bridge of his nose, as if dozens of sharp needles had been pounded through his face. He passed out.

43

He was not unconscious a long time. Only a few seconds. A vision of Heather, obscenely pinned under Roy, flashed through the blackness in which Colin drifted, and that terrible image propelled him out of the darkness.

Heather screamed, but her scream was cut short by the sound of a hand striking her face.

Colin's glasses were gone. Everything was blurred. He sat up, expecting Roy to leap on him, and felt the floor around him. He found his specs. The frames were twisted, but both lenses were intact. He put them on, bending them to make them fit.

Heather was on the floor on the other side of the room, flat on her back, and Roy was straddling her, facing away from Colin. Her blouse was open, and her breasts were bare. Roy was trying to pull off her shorts. She struggled, and he hit her again. She began to weep.

Groggy, hurting badly, but given strength by his own anger, Colin flung himself across the room, grabbed Roy by the hair, and pulled him off the girl. They staggered backward, then toppled sideways and rolled apart.

Roy scrambled to his feet and seized Heather as she ran for the door. He turned her away from the exit and shoved her toward the wall. She

335

tripped and fell on the hidden tape recorder.

Colin was lying on something hard and sharp-edged, and, as dizzy as he was, he needed a moment to realise that it was the pistol beneath him. He pulled it from under him and rose to his knees and fumbled with the safeties as Roy started toward him again and as sparks of pain flashed before his eyes.

Roy laughed with vicious delight. 'You think I'm scared of an unloaded gun? Jesus, you're a wimp! I'm going to kick your head apart, you stupid little creep. Then I'm going to fuck your stupid girlfriend till she bleeds.'

'You're a filthy, rotten bastard!' Colin said, burning with rage, more furious than he'd ever imagined he could be. He staggered to his feet. 'You stop. Stop right where you are. The safety catches were on. Now they're off. You hear me? The gun's loaded. And I'll use it. I swear to God, I'll blow your guts all over the wall!'

Roy laughed again. 'Colin Jacobs, the big tough killer.' He kept coming, grinning, confident.

Colin cursed him and pulled the trigger. The shot was deafening in the shuttered room.

Roy stumbled backward, but not because he had been hit. He was only surprised. The bullet had missed him.

Colin pulled the trigger again.

The second shot missed too, but Roy cried out and threw up his hands placatingly. 'No! Wait! Wait a minute! Don't!'

Colin advanced on him, and Roy backed into the wall, and Colin pulled the trigger again. He couldn't stop himself. He was hot, white hot, burning with anger, seething, boiling, so hot with rage that he felt as if he would start melting, flowing like lava, his heart thumping so hard that each beat was like the explosion of a volcano. He was not human any more, just animal, savage, barbarian, fighting a brutal territorial battle with another male, driven to attack until he drew blood, powered by a terrifying but irresistible primitive lust to dominate, to conquer, to destroy.

The third shot grazed Roy's right arm, and the fourth bullet took him squarely in the right leg. He collapsed as dark blood suddenly stained his sleeve and soaked through one leg of his jeans. And for the first time since Colin had known him, Roy looked – in the face, at least – like a child, like the child he actually was. His face was contorted by a look of helplessness, an expression of stark terror.

Colin towered over him and lined the sight up with the bridge of Roy's nose. He almost pulled the trigger one last time. But before he could take that final step into total savagery, he became aware that there was more than fear in Roy's eyes. He saw despair, too. And a pitiful, lost look, a deep and abiding loneliness. Worst of all, he saw that part of Roy was beseeching him to squeeze off one more shot; a part of the poor bastard was begging to be killed.

Slowly, Colin lowered the gun. 'I'll get help for you, Roy. They'll fix the leg. And the other things, too. They'll help you with the other things. Psychiatrists. Good doctors, Roy. They'll help you get well. Belinda wasn't your fault. It was an accident. They'll help you understand that.'

Roy began to cry. He gripped his shattered leg with both hands and wept uncontrollably,

337

moaned, wailed, rocked back and forth – either because the shock had worn off and his wound was hurting him . . . or because Colin had not put him out of his misery.

Colin was unable to hold back his own tears. 'Oh God, Roy, what they did to you. What they did to me. What all of us do to each other every day, all the time. It's terrible. Why? For God's sake, why?' He threw the gun across the room; it hit the wall with a crash, clattered to the floor. 'Look, Roy, I'll come visit you,' he said, through tears that wouldn't stop. 'In the hospital. Then wherever they take you. I'll always come. I won't forget, Roy. Not ever. I promise. I won't forget that we're blood brothers.'

Roy didn't seem to hear. He was lost in his own pain and anguish.

Heather came to Colin and tentatively put one hand against his battered face.

He saw that she was limping. 'Are you hurt?'

'It's nothing serious,' she said. 'I twisted my ankle when I fell. What about you?'

'I'll live.'

'Your face looks awful. It's swollen where he hit you with the gun, and it's turning all dark.'

'It hurts,' he admitted. 'But right now we've got to get an ambulance for Roy. We don't want him to bleed to death.' He reached into a pocket of his jeans and took out some coins. 'Here. Take this. There's a pay phone at the service station at the bottom of the hill. Call the hospital and the police.'

'You better go,' she said. 'I'll take forever with this bad ankle.'

'You don't mind staying here with him?' Colin asked.

'He's harmless now,' she said.

'Well . . . OK.'

'Just hurry back.'

'I will. And Heather . . . I'm sorry.'

'For what?'

'I said he'd never get his hands on you. I failed you.'

'He didn't do anything to me,' she said. 'You protected me. You did very well.'

Tears shimmered in her eyes. They held each other for a moment.

'You're so pretty,' he said.

'Am I?'

'Don't ever tell yourself you aren't. Don't ever again think you're ugly in any way. Not ever. Tell them all to go to hell. You're pretty. Remember that. Promise me you'll remember that.'

'OK.'

'Promise me.'

'I promise.'

He went to call the ambulance.

Outside, the night was very dark.

As he walked down the long hill, heading for the phone at the service station, he realised he could no longer hear the voice of the night. There were toads and crickets and the distant rumble of a train. But that low, sinister murmuring that he had always thought was there, that sound of supernatural machinery laboring at evil tasks, was gone. A few steps farther on, he realised that the voice of the night was now within him, and that in fact, it always had been. It was within everyone, whispering maliciously, twenty-four hours a day, and the most important task in life was to ignore it, shut it out, refuse to listen.

He called the ambulance, then the police.

DEAN KOONTZ

THE DOOR TO DECEMBER

Six years ago, Laura McCaffrey's three-year-old daughter Melanie was kidnapped by Laura's estranged husband, Dylan, and seemingly vanished from the face of the earth.

Now Melanie has been found, a nine-year-old wandering the Los Angeles streets with blank eyes and a secret in her soul she will not or can not reveal.

Dylan has been found too – or at least his mangled remains.

Melanie is home again. But can she ever truly be safe – as the floodgates of terror open and the bloody torrent comes pouring through . . . ?

FICTION / GENERAL 0 7472 3705 0

More Thrilling Fiction from Headline Feature

DEAN KOONTZ

HIDEAWAY

Although accident victim Hatch Harrison
dies en route to the hospital, a brilliant
physician miraculously resuscitates him.
Given this second chance, Hatch and his wife
Lindsey approach each day with a new
appreciation of the beauty of life – until a
series of mysterious and frightening events
brings them face to face with the unknown.
Although Hatch was given no glimpse of an
After-Life during the period when his heart
had stopped, he has reason to fear that he has
brought a terrible Presence back with him . . .
from the land of the dead.

When people who have wronged the
Harrisons begin to die violently, Hatch comes
to doubt his own innocence – and must
confront the possibility that this life is just a
prelude to another, darker place.

'Fiercely exciting' *Kirkus reviews*

'Brilliant' *Mystery Scene*

'A wonderful story. His prose sparkles as it
speaks' *Daily Mail*

FICTION / GENERAL 0 7472 3815 4